PRAISE FOR *Solomon's Crown*

"I cannot believe this book exists. I want to wrap myself in velvet to read passages aloud beside a blazing hearth that's taller than I am. . . . The prose thrums with the best kind of heartbreak. . . . There are moments of breathtaking loveliness."

—*The New York Times Book Review*

"Riveting, haunting—two powerful rulers in a battle for love and respect."

—TAMORA PIERCE

"Absolutely captivating and wonderfully romantic . . . I didn't want to put this book down, even when it had ended."

—RAINBOW ROWELL, #1 *New York Times* bestselling author of The Simon Snow Trilogy

"Glorious, heart-wrenching, and, above all, hopeful, *Solomon's Crown* is a meditative, startlingly lovely examination of love, rivalry, and what makes a legacy, and Natasha Siegel has crafted a triumph of a debut."

—GRACE D. LI, *New York Times* bestselling author of *Portrait of a Thief*

"An utterly delightful reimagining of medieval Europe, where a romance between two kings unfolds across enemy lines . . . Natasha Siegel's sweeping tale full of heart and historical optimism will make you believe the impossible."

—C. S. PACAT, *New York Times* bestselling author of *Dark Rise*

"I savored every page. These two kings will wreck your heart, and you'll ask them to do it again. Natasha Siegel's is a voice I craved in historical fiction."

—HEATHER WALTER, author of *Malice*

"*Solomon's Crown* has the mixture of sweeping scope and lush sensory detail that makes for the best historical fiction. I turned the last page and immediately itched to read it again, more slowly, so that I could roll around in the aching romance and assured prose. This is a joyful debut from a remarkable talent."

—FREYA MARSKE, author of *A Marvelous Light*

"A breathtakingly intimate love story set against a sweeping historical backdrop . . . an unforgettable delight."

—S. T. GIBSON, author of *A Dowry of Blood*

"*Romeo and Juliet* meets Oscar Wilde in twelfth-century Europe. *Solomon's Crown* is a work of supreme imagination, wit, and forbidden love that feels timeless, and Natasha Siegel's lyrical language sings. This is truly a unique work and one to be savored."

—MARGARET GEORGE, *New York Times* bestselling author of *The Splendor Before the Dark*

BY NATASHA SIEGEL

The Phoenix Bride

Solomon's Crown

THE
PHOENIX
BRIDE

THE PHOENIX BRIDE

A Novel

Natasha Siegel

DELL

NEW YORK

A Dell Trade Paperback Original

Copyright © 2024 by Natasha Siegel
Book club guide copyright © 2024 by Penguin Random House LLC

Published in the United States by Dell, an imprint of Random House,
a division of Penguin Random House LLC, New York.

DELL and the D colophon are registered trademarks
of Penguin Random House LLC.
RANDOM HOUSE BOOK CLUB and colophon are trademarks
of Penguin Random House LLC.

LIBRARY OF CONGRESS CATALOGING-IN-PUBLICATION DATA
Names: Siegel, Natasha, author.
Title: The Phoenix bride / Natasha Siegel.
Description: New York : Dell, 2024.
Identifiers: LCCN 2023042643 (print) | LCCN 2023042644 (ebook) |
ISBN 9780593597873 (trade paperback) | ISBN 9780593597880 (ebook)
Subjects: LCSH: Great Plague, London, England, 1664-1666—Fiction. |
LCGFT: Historical fiction. | Romance fiction. | Novels.
Classification: LCC PR6119.I325 P58 2024 (print) | LCC PR6119.I325
(ebook) | DDC 823/.92—dc23/eng/20230928
LC record available at https://lccn.loc.gov/2023042643
LC ebook record available at https://lccn.loc.gov/2023042644

Printed in the United States of America on acid-free paper

randomhousebooks.com
randomhousebookclub.com

2 4 6 8 9 7 5 3 1

Book design by Caroline Cunningham

To my father, Kim

Up then, fair phoenix bride, frustrate the sun;
Thyself from thine affection
Takest warmth enough, and from thine eye
All lesser birds will take their jollity.
Up, up, fair bride, and call
Thy stars from out their several boxes, take
Thy rubies, pearls, and diamonds forth, and make
Thyself a constellation of them all;
And by their blazing signify
That a great princess falls, but doth not die.

—John Donne

1665

CHAPTER ONE

Cecilia

Three springs had passed since the king's return to England, when I married William Thorowgood. I loved him, and still love him, as a swallow loves the wind.

It was the first marriage in my family since my sister's two years beforehand, and I was terrified and exuberant in equal measure. I felt as if I were weightless, as if too heavy a breath would send me spinning down the aisle. Meanwhile, Will was blissful and unafraid. He had always lived a life unflinching; his love for me was not diminished by the promise of its permanency. As the priest droned his sacrament, Will linked his hand in mine, and he drew his thumb over my palm in a silent vow.

We returned to the Thorowgood manor afterward to celebrate. I was wearing a gown of eggshell blue, pink pearl earrings, columbine woven into my hair. Will had a handsome navy coat and a gap-toothed grin. He'd never been graceful; he couldn't have danced well if the king's head had depended upon it. He whisked me about the grass like a housemaid with a broom. The musicians were breathless trying to keep up.

"I can hardly believe I have you, Cecilia," he said as we spun across the daisies.

I could hardly believe I had him, either. Will was radiant that day, hair glinting guinea gold in the sunlight; I felt as if I held a treasure, one all the more precious for having almost slipped away. This marriage had once been intended for my sister, Margaret. Now she was watching and smiling from the crowd. Her husband—sneering, pork-faced Robert Eden—loomed behind her. He was wealthier and more high blooded than anyone else present, and his proposal to my sister had led to the dissolution of her betrothal to Will. Now I was marrying him in her stead. I pitied her for the loss, but I was grateful for the gift fate had given me.

I was far more grateful than sorry, and perhaps that was a sin of mine.

After the dance, we staggered to the cake, panting and laughing. I took a second slice, and then a third. At the table, I fell into competition with Will's younger brother to see who could eat more. The second of five, Will was named for his grandfather, but his siblings were all burdened with virtue names. After his sisters—Pleasance, Clemency, and Honor—the well of inspiration ran dry, and the youngest was saddled with the delightfully terrible Good Thorowgood. Good was a sweet boy, if overcompetitive. He was fourteen years old at the time, and he had the stomach of a half-starved whale. He would have beaten me soundly, but by the fourth slice of cake, we were both giggling too much to swallow.

The combination of wine, food, and joy soon overwhelmed me. I've always had a sensitive stomach; I ran off to be sick in the heather. As I stood and wiped my mouth, I found my sister hovering at my shoulder. She rubbed my back, saying, "Temperance, Cecilia."

"Hush, hush," I breathed, half laughing. I leaned into her and dropped my head to her shoulder. "There are other days for temperance than this."

"You shall take ill."

"I already did." I gestured to the bushes. "And now, I am not."

"You are not?"

"Ill. I feel as well as any woman could."

Margaret smiled at me, indulgent, petting my hair. "You are overjoyed," she said. "Overwined, overfed, overloved."

"Contented."

"Yes."

"I am *sick* with contentment, Maggie," I said. "I must be happier than the king himself. Restored! Just as he is. We are all restored now, are we not? Our family, pulled from the ashes?"

"Of course," she replied. But when I turned and saw her face, her teeth were worrying into her lower lip.

"You are upset," I said. "What is it? Are you unwell? Your menses?"

She was prone to such troubles: stuttered courses, painful cramping, even the cruelty of phantom pregnancies. It burdened her, and I was one of few she was willing to speak to of it. But this time, she said, "No, it isn't that."

"Then what?"

"Don't trouble yourself upon your wedding day."

"What's the matter?"

"It is only—soon I shall go to London with Robert, but you will be here, without me."

"We will visit."

She replied, "Yes, I hope so. If you are not too distracted by your new husband."

"I will miss you, also, you know," I told her. "Of course I will. Forgive me for not saying so earlier."

She sighed, pale lashes creeping like frost over the planes of her cheeks. "You needn't apologize," she said. "God made us two, and in doing so gave part to me, and part to you. It often feels as if I am missing some of myself when we are apart. I suspect it will always be so." She took my hands. "Regardless, here is my advice to you, Cecilia, on your wedding day: Allow yourself happiness. Feel worthy of this, and worthy for all that comes after. You and Will deserve each other. You deserve a good life together. You have waited so long for it."

I smiled at her. "Thank you."

Margaret led me by my wrist back to the crowd. When we saw Will, she pushed me toward him; the shove was strong enough that I stumbled, and everyone laughed. We danced again together. Then Will pulled me away, to the other side of the gardens. Others smirked at us, but no one intervened. He kissed me by the rosebushes until I could hardly breathe.

"I am glad to be alone with you finally," he said. "I have missed you desperately."

I swatted his shoulder. "It's only been a week since we saw each other last. And now you will see me always."

"Our bed is newly made upstairs."

"We can't leave."

"Yes, I know." He ran his hands through his hair, and he grinned at me. "You provide me much distraction."

I tugged at his collar. "I like you in blue, Master Thorowgood."

"And I you, Mistress Thorowgood," he replied.

We giggled together at that, giddy. Will kissed my cheek. "Do you think it was fate that led us here?" he asked me.

"Fate, or Robert Eden."

"I never thought I would be glad of such a man. But for so long, I believed that I would love you from afar."

"But now, you will not," I said.

"Now, I will not," he echoed. "And there is no man in England as happy as I."

Flushing, I kissed him again to silence him. Will had been in possession of a constant earnestness, an insistent, innocent honesty, which had always disarmed me. His happiness often seemed greater and more genuine than mine could ever be.

We returned to the house. At our entrance, Margaret—who had been keeping court at the center of the foyer—clapped her hands together. Beside her stood a canvas upon an easel, covered with white cloth. She said, delighted, "Come, Thorowgoods! The portrait must be unveiled!"

I have always had a poor estimation of my appearance, particularly when painted, and it was with some reluctance that I pulled the cloth from our wedding portrait. Still, it was a fair thing, a kind thing: I looked much like Margaret in it, enough that we might have passed as identical. We were born just fifteen minutes apart, and yet we bore only a passing resemblance—not so in the portrait, however. The painter had lightened my hair, almost enough to match hers and Will's. My nose had been made smaller, my mouth bigger. My eyes were bluer than they are in reality. I was pretty, but there was no life within me; I looked very much like a painting, and very little like a woman. Will's likeness, meanwhile, was all sunlight and splendor. He had a face born for portraiture. He seemed as if he would burst from the canvas and take me in his arms.

The guests cooed and applauded. Will said, delighted, "A fair picture! Don't you agree, Cecilia?"

"A good likeness," I lied.

Satisfied, Margaret—who had paid for the portrait as a wedding gift—instructed its placement upon the wall. We returned to the banquet afterward for the final toast. By then, Will and I were itching for the others to leave. It was a great relief when the guests trickled out, one by one, until only my sister remained. She embraced me.

"I am so glad," she told me. "Be happy, Cecilia. You are blessed."

I was blessed, indeed. That day was unquestionably the most wonderful day of my life. For Will, too, I could tell that it was. Before bed that night, we danced again, humming and pacing shoeless upon the rug. We fell to the mattress half asleep, pawing at each other, laughing; for we were restored, and the king was restored. We had each other. Nothing else would ever matter again. All would always be well.

One day that summer, as we lounged in the sweet-dry grass of our unkempt gardens, Will asked me: "When was it, Cecilia, that you knew you loved me?"

The answers I could have given. For romance's sake, I could have said, *the day we met a decade ago, when we were thirteen, when you came to our house with your father to see my sister for the first time.* That day had been a humiliation for me. Maggie had risen to the occasion, of course; she was polite and pretty and she sang like a nightingale. But I had quickly established myself as an excellent foil to Will's would-be bride. I'd stayed up late the night before, reading in the library; exhausted, I poured half of the teapot onto the floor instead of into the cups. Thinking to mend the matter, I informed the horrified congregation that the rug required regular watering. Neither Mother nor Will's father were amused, although Will had laughed so much he had to hide his face behind his hand. I remembered watching that laugh. I remembered thinking, *Margaret is always the lucky one.*

Or I could have told him *later,* made ours a love forged in adversity. When Margaret had instead been wedded to Robert, my mother had sent an offer of me to the Thorowgoods as a replacement. I had been the one to suggest it, pleading with her, hands gripping her sleeves; she had capitulated, for pity's sake, but we'd both known there was no chance. "Why would Master Thorowgood agree, Cecilia?" she asked me even as she poured the wax to seal the envelope. "You have no dowry. Best to put it aside, and we will make you a decent match, with a merchant, or—or perhaps a doctor."

I had waited for the reply like a tragic heroine, pacing the corridors in my nightdress, staring longingly out of the window. I did not have to wait long. The response from Thorowgood Senior came swiftly: an emphatic no. That could have been the moment, when I'd thought that Will had forgotten about me—when I'd decided, heartbroken, to put him out of my mind. I have always been compelled toward the forbidden.

But it wasn't then. I didn't spend the next two years lovesick. In fact, I willingly met with merchants and doctors and lawyers, men who were wealthy but not noble, those who wished to climb the vines of high society by taking a pauper gentlewoman as a wife. Some I liked, some I did not. I even considered marrying some of them, but the matter was hardly urgent. We had what we needed from Margaret, and my mother wasn't particularly concerned with forcing them upon me. Her disapproval was mild and uninterested. She allowed me to live in relative independence. I took lovers from the village, and once I grew bored of them, I turned to poetry and music. I did not love Will then; my infatuation had faded. When my mother eventually told me that Will's father had died, I had considered this news of little consequence, and I hardly looked up from my stitching.

No, the moment I fell in love with William Thorowgood was two weeks after that, the very same day he proposed to me. I had been playing the harpsichord in the music room when I heard the sound of the carriage. I looked out of the window, expecting to see Margaret. Instead, it was Will at the door, about to knock, with a posy of bluebells in his hands.

I opened the window and peered outside. "Will!" I called, almost laughing in astonishment.

He looked up at me. "Cecilia!" he replied. "Hello! It has been too long!"

"It has! What are you doing here?"

He lifted the flowers, brandishing them at me like a rifle being aimed. "I thought I might marry you!" he said, grinning. And without responding, I slammed the window shut so I could run down the stairs and open the door to greet him.

Love is like that sometimes. We call it a burning, liken it to embers and flames, but often it is something less consuming. Like moon phases, waxing and waning, even disappearing entirely. But when that moon is full—oh, when it is full. It shines, and it shines, and it shines.

We had our house in Suffolk, near the sea air and the villages, but we went to London the spring after our marriage. We were not attached to court, but my sister and her husband were. We'd decided to visit them.

I wish we hadn't.

In the carriage on the way, Will read a comedy to me, and he put on voices for each character. I laughed so hard at his performance of Malvolio that I started wheezing, and he had to clap me on the back. I didn't notice that we'd reached London proper until I peered out of the window, to see townhouses looming over us, and to feel the stench of the river settle thickly on my tongue. My nose wrinkled, and Will pulled me into his lap.

"Country rose, wilting in the city," he teased, and I kissed him to keep him quiet.

My sister greeted us with great joy at her townhouse. Robert, who had never taken to either me or Will, was cool and detached. *I have a meeting at court,* he'd told us, and then excused himself from supper entirely. We had chicken boiled in butter and quince pastries and treacle-thick port wine, poured in such quantities that my sister became terribly drunk and had to excuse herself to sleep. Then it was just Will and me again, as it had been and as I thought it always would be. He said, "Let's go for a walk."

A walk, in London, in the muck and the heat! I had protested, of course, but only halfheartedly. Will sniffed out adventure, and there was no pointing him away from it. We rambled in a random direction, found a nearby park closed for renovations, a theater midperformance we could not enter; the city had closed its doors to us. But then, a bookseller's, still open despite the lateness of the hour.

Will had never been a great reader, so he lingered with the bookseller at the counter, petting the shop's tabby. Meanwhile, I stacked my arms high with books of music and philosophy and translated classics. The most expensive of them all, a first edition of Machiavelli's *Florentine Histories,* had cost more than our carriage. As we left, Will chided me gently for my exorbitance, but he hadn't really minded. We rarely spent much in Suffolk, where we had everything we needed and nowhere to indulge.

At the townhouse, we fell into bed, exhausted. Will kissed my shoulder and draped his arm around me.

"Back home tomorrow," he murmured to me, half asleep.

"Tomorrow," I said.

The next day was normal. We said our farewells, clambered into the carriage. I read my *Florentine Histories* as we drove, Will napping in the seat beside me. We got back late, and he fell asleep soon after dinner; the exertions of travel, he told me.

The next morning, he was sick.

I thought he had a simple ague. Where our arms touched beneath the blanket, the skin stuck with sweat. I unpeeled myself from him and went to fetch a cloth. He watched me leave the bed. Coughing, he said, "Water, too, love." When I returned, he was asleep. He had often caught chills, and I wasn't overly worried. Too much time in the carriage, too much stink in the city air. Our return to the countryside would stamp out whatever London rot had taken root within his lungs.

But he was still unwell the next day, then the next. It became clear it was serious. The fever worsened. Strange lumps appeared on his groin and his armpits. He became sallow and unresponsive. The doctor came.

Plague, he said behind a beaked mask.

It was a slow dying. I stayed so near him, and yet I didn't get sick at all; plague is often cruel in that manner. Sometimes, in the darkest moments, I leaned over him and breathed deeply, hoping I might somehow share his burden. I wrote to his sisters to come. We all huddled about the door and said, *Soon the worst of it shall pass.* I brought him bowls of soup with trembling hands. His cheeks hollowed, and his voice thinned. *Soon, the worst of it shall pass,* I told myself. *Soon, it will.*

He slept and slept. Then one day he did not wake up. It happened while I was sitting beside him, reading, holding his hand. He was asleep, but I read still. He had a rattling breath, like dice in a cup. He breathed in, breathed out, breathed in. There was a quick breath, a stuttering breath—and then the noise stopped.

I noticed almost immediately, and I dropped his hand. Perhaps he was still alive, slipping slowly away. Perhaps he was still aware, somehow, that I was beside him, and he felt my absence as he died. But I didn't stay with him, and I bear that burden still. I panicked and ran to the kitchen, where his sisters were eating. I said, *He is not breathing*. In response, his eldest sister, Pleasance, screamed. She did not wail, like a mourner. She shrieked in pain, as if I had hit her around the head.

Afterward, I went to the music room. The scores I had purchased at the London booksellers were sitting on a stool by the spinet. I opened one and I played it. I don't think his sisters have ever forgiven me for doing that. Will was dead, and I was playing the harpsichord. They must have thought me callous. They must have thought me cruel.

I was callous. I was cruel. I played and played and played, for hours and hours. Raw fingers, cold keys.

When was it, Cecilia, that you knew you loved me?

Spilled tea and sweet grasses and posies full of bluebells: *I always knew, Will.* I trusted too much in good things. The moon may shine, but the sun always burns it away.

CHAPTER TWO

David

My father has always been fond of proverbs. "Moses may be dead, but Adonai still watches," he once said, disapproving, when I stumbled over a prayer. As he embraced me when I obtained my diploma in Lisbon: "To beget a son is to spin gold." And as we boarded the ship to England: "No man is a prisoner, if he can escape."

The saying of his that has remained with me longest, however, is one he invented himself. "The first virtue of a physician is caution," he once told me, and he has told me the same many times since. "Courage is the surgeon's lot; for a physician, it is caution. Caution above all else, Davi. Never forget."

My father is a physician, just as I am. The men of my family have been physicians for centuries, and they likely will be for centuries more. But sometimes I wonder if I ought to have been a surgeon. I am fascinated by the structure of bodies, the mechanics of them, the coglike dependency of organ and bone. Such interests are better suited to a scalpel than a mortar. Had I become a surgeon, I might have been more than competent; I could have been extraordinary. As it is, I am as skilled as anyone might wish their doctor to be. But the spark of genius is not there.

I don't dwell upon it. Surgery is unsafe for both patient and doctor. A slip of the blade could mean the noose for a Jew. It is risk enough to be a physician, after all. Consider Roderigo Lopez, a *converso* who treated Queen Elizabeth. He was a self-professed Christian, converted decades prior, but still stained with a Jewish past. When a treatment did not work, he was accused of poisoning the queen, and he found the ax for it. In Portugal, it remains illegal to practice our faith at all. Such things are why my father kept a crucifix above his table; why my mother bought bacon at the butcher; why I have always kept that second virtue of caution strapped to my arm, like a duelist's buckler.

Now we have come to England, the farce is gone, but the fear remains.

I still find some satisfaction in the physician's art, at least. It is gradual and questing, a science of minutiae: in the recording of symptoms, measuring of ingredients, and application of treatments. Each measure is a drop, a teaspoon, a single swallow. There is an exceptional wealth of things to memorize. Myrtle berries calm a burning stomach, this is simple enough, but then the doctor must learn how to administer them. Bought dried or fresh; given in a julep, decoction, oil, or electuary; made into a conserve, preserve, troche, or pill; how much sugar to use, how often to administer. The remembrance of these things must be as habitual as prayer. And the plants themselves, their properties and their constituents—roots, vines, fruits, leaves, and barks—must be as familiar to me as the pattern of moles on my skin, the sound of my father's voice, the tying of my bootlaces. I am a walking herbal.

Physicians are gardeners, in both mind and body. Most of my

ingredients I buy, but the plainer sort—those that grow easily in an English climate—I maintain in a plot behind the house. When we first moved here, the place was nothing but a brick wall and a patch of dirt. At first we had pretentions of order. I sowed in rows and labeled each seed, as if I did not know each plant by sight. On the walls, we no longer needed the crosses we had hung in Lisbon, so we replaced them with hooks to dry herbs upon, and dangling beads of glass and feathers. They are still there. When the light hits them, they scatter color and chaos across the ground, and they clatter in the wind: half song, half shatter.

The rest of the garden is pandemonium. Great tangles of herbs burst over dead twigs; cracked clay pots compete with parasitic vines. The sole wooden bench is marked by a dozen names and talismans carved by my father's knife. My mother was the one who tended the herbs in Portugal, and *that* garden was a paradise. Every plant she touched thrived. She was particularly proud of her lettuce, which grew in great leafy hearts and blessed our table every Passover. When my father and I left, she gave me some seeds to bring with us. By that time, my parents were not speaking to each other. She folded my fingers over the pouch as I bade her farewell. "Tell Gaspar to plant them," she said. "He will know the best place."

I did not follow her advice, and I planted them myself. They never sprouted. Later, my father tried his hand at it with new seeds. They grew, but poorly. The bitter variety of lettuce we favor prefers a warmer climate, just as my mother does. My friend Manuel came to inspect the garden one day before Pesach—we were hosting this time—and the leaves were so withered he had to hide a laugh behind his palm.

I groaned. "It is the London air," I said. "The seder plate may have to go without."

"It isn't *that* bad," he replied, dark eyes dancing.

"It is."

His gaze softened. "You are too hard on yourself, David. You are providing so much for us." Leaning forward, he took my hand in his. "All will be well."

He'd always run hot; at that moment the heat of his touch—less a burning than an ache, a candle flame at a distance—seemed to run up my arm and into my neck, sit in my throat, make me swallow dryly. Manuel, patient and earnest and more trusting than any man I have ever known, saw my discomfort and assumed it was still about seder. "All will be well," he repeated.

Sara came out to the garden then, and he let go of me. She was gorgeous that day, as she always has been—dark skinned like her brother, with a crown of black hair that sprawled like a lion's mane. She wore a gown of ruby silks, made from fabrics their father had imported. "Gaspar says you must come inside," she said, and so we went, lettuce and all.

The Cardozos had come to England around the same time we did. They were from Andalusia originally, although they had lived in Amsterdam for some years before moving to London. We'd all soon become dear friends—Sara, Manuel, and I—sneaking into Royal Society lectures, arguing with beadles at shopping galleries, neglecting synagogue in favor of debates at coffeehouses. That spring—spring one year ago—I was preparing to introduce them to Jan, a new friend of mine whom I knew Manuel would adore. The meeting would never come to pass.

Seder that night was wonderful, despite the pitiful state of the lettuce. My father drank too much and argued uproariously with the Cardozos about the ideal amount of salt for pickling a cucumber; plates were picked clean, songs sung, blessings said. On occasion, Sara would smile at me from across the table and tuck her hair behind her ear. I was too distracted to realize what those smiles meant. I was busy watching Manuel, who was leaning forward in concentration over the Haggadah, a curl falling over his forehead and brushing his cheek.

Adonai forgive me, I must forget him entirely. That spring before the plague came, when we held hands beside the lettuce and prayed for joy and celebration: It is dead to me now. I have buried it alongside my mother's dead seeds. I cannot cope another way.

I left so much behind when I came here. I left behind our Lisbon garden, the winding streets of my childhood, the simple beauty of the ocean greeting me from my window each morning. But London permits me to live openly as a Jew without deception, to wear a beard and hang a mezuzah on our doorframe. It has given me great joy and even greater grief.

Was it all worth it? Perhaps I'll never know. Moses may be dead, but Adonai endures.

I wonder what he thinks of me now.

It is a stiflingly hot summer, one perhaps warm enough for my mother's lettuce. One year ago, I was in an oiled coat and a beaked mask, visiting plague patients and checking my armpits each night for buboes. Today, I tie my cravat and button my doublet in preparation for a morning free of appointments. Just as London did, I survived last year—and I will survive this one. I must.

I leave the house early, to request the rebinding of three books at my printer's near Fleet Street. Once I return, I examine my father. His heart quickens, but otherwise, he is well; he hasn't had his chest pains for some time. It is the fifth day of turmeric for his joints, but we see little improvement. It seems the ginger was better, and I may combine them. I have ordered bayberries to make an ointment.

Meanwhile, all else has been accounted for. The pantry and the herbal have been stocked, and the deliveries arranged. The new maid no longer hides behind doors to avoid me. Her name is Elizabeth Askwith. I ought to be calling her Mistress Askwith, really, but the first time I addressed her I was exhausted from a day of appointments, and I couldn't remember which English title was correct. Instead, I said her full name, and I established a precedent of such. So now, when I need her, I call "Elizabeth Askwith," and she thinks it is the manner of all Jews to use both names, so she replies, "Yes, David Mendes." Perhaps she is jesting, but she doesn't seem the sort to jest. She has the severity of a Puritan, if not their faith. Last week, I saw her stripping nettles for soup with her bare hands. I asked her why she refused to use gloves. She said the nettles made her fingers strong.

"A good maid must be stout, David Mendes," she told me as she threw the weeds into the cauldron. She has dark, curtain-like hair, in harsh contrast to her pale skin, and at that moment it looked something like a monk's hood. "My mother could wring two chickens dead at once, one in each hand."

I have stayed out of her way since then, but this morning I must find her. I am calling upon Sara, who sits shiva for her father, and I should bring food with me. I go to the kitchen, where Elizabeth Askwith is kneading dough. I say, "Where are the tarts?"

"In the pantry, David Mendes, I shall fetch them," she replies. She flings the dough down with unaccountable violence and goes to the pantry door. When she returns, she has a tray of four tarts.

I frown and scratch my beard. "Were there not six?"

"Gaspar Mendes had two of them with supper," she replies.

"Gaspar Mendes is not permitted to eat tarts with supper."

"Gaspar Mendes says that he is the head of the household, till you get you a wife."

I huff. "I am the one who pays you, am I not?" I ask.

She pauses at that. "Aye, David Mendes, that is true," she admits, but she makes no further comment as she wraps the tarts in cloth. She gives me a basket to carry them, and I take it with me to my father's room as I bid him farewell. He is whittling in bed, which I have often made complaints of, for it covers the sheets in wood shavings and gives him splinters. The thing he has produced seems to be either a wolf or an otter.

He sees my frustrated expression, and the basket in my hand. "I had only two," he says.

"Two is too many," I reply.

"But one is not enough."

"I have told Elizabeth Askwith to give you no more pastries. You get too many from your friends as it is. And your heart would do better without them."

He flaps his hand in the air and shrugs. He says, "Ach," in the back of his throat, with a good amount of spittle. "You'll take those to Sara?" he asks.

"Yes."

"She still has no husband?"

"Since you asked yesterday? I expect not."

"Ach."

I approach to brush wood curls from his blanket, and I pat him on the shoulder. "I will return tonight. I have appointments all afternoon."

He grunts in acknowledgment. "David," he says as I reach for the door.

"Yes?"

"Give Sara my blessings."

I sigh. "I shall."

"Did you pray today?"

"Yes."

He frowns. He doesn't believe me. He will never believe me when I lie, for he can see it on my face when I do. Ashamed, I hurry out of the room, closing the door behind me.

As I leave the house, I pause to look at the mezuzah affixed to the doorframe. It is a lovely thing, white marble tipped with gold. Despite its obvious value, it has never been stolen; perhaps potential thieves see the Hebrew and believe it is cursed. I have not been able to touch it, not since the plague. Instead, I raise an uncertain finger to it, and then I drop my hand without touching it. Perhaps it is somehow more blasphemous than disregarding it entirely. But I like to acknowledge it, at least.

It is not enough, but it is more than nothing.

Sara's home is only a couple of streets east of mine. It is as warm today as it was the day before. Sun broils the cobbles, my feet pounding the street in time with the cobbler hammering boot soles on his doorstep, the washerwoman beating her sheets from an open window, the horses' sullen hooves as they drag their burdens. Despite the dryness of the air, I can still smell the wet-brown river stench of the Thames, the ceaseless damp of it; we are near the bank here. On the hottest days I have seen boys jump into the water to cool themselves down, although I certainly wouldn't recommend it to any of my patients. On a morning like this, however, with the sweat pooling at my collar, I am almost tempted to try it myself.

I reach Sara's home in good time. I haven't seen her in almost a year; after Manuel's death, I think we both found the other's company too painful to bear. But she is a good woman, and now she has endured yet another death in her family. With her father gone, she is the only one left. I can no longer pretend we are strangers.

She has had many visitors before me. I lay my basket of tarts upon a table groaning with cured meats, fruit, and potted fish. Sara herself is sitting on the floor beside the fireplace, and she doesn't acknowledge my entrance. I set about making more space on the table, rearranging the offerings in case more come. As I straighten the cloth, she says, "David? Is that you?"

She sounds surprised, but not horrified, which I suppose is as much as I could have hoped for. "Yes," I reply. "I have brought you cherry tarts."

"Good. There is only so much salt herring I can stand." She stands up. "Pardon, the house is quite dusty."

I expected her to be angry with me for abandoning her, but instead she seems relatively at ease. It makes me distinctly uncomfortable. "Is your maid here?" I ask her, to distract myself from it.

"I told her to take leave for the week," she replies.

"Why?"

"I don't know," she says. "I am quite lost."

She looks down at the floor once more. As she drops her chin, her hair moves back to reveal the curve of her jaw, and the mole on the side of her neck. Unbidden, I remember her trying to kiss me the day after Manuel's funeral: *We need each other, David.* My stuttered apologies, my stumbling steps backward. My throat constricts in shame.

"I will leave you, if you wish," I say.

"No, it is good to see you." Seeing my frown, she sighs. "Truly, David, it is. It has been too long."

"Have you been eating?"

"As best I can. It is difficult to do anything but worry. Rabbi said I must allow myself grief, but all I can think of is the business, and how I shall manage it alone."

The Cardozos import Turkish fabrics. "Your father retired years ago. You have already been managing it alone."

"Certainly," she replies. "But now that Father is gone, I have no man's face to wear. I suppose I ought to marry."

I laugh nervously. "Perhaps."

There is an awkward moment of silence.

"Unpack those tarts, then," Sara says, and she goes to the couch. She returns with a cushion, which she puts upon the floor. As she sits on it, I retrieve the basket. I pull up a stool opposite her.

"Have you had many visitors?" I ask.

"The entire neighborhood, it seems. But I remain in need of good conversation. Do you have any stories to tell?" She bites into a tart, humming in appreciation. "This is excellent."

"Stories?" I ask. She seems genuinely happy I am here. I suppose I ought to be grateful for that.

"Perhaps of new patients, with odd ailments? I shall never forget the man who had been eating paint. What was his name?"

"Henry," I say.

"Did he ever tell you why he did it?"

"No, he couldn't. It was a compulsion."

"When I was young," she says, "and I saw the silks coming into port, all bright and shiny like fruit, I often thought they looked delicious. But I never ate them."

"We all have thoughts such as Henry did. Transient impulses. The trouble starts when we let them dictate our action."

"If only it were as simple as you make it seem." She makes a shooing motion. "If only one could say, 'Impulse, I see you, and you are absurd!' And then drive it away."

"Often, one can."

She snorts. "If you are David Mendes, I suppose."

"Well—I have no stories," I say curtly. "No patients, certainly, that are eating paint."

"There must be something you haven't told me yet. You've always spoken so little of your work."

There are things I haven't told her, of course. There are things I prefer not to think of, things it would hurt her to hear. "Not really," I reply.

Sara pouts, dissatisfied. Still, she doesn't press. She permits me my silence, as she always has done. It is a great relief.

A wood pigeon coos outside the window, and Sara cranes her head to look at it. In the early afternoon, the sun filters dusty gray and hot through the glass. The weather is already very warm, and the stink of the city is unconscionable. Sara has kept the windows closed, with sprigs of rosemary bunched in small vases on the sills. As we stare, a bee floats toward the flowers from outside. It smacks into the glass and bounces back, before beginning another adamant approach.

We finish eating in silence. There is a single tart left, and I leave it in the basket, returning it to the table. As I close the lid, Sara sighs, rubbing her eyes with her hand. I suddenly feel unwanted.

"Shall I leave you?" I ask.

"Soon. Will you sit with me first?"

I slide down to sit beside her on the floor. She presses her arm against mine.

"I am glad you are here," she says.

"As am I," I reply. "I am sorry I didn't come sooner."

She doesn't point out the lie, although she must recognize it. As time has passed, it has become more and more difficult to think of her. It is not that I resent her for what has happened, but rather that I resent myself when I am around her. I have made her into a fault of mine, one I must do penance for.

"I really am sorry, Sara," I say. "For everything."

"I know," she replies.

When I return home, Elizabeth Askwith is arranging flowers by the staircase. She curtsies perfunctorily and says, "A letter came while you were gone, David Mendes. On the table."

I thank her. In the kitchen, I see the letter, and I lift it up before I notice that the door to the garden is open. Outside, my father is sitting on the bench; Elizabeth Askwith must have helped him downstairs. He smiles to see me. The wind shuffles the gray-black hairs of his formidable eyebrows, and his hands run rapturously over the wood grain of the bench. What he lacks in physical strength is compensated by the ease of his joy, which comes swift and undemanding. He has a capacity for happiness I have always envied.

"You are home! The air is good today, Davi," he tells me.

"Yes, it is."

"The breeze moves quickly. It stirs the heart. Look at the lavender! A good crop this year."

"Are you cold?" I ask. "I could fetch a blanket."

He flaps his hand dismissively. "I have a scarf."

"Is your chest—"

"Honestly," he snaps. "Must we speak only of my ill health?"

Chastened, I go to sit beside him, the letter still clutched in my hands. The evening is warm but overcast. In the filtered light, everything is darker and deeper than usual. The soil is the color of dried blood, the green of the plants shadowed to a velvet gloom. Father is wearing his old silk doublet, a lurid slash of blue and black and white. "Who sent that?" he asks.

I look down at the letter, which remains sealed and untouched, pressed with red wax. It looks expensive. Breaking the seal feels somehow heretical. I open it and glance at the message.

"What does it say?" Father asks, impatient.

"A request for consultation."

"Obviously, Davi. From who?"

"A wealthy family, aligned with court. It is . . . surprising."

He frowns. "Where are they based?"

"Saint James's. The household of Lord Eden."

"Will you go?"

I reply, "Yes. The pay is generous."

"I would expect so." He sighs. "Perhaps not generous enough, considering what you risk."

"I will do nothing more than prescribe some well-tested medicines. And if they prove successful, my work might attract attention from others in the area . . ."

"Attention is good, for a doctor," he replies. He needn't continue with the disclaimer, for I know it as well as he does: but not for a *Jew*. Success must come to us as foxglove is administered to a patient. We may take enough to live, to thrive, even; but one ounce too much, and we are purged.

"I will be cautious," I say.

"See that you are," Father replies. "For the sake of all of us. Our community couldn't survive the blood of a lady on our hands."

"Yes, I know."

I understand his concern, but Father needs a good number of medicines for his heart, poultices for his joints, too, and his love of good wine leaves our purses lighter than I would like. We are not struggling yet, but the money can do us nothing but good.

We could lose everything we have in an instant, after all. What if England decides they don't want us here, and we are forced to flee again?

Besides, I am a doctor, and here is a patient who needs me. I can sense Lady Eden's desperation, in the slanting spikes of her hand, the half-smudged ink of her signature. It is hardly an obsequious letter—more patronizing than anything else, really—but I am inclined to sympathy. *My sister is suffering,* it says. *She will not eat, will not smile. She is a ghost of herself, and you, sir, are my final recourse. I fear that this is more than grief. She has a sickness, and it must be cured.*

"I will go tomorrow," I say. "Let us hope that this Mistress Thorowgood is not beyond saving."

CHAPTER THREE

Cecilia

I have been in London for 134 days.

It is summer here, sweltering and unrelenting. In Suffolk, summer was a litany of small comforts: the scent of dried hay hanging sweet in the air, Will's laughter in the orchard, lurid blooms of larkspur in the garden. But there are no such comforts here. In the city, summer means stink, and my window is shut fast to prevent the smell reaching my bedroom. Margaret has worked so hard to approximate my old life: she has put fresh flowers in the vases; given me silk sheets in the pale blue of an unclouded sky; strewn lavender across my windowsill.

When I close my eyes, I am permitted a temporary transportation to another time, another place. As brief as a breath, I am standing in the heather, and Will is waiting for me.

But I must open my eyes eventually. And then I am reminded of where I am: *here* is not Suffolk, with its hay and larkspur. *Here* is my sister's townhouse, sitting heavy as a tombstone in Saint James's. This is a hungry place, a starving one, sucking all of its surroundings into it. The sky pinches at its edges, pavement falling to meet its foundations, like water into a drain. In a city so crowded, it feels unimaginable that space could be found for such an enormous construction. And yet this neighborhood is full of identical buildings: layer cakes of stone and wealth, with iron fencing and red-coated footmen.

The interior of the townhouse is just as offensive, with narrow hallways and spiraling, white-stoned staircases. Every corridor grows another and another, closing like teeth, braiding like hair. The only part of it that doesn't threaten to swallow me whole is the courtyard, and that is where I spend most of my time. It is the nearest I can get to the past. Fresh air and the scent of linden, the soft burble of the fountain—eyes closed, head tipped back to meet the sky, I go somewhere else, somewhere three years ago. I hear my sister's voice. *Be happy, Cecilia. You are blessed.*

I have been in London for 134 days. I hate this place, I hate this city. I hate its crowds and its stink; I hate that I am trapped within it; I hate that it killed Will, and yet I have returned to it. I hate, I hate, I hate. And I hate Margaret sometimes, too, despite myself. I hate that she was given all the good fortune between us, to keep her husband, to be the eldest, to be pretty enough that a man as wealthy as Robert Eden took one look at her at a party and had her betrothal dissolved as easily and sweetly as sugar in tea.

I shouldn't resent her for it. She invited me here, and I came to London with open, searching arms, desperate for absolution. It hasn't absolved me, of course. Perhaps I have betrayed Will by ever hoping it would. But someday, the city might do the same to me as it did to him and lay me in my grave.

I hope it does. In that, at least, there seems some justice.

I have had many physicians in the time I have been at the Eden townhouse. My most recent was Master Percy. He was old and gaunt, with a round, moonlike face, surrounded by wisps of white hair like separated clouds. But when Margaret enters my room without him this morning, expression apologetic, I know that she has dismissed him.

Impatience: a trait we both share, and one that has been our downfall many times. "Again?" I ask, raising a brow.

"He wasn't helping," Margaret replies. "And you didn't like him, besides."

Of course I didn't like him: Who *likes* their physician? But Master Percy was less objectionable than some of the others, and I feel sorry to see him gone, if merely for the possibility of a worse replacement. Every time I get a new physician, I have to speak to them of my symptoms—the nausea, the occasional vomiting, the light-headedness, the shortness of breath—and hear them offer the same diagnoses in return: ulcers, colic, even hysteria. None of their treatments work. I don't know why Margaret expects they will. They are only physicians, after all, and medicine can't cure loss.

"I have discussed the matter with Robert," Margaret tells me, "and he felt it may be necessary to consult someone with . . . alternative expertise."

I'm not certain why Robert has a say—the man has spoken fewer than a dozen words to me since I came here—but I can hardly protest, considering he is providing my bed and board. "Alternative expertise?"

"The methods taught in England are sound, of course, but there are a great variety of physicians in London who have been trained elsewhere."

"You want to employ a foreigner?" I ask, surprised.

Her eyes flit guiltily to the corner of the room. "Robert found a man well known for treating disorders of the stomach. I wrote to him yesterday, and he shall be here soon."

I say, "I need some respite, Maggie. I don't want another doctor prodding me."

"If it is what you need, then you will bear it," Margaret replies.

I bristle. Margaret fears for my well-being—fears I am mad—and she doesn't trust me to take care of myself. I know that I am unwell, that is clear enough: I can't eat, can't smile, can't speak except either to be cruel or apologize. On the worst days, I am so terrified and furious that it sickens me as would poison, as would something rotten or curdled, and I vomit after I eat. But my body is my own, it always will be. I have had enough of strangers' interventions, and I am exhausted by the thought of more leeches and tinctures.

"I won't see him," I say. "I refuse."

Margaret scowls. "Be reasonable, Cecilia."

"I am being reasonable. I am so tired of it all. I am bled so often I can hardly stand; my food is bitter with medicine; I sleep so much I can't tell reality from dreams. What life is this?"

"*A* life, at least, which is more than you would give yourself without my help."

"I am not—"

"The world is passing you by," Margaret says, her voice wavering. "You are so young. My heart breaks for you. A few more weeks of suffering, for a permanent resurrection—it is worth it, surely?"

"I can recover in my own time."

She shakes her head. "Do you remember," she says, "how you got that scar?"

She means the silver line drawn upon my lower lip: a childhood injury from when I had bitten so hard into it I had bled. It had been caused by a night terror, one so violently frightening I had injured myself and screamed myself awake from the pain. Margaret, sleeping beside me, had awoken to find me with blood dripping down my jaw, and my hair torn and wild. She had wiped me clean and fetched me warm milk and honey. After, she had held my hand until I fell asleep again.

Margaret herself never had nightmares while we slept in the same room, except once, the night before she married Robert. I fetched her warm milk and honey then, as she had so often done for me. I will never forget the way she clutched the cup and began to cry into it. She is a very quiet and pretty crier, unlike me. Her face remains mostly blank, but her eyes go red and small. She said, *I do not know if I will please him,* and I hadn't known how to reply.

But that was the past. Now Margaret is determined, grim faced, and I know there is nothing I can say. "Let me help you," she begs of me. "As I always have. A new life awaits you. It is time you seize it."

She doesn't give me time to reply. She turns around and sweeps out of the room. I haven't the energy to give chase. Instead, I fist my hands in the bedspread, feeling the silk run like water beneath my fingers. I breathe a rattling, shuddering breath, attempting to calm myself down. I must forgive my sister her rudeness. She works so hard to make me well. I could tell her that her efforts are pointless, but she would never understand. Margaret can't comprehend what I have lost, for she hasn't loved as I have, and perhaps she never will. She *does* love Robert, but it is in her curious, measured way; I think she must portion out the love each day, so it doesn't run out too fast.

I slip out of bed and stand on shaky legs. My book of poems is on my desk, and I go to retrieve it. The afternoon sun casts a glowing square through the window. I pause to bask in its warmth. Outside, the street is quiet and empty; in this area, there are few walkers, only the gilt carriages of the homeowners as they return from Whitehall. I peer down at the cobblestones, watching the furtive movements of a pigeon by the iron fencing. Glancing toward the house opposite—a building near identical to the Edens'—I notice that someone is standing in the window directly opposite mine. It is difficult to make out any features, considering the distance and the glare of the sun, but the figure is certainly looking back at me. It appears to be a man, in breeches and a coat, the curling shape of his wig visible even as a silhouette.

The man waves. Bemused—*fascinated*, for the first time in months—I wave back at him.

Someone knocks at the door; it is likely food. I take a step back from the desk, book in hand. My stomach churns, queasy, in anticipation of the effort of eating. Still, it has been a relatively good day, unplagued by dreams. So I will have three bites. I will see this doctor, hear his useless recommendations, and watch him leave. I will stitch and go to the library. I will play the spinet and I will eat dinner. Tomorrow, I will do it all again.

I have been in London for 134 days.

Perhaps, eventually, I shall lose count.

After my meal—attempting to avoid my sister and her doctor— I go to the courtyard. The linden tree is heavy with spring blossoms. It reaches devotedly toward me, greeting me like an old friend, its scent sweet and heady. When I breathe, its perfume clings to the back of my tongue. I make loops of the tree, over and over, faster and faster, until the rise and fall of my chest becomes labored, and the movement of air in my lungs feels like the opening of a wound. I lean against the trunk and attempt recovery, rolling my fingers against the bark in a mockery of a harpsichord piece.

Minutes pass, perhaps hours—I cannot tell. Then the door to the house opens. It is Margaret. For no cause except instinct, I duck behind the tree so she can't see me.

It is a ridiculous gambit. If she takes even a single step into the courtyard, she will notice me. But she doesn't come further inside. She calls, "Cecilia?"

I don't respond.

Margaret makes a noise of vexation. "Pardon," she says, and for a moment I think she is apologizing to me; then I realize someone is accompanying her. "She must be in her room," she says. "I'll fetch her. Take a seat, I shan't be long."

I hear no reply. But Margaret walks away—I hear the harsh clip of her heeled shoes, like nails being hammered into the floor—and someone else walks into the courtyard. Their footsteps are softer, more measured. They sit in one of the iron chairs beside the fountain, and it rattles.

Silence. The fountain trickles. The wind rustles the linden tree. A bird trills above us. Very slowly, I inch sideways and peek past the tree, toward the stranger.

It is a man: olive skinned and short bearded, with dark, curly hair tied back with ribbon. His face looks like none I have ever seen before. I didn't know that someone's features could be so brazen. His nose begins at a steep angle and changes its mind halfway through; his neck is broad; his eyebrows are anvil heavy, the eyes beneath so dark they have no pupil, just circles of empty space. The physician, no doubt. I don't know what I imagined he would look like, but it wasn't this.

His gaze meets mine directly. Aghast, I lurch back behind the tree, spinning on my foot so I am turned toward the wall.

For an intensely awkward moment, neither of us speak. Then the man says, "Mistress Thorowgood, I presume."

I expect some hint of insult or confusion in his tone, but he mostly sounds concerned; he has a deep voice and a warm, rolling accent. The cadence of it is songlike, and entirely foreign.

"Are you in distress?" he asks.

A short, bitter laugh rises in my throat. It emerges before I can stop it. "Constantly."

"Do you require assistance?"

"Not for the moment. I would rather remain behind this tree."

"Very well," he replies.

He goes quiet, looking away from me, staring ponderously at the fountain. I peer out again to watch him. He has a notebook and pen in his pocket, and he wears simple, utilitarian clothing: a vest, jacket, and long breeches. "You are the physician," I say.

"Yes. My name is David Mendes."

"I am Cecilia Thorowgood," I tell him. "Which you are already aware of, evidently."

"Is there a reason you wish to remain behind the tree, Mistress Thorowgood?"

I do not reply. I am still out of breath, and I have been suddenly struck with a terrible anxiety; it has been so long since I was alone with a stranger.

Eventually, he asks, "Are you frightened of me?"

I snort. "Of course not. But if it's all the same to you, I'd rather you didn't prod me with torture instruments and tell me I ought to be bloodlet."

"Is that what other physicians have done?"

"Yes."

"That is a shame," he says. "I swear I shall never touch you without your permission, using instruments or otherwise."

"Then you shan't ever touch me at all."

"If that is what you wish."

I step out from behind the tree. Mendes smiles at me. "Good afternoon," he says.

"Good afternoon," I reply automatically. Then, "I have no need of a new physician, you know."

"Your sister requested my presence."

"Her request was foolish. And she'll have you dismissed within the week, so you really ought to spare yourself the trouble and leave now."

Mendes offers me a strange expression, part amused, part perplexed. Then he passes his hand over his face, scrubbing the twitch away from it, as if polishing a spoon. His beard is so neatly trimmed I wonder if he has used mathematical instruments to accomplish it. His jaw is a little lopsided, and he has a few tiny pox scars on his upper neck, like a scattering of stars. He seems young for a physician. He can't be much older than I am.

A wave of dizziness hits me, and I lean further against the tree. Mendes gestures to the other chair. "Would you like to sit?"

I sit at the roots of the linden, partially out of petulance, and partially because I feel so woozy I don't trust myself to walk to the table. Breathing deeply, I rest my head in my hands, ignoring the black spots in my vision.

"When did you last eat?" he asks me.

"If I answer your questions, will you leave sooner?"

"I suppose so."

I say, "I tried to eat this morning."

"And you vomited?"

I shrug.

"Were you hungry when you ate?"

"I can't remember."

"Do you become hungry?"

"Sometimes."

"If you are hungry, and you attempt to eat, what happens?" he asks.

"I lose my appetite," I reply. "And if I force myself to swallow, it comes back up."

"When did you last leave this house?"

One hundred and thirty-eight days ago. "I don't know."

"Truly?"

"I don't know," I repeat. I feel as if I am before the bailiff. Observing Mendes more fully, I consider his beard, his foreign features, his accent—and the conclusion I draw makes my eyes widen in shock. "Are you a Jew, Master Mendes?" I ask.

"Yes, I am," he replies.

That is surprising. Margaret is an unwavering Christ lover. She must be in an extraordinary state of concern to allow a Jew into her home. Although, she mentioned that Robert was the one to locate him; perhaps she didn't know.

He stares at me. I stare at him. Perhaps he is expecting me to comment on his Jewishness, somehow, but I don't have much to say about it. I've never met a Jew before and I am unlikely to again. He is a man as much as any other, and as with most men, I am little inclined to trust him.

I settle on, "At least you are not a Catholic. If you were, I think my sister might have already called the constables."

He opens his mouth, closes it, and then covers his face with his hand. I wonder if I have insulted him, but then I notice his eyes crinkling, and I realize he is trying not to laugh.

I find my own lips twitching, too, and I glance away. "Look, regardless," I say, "I am being sincere when I tell you this isn't worth the effort. I have told my sister, but she didn't listen to me:

I do not want another doctor. You surely must have other patients?"

"I do," he says.

"No doubt they are more welcoming than I."

"Undoubtedly," he replies, still clearly amused.

This conversation feels like playing tennis. I pause to think, then serve. "You are unsafe here, you know. My sister calls Jews Christ killers."

"Your sister overestimates my age."

I afford him a small laugh at that. "She must," I agree. "But still, you are welcome here only because she believes you will help me."

He asks, "And I cannot help you?"

"Such a thing would be impossible."

"I disagree," he replies, ball across net. "And I doubt that is what you really believe. It is more likely you are frightened by the thought of recovering; many patients are."

I gape at him. The score swings to his favor. "That's absurd," I say weakly. "I want to be left alone. It is only that. I dislike having someone prodding at me, asking me endless questions, attempting to cure me of the incurable."

"And what is this incurable ailment you believe yourself afflicted with?"

"Loss," I say. "It is loss. I am grieving, and there is no doctor on earth who might undo that."

This is enough to win me the match. He can't counter. Wordless, he presses his mouth into a thin line, staring at me in mute frustration.

I can't tell what he is thinking. He has a strange, fastidious sort of chaos about him. There is a fascinating opposition between his careful grooming and the inherent disorder of his features. His face carries a mournful heaviness that is almost charming; he reminds me of a bloodhound, with his broad brows and large, dark eyes.

Finally, he says, "I am sorry that you have suffered such a thing. I wish that I could afford you greater room for grief. I don't know what has happened. Lady Eden has told me very little. But she did tell me that she is concerned, and I understand why."

"I'll manage," I say.

To my horror, he stands up from the chair and approaches me where I sit beneath the linden. For a foolish moment, I think he will sit with me in the grass. Then he turns around and leans against the tree beside me, still standing, arms crossed. We both stare at the fountain as it trickles.

"I do not know you," he says, "nor you me."

"Exactly."

"So let me know you, at least a little," he continues. "You could provide me that much. Answer my questions, and if it really does seem you can't be cured, I will leave."

"Fine."

He makes a pleased noise. "Very well. When you awaken, Mistress Thorowgood—"

"Cecilia," I say. I can't stand to hear my married name spoken aloud. He has said it too many times already.

He winces. Perhaps the thought of such familiarity pains him. "Cecilia, then. When you awaken each morning, how do you feel? Drowsy? Nauseated?"

When I awaken each morning, I open the curtains, and then sit upon my mattress and stare at the wall. Sometimes I am quiet. Sometimes I think I am quiet, and then a realization comes, slow and inevitable, that I am sobbing without tears. When that happens, I find myself disgusted by my own pitiful-ness. I scrub my face with my hand as if I can erase myself like chalk on a board. It doesn't work. I score scratches against my forearm as if I might peel away my skin and find another woman beneath. It doesn't work. Nothing works.

"Cecilia?" he says when I don't reply.

"Forgive me. I—I don't—" I gasp. "I don't know."

Alarmed, he stoops beside me. I turn my head to look at him. How dark his eyes are, how alarmingly wide. Will had eyes like the surface of frozen water: you could skitter across them, dazzled by the light reflected. Not this man. His gaze threatens to swallow me whole.

"I'm sorry," he says softly. "You have been deeply wounded, I think."

"We all have wounds, Master Mendes."

He looks down at his own hands, curled around his knees. "Yes," he replies. "We do."

The door to the courtyard opens, and my sister enters. Mendes stands up and steps back from me.

Margaret seems quite panicked, clutching her elbows with her hands; when she sees me, her fear becomes annoyance. "Oh, Cecilia, honestly," she says. "I have been looking everywhere for you."

"I was acquainting myself with Master Mendes," I reply.

She turns to give him an accusatory look. He seems more embarrassed than frightened, flushing under her gaze.

"We only spoke of her symptoms," Mendes says. It is true—theoretically—but still a deflection. He wears deceit uncomfortably, his gaze ricocheting across the courtyard.

"Fine," Margaret says. "I was going to call for tea, but perhaps now it would be best to proceed with the examination."

I blink at her. "Examination?"

"Cecilia, he is a physician. He must examine you if he is to help." She grimaces and gives Mendes a look of unconcealed disdain. "Pardon. I know it's not . . . ideal."

"It's fine," I say.

She blinks. "It—it is?"

"But if I agree," I say, "and you still find him lacking . . . then no new physicians. Swear it."

"But—"

"No more, Maggie."

"Very well."

She gives me a watery smile, and her gratitude fills my mouth like gristle. Smiling back, I resist the urge to spit it out.

Master Mendes offers me an arm. I take it, despite her glower, and we go inside. As we walk up the staircase, I sneak glances at my new physician, and each step we take seems more and more like a dream, in which we will ascend forever and never reach my rooms at all.

Men like David Mendes don't exist, not in Cecilia Thorowgood's life. My life is silk and sorrow, spinets and portraits and tea tables. My physicians are old men with jars of leeches and trembling hands. They are not Jews with gazes like ink and musical voices. I think of the tremble of his hands on his knees, the sudden vulnerability in his eyes as he crouched beside me—those extraordinary eyes, black on white.

He has seen loss, too, I am sure of it. He is printed with his past, but the words are in a language I cannot read.

We all have wounds, I think. *Even doctors cannot cure an injured heart.*

CHAPTER FOUR

David

I have agreed to meet Jan at Saint James's Park this afternoon, to see the canal they have opened there. Despite the strange sense of unease I feel after my first appointment with Cecilia Thorowgood, Jan is my closest friend, and I can't disappoint him. Besides, the park is only a short walk from the Eden townhouse.

Jan is waiting outside the gate of the park. Prodigiously tall and vexingly handsome, he is all elbows and ears, with ginger hair and eyes the color of the summer sky. A pair of ladies pass by as they enter, and they giggle at him behind their hands. He doesn't notice. "David!" he cries, sweeping me into an embrace. "See? I am on time."

"The stars are in alignment," I reply.

"Ha. Are you well? You look troubled."

"I had an odd appointment."

He grimaces. "How so?"

"It was a new client. A young woman."

His eyebrow raises. "Oh?"

I describe my new patient's symptoms in vague terms, cautious not to reveal her identity. The entire appointment still feels utterly incredible, a memory I have somehow exaggerated. Speaking to Cecilia Thorowgood felt like weaving through pikes, a single stumble risking injury. Her appearance, too, had been almost unreal, so severe and arresting—a face like pyrite, sharp and steel-eyed and furious—that when I looked at her, I felt as if I would cut myself. It felt as if I had been the patient, not her.

"It seems as much a disease of the mind as the body," Jan says.

"Yes."

"Is there something to be done for that?"

"Perhaps. I believe some medicines can help ease melancholy, but many physicians would disagree."

"Hm. Well—don't trouble yourself over it," he says. "You will do what you can, and that is enough."

He seizes me by the arm, steering me into the park. I follow, stumbling after him, trying to match his gait. The renovations made to the park are impressive, opulent and effusive, paths studded with square-trimmed hedges and white gravel. It is still odd to see such pride in luxury. I came to this country at the height of its commonwealth severity, but now the king's return has transformed it entirely. London is beholden to its master, as are its people; just as fashion now strides toward wigs and lace and ribbons, the city, too, adorns itself in finery.

"How goes *your* business?" I ask Jan as we meander toward the square. "Did the new shipment of beans arrive?"

"It is in France!"

"France? Why?"

"I shall tell you," he says, launching into a story.

He speaks incessantly as we continue. We earn some sneers from passersby; Jan and I make a mismatched, almost comical pair—our coloring is in such intense opposition—and we wear our foreignness unashamedly, having long realized the futility of hiding it. We have been teaching each other our mother tongues, and we speak in a bizarre mixture of Portuguese, Dutch, and English. This only further serves to displease the genteel crowd in the park, and it is little help that my heritage is so apparent in my features. One woman crosses herself when she sees me. I make no reaction.

Noticing her, Jan mutters a curse under his breath. "I hope she falls into the canal."

"Jan, come. Such things happen."

He sighs. "I wish you weren't so resigned to it. I mean—I wish you did not have to be."

I don't respond. We fall into silence, interrupted only by the crunch of the gravel beneath our feet.

Eventually, we reach the main square, which has been fenced off with iron. It contains a horde of visitors. Ladies bunch together in laughing splotches of pink and green, while gentlemen brandish canes at each other. Between them, children dart back and forth, shoving hands into the water, spraying anyone who dares cross their path. It is hot enough that such play invites mere grumbling rather than seething rage.

The crowd provides the wondrous sort of anonymity unique to large cities. Jan and I invite nothing more than hazy glances before attention is subsumed by the noise and color of the summer. A pamphleteer standing on the fountain's edge spots us and shouts, "Sirs! A moment of your time, I bid you!" We ignore him. The pamphleteer, disappointed, waves a fistful of papers at another pair of gentlemen. "Sirs, consider the Trinitarians—" he says. One gentleman interrupts, "Bollocks to your Trinitarians," earning a hooting laugh from his companion.

We move on, pausing to rest by the southern gate.

"It is a fair fountain," Jan says. The sculpture is of naiads dancing, water spouting between them to rise in eight arcs. The base is set unusually low to the ground, providing an opportunity capitalized upon by some of the children: One young girl splashes shoeless in a corner, notably grimy in contrast to the well-to-do crowd. As we watch, she bunches her skirts to her knees, revealing ankles made blade-sharp by malnutrition. Scandalized glances don't dissuade her. She is unaccompanied, and she will be removed by a beadle soon enough. For now, she tips her head downward, laughing at the water between her toes.

A hawker passes by with a tray of pies. Jan's head turns to follow her.

"Go on," I say. "I'll wait."

He makes in the direction of the hawker, hand hovering over his purse. I watch him for a few moments before I look back to the fountain. A summer breeze passes through the square. It brings with it the scent of sap and brief coolness.

My father would love to see this place. If only I could take him here. He adores crowds, adores the variety of London, the noise of it. *Everyone and anyone,* he would say. *Look, Davi: At least for now, we are the same as them. We are all united here, in Saint James's Park.*

Someone walks directly into me. I stagger back and meet a pair of startlingly green eyes. It is a young man, dressed in pastel-colored clothing covered in ribbons, so that he streams like a kite in the breeze. He is soft featured, pale skinned, with a long wig that flows in light brown curls to his middle back. While well groomed, his sparse mustache seems somewhat halfhearted in its countenance.

"Pardon, sir!" he exclaims. "It seems my feet are most stubborn today; they refuse to cooperate with the rest of me. I have been stumbling every which way and what way and find myself most perplexed by the entire affair."

"I—no matter," I reply, puzzled. He sweeps a very deep bow, looks about himself with great confusion, and then wanders into the crowd. I follow his progress with some concern, frowning to myself.

Jan returns. "Are you well, David?" he asks, seeing my baffled expression.

"Yes, fine."

He has settled with the pie hawker, it seems, for he clutches two pastries in his hands. He offers me one. "Apple," he says.

"I can't have a pie, Jan," I say. "There is lard in it."

"Oh. I am arse brained sometimes."

"Give it here." He passes it to me, and I walk over to the fountain, where the young girl is still splashing in the water. When she notices me, she takes a step back, frightened; I suppose that isn't surprising.

I offer her the pie. "Here."

She is wary, but too hungry to refuse. Her hands dart out with the speed of a comet, and she snatches the pie from me.

"Thanks," she mumbles, and she crams half of it into her mouth.

"Eat slowly, or your stomach will ache."

Ignoring the instruction, she chews the pastry openmouthed, crumbs falling into the water below. I sigh and leave her be, returning to Jan, who is smiling at me.

"We ought to return here soon. And let's go out tomorrow evening, also," he says. "I know you have no appointments then."

"I shouldn't," I reply. "I told my father I would go to synagogue."

"Will you?" he asks, and I wince.

"I ought to."

"We could always go another evening—"

"Not— I don't know," I say. Unimpressed, he stares at me, eyebrows raised. "I . . . Very well. Tomorrow. But not Mother Tiffin's."

"Why not Mother Tiffin's?"

"I'm not in the mood, Jan. Just an alehouse, please."

He claps his hands. "Very well!" he exclaims too loudly. "An alehouse it is."

He seems so relieved that I am willing to spend time with him, and I feel somewhat ashamed by it. I know that I have been solitary as of late. I have kept myself busy, kept myself distracted. Somehow, the simple act of living has become exhausting; it has led me to neglect him.

Driven by guilt, I ask Jan if he will have supper at my home. He agrees very happily. We take a cab together. As we drive, he talks of coffee and the fountain and his current Great Love, Peter, who has been his Great Love thrice before and shall no doubt soon cede the position to someone else. I pretend to listen, but I am dwelling upon the shock in the eyes of the girl in the fountain, and Cecilia Thorowgood's shuddering breaths, and the woman crossing herself as I passed her. I should be used to such things; I should be accustomed to both grief and prejudice. It feels a failing of mine when I allow them to trouble me so.

We pay the fare. I open the door to allow Jan into my house, and he passes through. I pause to glance at the mezuzah, raising my fingers to it. For a moment, I believe I will touch it, but I don't. Instead, I drop my hand and follow him inside.

I am picked up by a carriage the next morning for my return to the Eden townhouse. It is a marvelous thing, gilded like a Bible, with the initials R. E. emblazoned upon the door. The horses are white, and the driver has a blond wig with ribbons tied to its ends. We rattle through the city, people staring as we pass.

The gates of the townhouse are opened for us, and we are brought into the courtyard. I step down to the cobblestones and look back to the fence. I hadn't noticed yesterday, but the gates are crowned at either side with bizarre stone objects. They look something like pinecones with hats. I frown at them, trying to decipher their meaning, but I find no answer.

The footman leads me inside. The foyer is as horrifyingly gauche as it was the last time I saw it: decorated in a gaudy and expensive combination of green and gold, a large portrait of a frowning Cavalier glowering at me to the left of the stairs. Beside it stands a tall case clock, inlaid with mother-of-pearl, which shows the tides of the river on its face rather than the time. Countless mirrors glitter on the walls, expanding the room from enormous to gargantuan.

Lady Eden appears at the top of the steps. I am once again struck by how dissimilar she looks to her sister. Mistress Thorowgood was almost cruel in her features; there was a sense of defiance inherent in her sharp chin and small, pointed nose. Lady Eden, by contrast, is soft featured, wide waisted, with broad shoulders and deep dimples in each cheek. It is a welcoming face, but it still becomes distinctly hostile when she notices me, and she pauses halfway down the steps. I do my best to hide my unease. I have become unfortunately accustomed to detecting disdain, despite a sincere desire to remain ignorant to it. There haven't been Jews in this country for more than three centuries, after all; I don't expect that the good lady was one of those calling for our return.

"Master Mendes," Lady Eden says.

I bow. "Greetings, my lady. I have brought with me some medicines for Mistress Thorowgood, as promised."

"I see. You can leave them with the footman."

"I would like to explain their administration to her, if it pleases you."

She replies archly, "You might as well explain it to me, as I shall be in charge of giving them to her."

"Medicines are most effective when taken with full consent of the patient."

"Why is that?" she asks. "Her previous physicians felt no need to consult her. I have given Cecilia many medicines in her food without her knowledge, and it was for the best, I feel, as she would have refused them otherwise."

I am quite horrified by this, and I do not know how to respond. If I were a braver man, perhaps—a better one—I would admonish her. Instead, I say in a pleading tone, "I understand that the other physicians had their own methods, as I have mine. I have been trained as a physician since I was a boy; I am accredited by the Royal College in Lisbon. If I am to help your sister, you must have faith in my recommendations."

Her grip on the banister tightens, knuckles whitening with the force. She glares at me. For a moment, I wonder if she will order me to leave. Then she closes her eyes and shakes her head, recentering herself before she descends the steps to stand in front of me.

"This is of the utmost importance, Master Mendes," she says. "My sister's recovery is paramount, do you understand?"

"Of course."

"Do you believe she will soon be well?"

"I . . . It is difficult to say as of yet, my lady."

She considers me for a moment, eyes narrowed. "As your employer, I trust I have your confidence, sir."

"Of course," I repeat, confused.

"She must be better by the end of the summer. She is to be married before the fall."

I raise my brows. Cecilia Thorowgood had hardly seemed the picture of a blushing bride. "I hadn't realized she was betrothed."

"She isn't—not yet. Once she is prepared, I shall introduce her to her suitor. He is a relative of my husband's, you see. Robert was rather keen on introducing them; he never would have consented to her presence here otherwise. And if she remains so sickly . . . Well. I have been begging Robert to give her more time, but there is only so long a wife's pleas may be heard." She seems genuinely aggrieved by this, wringing her hands, but her gaze remains sharp and calculating. "We wouldn't want Cecilia sent back to solitude in Suffolk, would we? I think both of us know how disastrous such a thing would be for her delicate constitution."

Astonished, I don't know how to reply. Lady Eden takes my silence as acquiescence, and nods curtly at me, taking a step back.

"Cecilia is in the courtyard," she tells me. "Give her your medicines; explain them to her. I will be watching from the windows. She will trust you more if she thinks I am not there."

A marriage Mistress Thorowgood is entirely ignorant of; I ought to inform her, surely? I can imagine how Manuel would have reacted to such a thing: his grave face, solemn eyes. Always so unflinching in his principles, even when he risked disaster. *You must do what you feel is best, David,* he'd say, but we'd both know what he really meant. To him honesty was worth more than gold.

But Manuel isn't here—not anymore—and I must make this

decision alone. If I did tell her, what would be the outcome? My dismissal and her expulsion from the townhouse? When she meets her suitor, she will be able to refuse him if she wishes—her sister could hardly force the matter, could she? Besides, my position is too precarious. The Edens have the ability to see me utterly destroyed, if they so wish.

I decide to remain silent, but I hate myself for it.

Perhaps Father was right. I ought never to have answered that letter at all.

In the courtyard, the first thing I take note of is the linden: I had been nervous enough on my first arrival here that I hadn't taken time to inspect it. It is an impressive specimen, blooming early. Beneath its canopy of white flowers, Mistress Thorowgood—Cecilia—stands in the grass, her bare toes rippling against the soil, raising her chin to the sun. Her hair hangs in a dark-gold sheet to her elbows, uncurled and uncombed. She is wearing only a chemise; it is too large, gaping at the neck. Her feet are bare. I am stricken once again by her thinness, which—while not quite yet to the point of danger—still lends her a fragile, serrated quality. She is like a glass knife, sharp and brittle, as likely to shatter as to cut.

Blue-gray eyes meet mine. "Master Mendes," she says.

I am disarmed, by both her state of undress and the intensity of her gaze. "Mistress Thorowgood. Forgive me, I . . . Are you not cold?"

She glances down at herself. The chemise slips lower, revealing the slope of her shoulder, and I glance studiously away. "I am fine," she says.

I step forward and shrug off my jacket, offering it to her. It is a favorite of mine, silver-green wool, softened with use. She gives it a disdainful look. "I said I was fine."

"You will catch a chill."

She ignores this and turns around, walking a loop of the tree. Tucking the jacket beneath my arm, I sit down on one of the iron chairs and gesture to my case. "May I show you the medicines I have brought?" I ask her once she is back in view.

She doesn't respond. A breeze passes over us, and she shivers.

"Take my jacket," I say.

"I don't want it," she repeats, but her tone is uncertain. She curls her arms around herself.

I toss the jacket at her. She catches it and huffs in annoyance, but she still puts it on. Meanwhile, I open my case and put the bottles on the edge of the fountain. She watches me, but still doesn't approach.

"May I ask you a question?" I say.

She narrows her eyes. "That depends on what it is."

"On the gates of the townhouse, there are carved some strange pinecones. I couldn't identify them. Do you know what they are?"

"Pinecones," she says, frowning. She spends a good while considering this. Then she splutters. "You—you mean the pineapples?"

"Pineapples," I repeat, mystified, and she nods. "These are a fruit?"

"Yes."

"Are they common in England? All my years here, I have never seen them."

She shakes her head. "They are foreign."

"From where?"

"I don't know. Robert had one imported last month. China, probably."

I say, "China must be a country even stranger than I had imagined, if they are able to grow apples on gates."

At that she laughs properly, turning her head away as if to stop me from seeing. As she does so, her hand flutters over her belly as if it hurts from the movement; I make a mental note to revise the dosage of the centaury decoction.

Once she recovers, she says, "May I ask you a question, Master Mendes?"

"Of course."

"Where do you come from?"

"Aldgate." Seeing her suffering look, I relent. "I was born in Portugal. Have you ever been?"

"Oh no. I've never left England. I imagine you're far better traveled than I."

"I haven't traveled that much. I have only seen Lisbon, and Granada, and here."

"Granada?"

"Yes." She is inching closer now—clearly compelled by the topic—so I continue. "A city in the south of Spain. It is very beautiful."

She sits down in the chair opposite me, cocking her head. "Is it different from London?"

"Extremely so. Different from Lisbon, also. There is nowhere else like it. There is a castle there, called Alhambra, a Moorish building with walls of orange and white. When the sun falls upon it, it lights the land gold. There are great plains beneath, and mountains of orange stone. Their color spreads across the grass."

Her eyes pass beyond my shoulder, as if looking somewhere far away. Her lashes flutter, lids drooping; it occurs to me that she is very beautiful, and—horrified I would allow myself such a thought—I look down at the curlicued ironwork of the table.

She says, "It sounds wonderful."

"It is."

"I'd like to see it," she says. "I'd like to see something beautiful again."

I clear my throat, gesturing to the bottles on the table. "I have three decoctions for you."

"Decoctions?"

"Mild medicines, made by boiling herbs in water. The first is mint and centaury; one swallow to be taken before meals, one after, to settle your stomach. The second is ginger and gentian, two swallows in the mornings. That should, I hope, provoke your appetite."

"And the third?"

"Epithymum. One swallow. It is best mixed with ale."

"What is that?" she asks.

"It's a parasitic plant," I reply with inordinate pride; it is difficult to grow, and I was glad to find it in my garden that morning. "It grows on thyme, and it soothes melancholy."

"Melancholy," she repeats, face twisting into a scowl. "I am not mad, Master Mendes."

"I didn't imply you were. Grief causes melancholy. Would you deny this?"

"I . . . I suppose that I wouldn't."

I ask, "And would you deny that you are grieving? You told me yesterday that you were."

"I did," she says. "But to call me *melancholy*—that is too much, surely."

"Even so, there is little harm in taking the decoction."

She stands up and leans forward, looming over me, her hands planted on the table.

"Herbs can't cure loss," she says. "They can't remove memory."

"I never claimed they could."

"Suppose I refused to take this epi—ep—plant. Would you force it upon me?"

I feel another moment of resentment toward Lady Eden. She has taken advantage of her sister's weakness, and her actions have made my work immeasurably harder. "Of course not," I say.

"Then I won't take it," Cecilia tells me.

"Very well."

My agreement deflates her, and her shoulders drop. I wish I could convince her otherwise, but I know a lost cause when I see it.

Still, it's a great shame that she won't take the epithymum. I suspect it would help her, as it is clear she is suffering attacks of panic, and that is what leads her to vomit. This isn't surprising, as many issues of the gut are the result of the mind. We think of the heart as the house of emotion, but that burden is shared with the stomach—and, indeed, every other part of ourselves. We could never feel something as powerful as love or hatred without the aid of every organ available to us.

Cecilia blanches, and she sways in place. Alarmed, I step forward, offering her my arm. She takes it instinctively, then frowns, as if chiding herself for it. But she allows me to lead her out of the courtyard and back to her rooms. As much as I'd like to keep her in the fresh air longer, it is clear she needs to eat.

Once we reach her chambers, she slides into the bed. I pour her a glass of water.

"Is there something else wrong with me?" she asks. "Is it something more than grief?"

"It needn't be more than grief."

"What do you mean?"

"They are great burdens to bear, these bodies of ours," I say. "Miracles, but burdens, also. They are complex machines, and each part must work together for them to function. Just as an injury to an organ might cause the machine to fail, so might an injury to the soul."

"It wasn't only an injury," she says. "It feels worse than that. It feels like a death. I feel like I died with him."

I don't know who Cecilia is speaking of. But I understand her meaning, far better than I wish I did—and reflected in her face, I see myself as much as I see her. I see myself the day I lost Manuel, the day I left Lisbon; I see David Mendes one year ago, looking at himself in the mirror as the city died around him. Sometimes I tell myself I have left that haunted man behind. And yet he is here still, in a stranger's home, with a stranger's blue-gray eyes, and a stranger's grief pulled around him like a tallith.

I approach her, placing the glass of water on the bedside table. Reaching forward, I take her arm very gently, pressing my fingers to her wrist.

She stares at me until I pull away.

"Your heart beats, Cecilia," I say. "You are living still."

She doesn't respond. I gesture to the water and tell her, "Drink. I will send for breakfast. What would you like?"

"Nothing," she replies. I frown, and she sighs. "Some bread and cheese, I suppose."

I bow to her. She is still wearing my jacket, but I can't bring myself to demand its return. She is shivering, frail and exhausted, paler than ivory. It is warm enough outside; I shall retrieve it when I next come to examine her.

Cecilia exhales a long, shuddering breath. She stares down at her wrist, where my fingers had pressed against her pulse. "Forgive me," she says. "I acted childishly today. I have enough enemies in my mind alone; I needn't create another in you, Master Mendes. You have done nothing to deserve the misfortune of my company."

This is so unexpected I gawp at her, and reply with only, "Oh." A smile flickers over her face, brief as a gust of wind.

"I am cruel, sometimes," she says. "Forgive me for it. There is an anger inside of me, and it is eating me alive. Like your parasite growing upon the thyme. I wish I knew how to remove it."

"We will find a way," I reply. "Will you take the decoctions?"

"I don't know. Some of them. Not the one for melancholy."

I nod—it is the best I could hope for, considering. "Will you allow me to return?"

"Yes," she says, plucking at the sheets with her fingers. "Very well. If you must."

"Then I shall."

She gives me a wary look, eyes searching. It is as if she has sensed my inadequacy, as if she has realized I am afflicted by the same sickness she is. Loss, grief, melancholy—perhaps she is correct, and these are all symptoms without cure.

Then the suspicion fades from her expression, and she smiles at me hesitantly. I smile back. Something like peace passes between us. Her face no longer seems cruel to me, not as it did the first time we met. Her features are still sharp, and yet they are now softened, like sea glass, weathered by the tides. A victory, no matter how small.

Then, unbidden, I remember her sister in that jewel-carpeted foyer, the ticking of the pearl-faced clock. *Married before the fall,* Lady Eden had said.

Perhaps not a victory, after all.

CHAPTER FIVE

Cecilia

David Mendes returns three more times that week. We meet in the courtyard, upon my insistence, where he ensures I take my decoctions—except the one for melancholy, which he will not force upon me, although I can tell he wishes to. He watches me walk around the linden tree, asks me how I am feeling, and then leaves. All in all, we spend less than an hour together each day. We remain only oddly familiar strangers, with Margaret watching us from the side of the courtyard, pretending to scribble in her commonplace book.

One morning, as usual, I take my decoctions and begin my circuits around the tree. Mendes stands beside the fountain and watches me. He always waits a little while after I have taken the medicine; I suppose to see if I will keep it down.

"Why do you always do that?" Mendes asks me as I finish my first loop.

"Do what?"

"Walk around the tree?"

"If I didn't, I would forget how to walk at all," I tell him. "There is nowhere else to go."

When I make another turn and see his face again, he looks perturbed. "What about outside?"

"We are outside."

He sighs. "Outside the townhouse, I mean."

"Why?" I ask. "There is little point in leaving. Best I stay where I am."

"You can't remain here forever."

"Why not? I have seen London before, and I know what it is like. It is full of stink, and crowds, and disease."

He makes a galled noise. I cannot see him—I am currently on the other side of the tree—but I can imagine the aggravation in his expression, and it makes me smile.

"If you dislike London so much," he says, "then why did you come here in the first place?"

"I didn't have much choice," I reply. "It was this or a grave; but that doesn't mean I have to like it here. That doesn't mean I have to be *grateful* for it."

"This or a grave," he echoes. "What do you mean?"

"I was alone in the estate, after my husband died. I had visitors, but . . . I was unwell. Even more so than now."

Still making my slow loop of the linden, I look to my hand, sprawled across the tree's trunk. My fingers are curled, as if clinging to something, to prevent me from falling.

There was a well at the base of a hill near our manor. Five times, I sat on the edge and stared down into the hungry dark, imagining pushing myself forward. I never did. Perhaps I would have, had I stayed. I suppose I should be grateful I left when I could.

I walk into something. Startled, I stumble back: Mendes

has looped the linden in the opposite direction, and we have crashed into each other. He grabs my arm to prevent me from falling.

I look down at his hand, and then cast a warning glance to where Margaret is standing at the courtyard's entrance; she is on the other side of the tree, thankfully, and she can't see us.

Chagrined, Mendes releases me. His face is flushed. "Pardon."

"It's fine."

I am unaccountably flustered, and for a moment all I can do is shuffle my feet and look at the ground.

He clears his throat. I glance back up. "Do you ever consider remarrying?" he asks.

This is such an abrupt question that I snort. "Who would marry *me*?"

Something guilty passes over his face, but I can't begin to speculate why. "I didn't mean to imply . . . Forgive me. It's only—do you intend to spend the rest of your days here, in this house, alone?"

It sounds so awful when he puts it like that; it isn't as if I have *planned* to spend my life grieving. It just seems so impossible that I could do anything else.

He continues. "Even if London scares you, the answer is not to shut yourself inside this place and force yourself to malady. Find somewhere else to go instead. Meet new people. Swear to me that you will consider it?"

I look at his face. He is a handsome man, I see that now. He has a complicated sort of beauty, not the sort of open, smiling gorgeousness of Will, or the gentle prettiness of my rose-cheeked sister. His is the sort of face that, like a well-read book, is somehow lovelier for its cracks and lines, that invites you to study it for hours, until you can look at and think of nothing else.

We stare at each other, silent. A linden flower falls from the bough above him, landing on his hair. Acting on instinct, I reach forward and remove it, combing the petals out with my fingers.

He blinks at me. Perhaps I should be embarrassed, but I only feel relieved he didn't flinch.

I drop the flower. It is often said in fairy stories that it is impossible to tell a lie beneath a linden tree, and I know as I reply to him that I will have to keep to my word.

"I will consider it," I tell him, and his baffled expression softens.

"Good."

"How many appointments do we have left?"

He says, "Just one. Next week."

"Next week," I say. "And then you shall be free of me."

I say it with a small, bitter smile—a lamentation as much as a joke—but Mendes shakes his head. "You are not a burden, Cecilia."

It is such a simple statement, an inane comfort, and yet something about it almost brings me to tears. I look at the linden flower I pulled out of his hair, pinched between my thumb and forefinger. I have crushed the bulb; sticky, sweet-smelling sap glues the petals to my skin.

My sister calls my name. I wipe my hand on the tree's trunk.

"Thank you," I say to him. "For everything."

He watches me in silence as I walk away.

Over the next week, I decline to take the decoction for melancholy, although the other medicines do seem to have done some good. I have found my stomach has settled a little, and I haven't vomited again. But perhaps that is simply due to the easement of my loneliness, a reprieve I will soon lose once Mendes is dismissed.

The day of my final appointment with him, I wake up to see that a storm has brewed overnight. Crawling out of bed, I run my hands over the shutters of the window. The sky is ashen, in contrast to the idyllic blue of the day before. Rain smacks against the glass in obdurate handfuls. It is as if nature herself admonishes me for not staying asleep.

I *could* sleep more if I wanted to. But I feel oddly impatient, as if there is something I should do, but can't remember. The three decoctions Mendes gave me sit expectantly upon my desk. I ignore them.

The clouds outside rumble. Something in the construction of the townhouse's roof amplifies the noise, and the rain sounds like falling rubble, the thunder cannon fire. It feels closer to a siege than a storm. To soothe my anxiety, I walk in a circuit around the room, taking each step slowly and methodically, eyes following the movements of my feet. I pause at the window, staring at the house on the other side of the street. There, a figure shifts behind a pane of glass: the same silhouette I have seen before. It pauses, also, and it raises its hand. I wave back. We are twin shadows, greeting each other across the void.

I am startled by the sound of the door opening. Margaret enters, bearing a tray of pastries and a tea service.

"Good morning," she says with false cheer. "Are you well, Cecilia?"

"Well enough," I reply. It is not a bad day, I think, although perhaps it is too early to tell.

She lays out breakfast on the table. "I thought we could eat together."

I make a noncommittal sound and sit on the mattress. Meanwhile, Margaret continues to babble about the weather and the newest fashions at court. When she compels me to join her, I prod the food, silent, as her voice fills the space between us. It is not a conversation. It is a performance I am watching.

It has been like this since Margaret married Robert. The first time I came to visit her in London, for instance, I brought honey cakes. She nibbled around the edges of one like a hare, leaving the center untouched on her plate. Once, I would have snatched the rest from her, but I couldn't make myself reach across the table to do so. Some new sense of propriety had leashed me to the chair. She poured me tea, but only after asking, *Tea, Cecilia?* Once, she would have simply gestured to the pot. Our conversation now required effort to maintain. We were sisters still, but no longer friends.

Watching her now, chattering nervously to prevent me from speaking, I suddenly feel the loss of our childhood connection very keenly, like a splinter being pulled from skin. Margaret wants me to live with her, I think, because she wants a project to work on, someone to care for in the absence of a child. But I am not a child anymore; neither of us is. She has lost most of me, and now she clings to the small part that is left. It won't work. I know what loss is like, and she can't prevent it. Nothing can prevent it.

". . . a new portrait," she was saying. "Myself as Diana. Won't that be wonderful?"

"Oh, yes, very."

"We could have you painted, also, Cecilia."

I look down at my wrists—the way they jut out flintlike beneath the skin—and say wryly, "There isn't much of me left to paint."

"Hush, you'd make a lovely subject." She pauses. "What have you done with it?" she asks, voice gentle. "The wedding portrait?"

"I left it at the estate."

"You'll want it returned."

"I will not," I reply. "It feels vulgar to look at it; some foolish way of pretending, as if all is as it was."

"You must want some memory of him."

"I remember Will already. Sometimes I wish I didn't."

This shocks her. "You shouldn't say such things," she says. "You are permitted to miss him. You can do so and still move forward."

"Move forward?"

"Surely you will not spend your life a widow?"

First Mendes, now her. What is this obsession with my re-marrying? Who would want me now? Will is with me always; I can hardly remove his touch from my skin, like peeling the rind of a fruit, and offer my flesh anew. "I don't want a new husband," I tell her.

She links her hands in her lap and wrings them. "Cecilia, I am allowed to be concerned. As long as you live here, I will care for you."

"I don't see what that has to do with my marriage."

"There are so many eligible men at court. Wouldn't that be wonderful?"

"Wonderful for *you*—to have your sister a lady, and your status affirmed."

She sighs. "It isn't that," she says, admonishing. "You know I speak only out of concern for your well-being. You could be very happy, I think. If you were to marry a lord, you could play harp-sichord for the *king*, just as you always dreamed of—do you remember?"

Playing for the king: a childhood fancy, long discarded. I scowl, but I don't bother replying. Instead, I stare stonily at my plate.

Margaret follows my gaze. Her face pinches. "You've eaten nothing. Have one bite, I beg of you."

One bite. It is doable. I raise the cake to my lips, and I make an incision with my teeth, cutting a wafer-thin slice. It sits heavy in my mouth, doughy and cloying.

"There," Margaret says, satisfied.

I swallow, and I smile at her without feeling, using my tongue to scrub the crumbs away from my teeth.

Afterward, I go to the music room. It is early evening; the sun is setting, and its light bronzes my skin. All is very quiet, and the air is still. It almost feels as if the townhouse outside this room is abandoned, as if London itself has been emptied of people. All that exists is me and the spinet: my dearest friend in this place. It is a shrunken version of the harpsichord I grew up with, and I have grown quite fond of it. The compulsion to play is one of few things that still draws me out of bed.

The spinet's case is very fine, veneered in dark wood. The ivory is still glossy. I hover my hands over the keys, and I smash down, vindictive, producing a dissonant holler that seems to make the very walls tremble. It is intensely gratifying.

I arrange my fingers for an old pavane my mother made me learn. I begin, think better of it, and begin again. The movements bring forth memories of dismal hours spent practicing it as a child, when each note had been embossed upon my skull, and my hands turned to claws. But even this song now presents an escape, in this miniature life I am living. By resurrecting it, I briefly become Cecilia at twelve years old, for whom this pavane was the greatest evil she had ever known. And despite the hatred I once had for it, I realize now that it is a very sweet song. It seems to follow itself, ebbing and rising. I begin it again, and then a third time. Upon this third playing, the music feels complete. The spinet strikes each note cleanly and harshly; when I finish, the silence covers me like cloth over a birdcage.

Someone clears their throat. I look over my shoulder to see my sister and Mendes in the doorway, watching me. Margaret is wearing an awful expression, pitying and nostalgic. I can only imagine what she must think of me, playing childhood songs on her husband's spinet, a ghost in a dressing gown. But beside her, Mendes is smiling with neither sympathy nor horror. He seems quite impressed.

"You play beautifully," he says.

Embarrassed, I look back to the keys, pressing a high note. "Thank you."

My sister wavers in the doorway, fiddling awkwardly with her skirts—clearly wanting to intercede, but uncertain how to do so.

A voice calls her name from downstairs: her husband's. The timing feels like providence. Grimacing, she glances at the door.

"You needn't stay if you'd rather leave, Maggie," I tell her. "I'm certain Master Mendes just wants to ask about the effects of his medicines. It won't take long."

She gives me a suffering look, but Lord Eden's wishes must trump either of ours; it has always been so. "Once you are finished, go directly to our steward," she tells Mendes, opening the door with some reluctance. Sir Eden shouts for her again, and she cries, "Yes, darling, one moment!" as she leaves.

Once she is gone, Mendes gestures to the spinet. "You really do play beautifully. How long . . . ?"

"Since I was a girl. Margaret sings along, sometimes." I tap at a key absentmindedly, feeling the spinet hum in response. "At first, Mother thought to have us duet, but my voice is terrible.

She soon lost hope, and she set me upon the harpsichord instead."

Mendes sits on the chair by the desk, folding one leg over the other. I play another note, considering a fantasia, but I can't commit to it.

"I haven't taken the cure for melancholy," I say. "But I've attempted the others."

Mendes frowns. He has trimmed his beard, and I can see his lopsided jaw more clearly. Despite the asymmetry, his chin is quite square and sharp, the sort one might find upon a Roman bust. His nose, too, is an emperor's nose. With his dark curls, he might pass for Hadrian.

He asks, "Have you seen any improvement?"

"My stomach has been calmer," I reply begrudgingly. "I won't take anything else, mind you, but—"

"I didn't intend to prescribe anything else."

"Oh?"

"As you have responded well to the medicines," he says, "I doubt we need to meet again. It is my hope that eventually you will take the epithymum. I shall send more decoctions, once you finish them, but apart from that, there is little else I can do for you."

"Is that all?" I ask, surprised. "You're leaving for good, after three bottles of medicine and a brisk farewell? My sister's money might have been better spent elsewhere."

Rather than being insulted at this, he shrugs, as if it is a fair criticism. "If you seek further improvement, the best treatment would be a change in location," he says. "I still don't believe you are happy here."

"Margaret takes care of me."

"Does she," he says in an unreadable tone.

"Yes, she does. If I were left alone—I don't know what I would do. I am incapable of making myself happy."

"Are you incapable of it," he replies, "or has your sister convinced you that you are?"

I splutter in consternation. "You shouldn't criticize her. She is the one paying your wages."

"But you are my patient. Your recovery is more important than her satisfaction."

"Then *treat* me, instead of leaving."

"I thought you didn't want me to treat you."

"I—" Sighing, I tip my head back. "I don't know what I want. I would like someone else to do the wanting, for once."

Mendes says, "Then this is my final prescription to you, Cecilia: freedom, in as large a dose as you can manage. Leave this awful house and go into the city. Find somewhere you enjoy being. Drink coffee, make friends, visit theaters. *Live*."

"You say that as if it is easy."

"It isn't easy," he says. "But it is possible."

Possible for some. I snap, "Oh, indeed. I suppose *you* must be very happy, Master Mendes, with your perfect life, full of coffee and theaters and friends. I suppose your freedom has erased all the grief you have ever felt, and London has cured you of all the sickness you have ever suffered."

I expect him to retort, but he doesn't. He opens his mouth, closes it, and then goes quiet.

In the wake of his silence, I feel ashamed at my petulance. I tap mournfully at a spinet key. "Forgive me. I know . . . I understand why you feel I should leave. My life here is so small; I must seem so pitiful to you. But I was worth something, once, I swear. Before . . . before it all."

"You are still worthy," Mendes says.

I reply, "Not enough."

He doesn't respond. He is looking at me with something deeper than pity. In his expression, I see some element of understanding that feels unlike anything I have seen since Will's death. I have a sudden urge to step closer to him, but I don't. We regard each other in mutual regret.

"My husband's name was Will," I say. "He died last spring. Plague. It was—difficult. He suffered. I stayed with him the entire time, but I didn't get sick at all."

Mendes says quietly, "Plague is cruel, in that manner. It does not always share its burden."

"You lost someone, too?"

He pauses, bites his lip. "A friend."

The word seems to carry some hidden sort of weight, a second meaning I can't fully comprehend. "What were they like?" I ask.

"He was . . ." Mendes sighs. "Good. Kind, and honest, and principled to the core."

"Like you," I reply.

He makes a shocked sort of laugh, as if I have said something utterly absurd. "And your Will?" he asks. "What was he like?"

"Good, also. Joyous and loving. He was so much better at being happy than I am." My stomach twists. I hunch over the spinet. "Pardon. It hurts to remember him. I usually don't speak of it."

"I know."

"It's only . . . sometimes I feel as if I am being cruel to him, for being as I am. I know he would want me to be happy, but I can't be. I loved him so much. I don't know why this happened to me. Why was I the one burdened with survival? Why was he the one who went away?"

His hand raises slightly, then falls. "I . . ." he says, and his breath stutters. "I wish I could give you an answer. I can't. But you are not being cruel to anyone by being unwell. The only person you owe your happiness to is yourself, Cecilia. Remember that."

I bow my head, blinking back tears. Clearing my throat, I say, "No matter," and drag a finger across the spinet. "Shall I play another song?"

"If you wish."

I play a toccata. The piece is monstrously difficult—I have struggled over it for years—but it is still a fair rendition.

"I can't perfect that song," I admit to him once I have finished it. "Something is missing. I don't know what."

"It sounded perfect to my ear," Mendes says.

"Then your ear is terrible."

He chuckles. "How does it work?"

"How does what work?"

"The spinet," he says. "How does it produce sound?"

"You don't know?" I ask, astonished. "Aren't you a man of learning?"

He flushes. "I've never had occasion to read upon the workings of instruments. If it were a tree, or a shrub, I might be more knowledgeable."

"It isn't a shrub, certainly. Come here."

I shift to make room for him beside me. He approaches and stares down at the keys.

"When you press down, it moves one of several levers inside," I tell him. "And the lever plucks a string."

"As a lutenist does?"

"Yes, I suppose so."

He hovers a finger over a key, giving me an inquisitive look. I nod, and he presses down. The spinet sounds a note as Mendes smiles, pleased; my own hands are still on the keys, and the vibration of it seems to travel up my fingers and through my arms, to the center of my chest. I play the same note, an octave lower. His smile widens.

He plays another, and I echo again.

"*I* ought to be mimicking *you*," he says. "As you are the musician."

"You are also a musician now," I reply. Still, I say, "Try this," and play him the simplest section of the toccata: a straightforward melody, albeit deceptively ornate to the ear. He looks so horrified in response I almost laugh at him.

"I can't do that."

"You can." Without thinking, I stretch sideways to lay my hand upon his, right over left, the tips of my fingers pressed against his knuckles. He freezes. I realize too late that I have been impulsive—overfamiliar—but I see no recourse except to forge ahead and tolerate the embarrassment.

As gently as I can, I use my fingers to press his against the keys, playing the same melody again by proxy. "There," I say, pleased, looking sideways at him.

Our positions have brought us quite close together. I find myself cataloguing details I haven't noticed before: he has another tiny pox scar where his right ear meets his hairline, barely visible beneath a dark curl. His ears are small and round; he smells of garden herbs—rosemary and thyme—their perfume overlaying that intangible sort of heat men sometimes have, a scent that makes me lean slightly closer and my breath catch. He is still looking down at our hands upon the spinet, smiling slightly. Then his eyes meet my own, and suddenly all is very silent.

We are both frozen. The room is a book we have been pressed within, preserved like flowers. The only thing of substance is his touch, an unbearable warmth where his skin presses against my own.

I open my mouth to speak, but I make no sound. Instead, I play the notes again with his fingers, uncertain what else to do. The sound is soft, more a sigh than a song. Beneath my palm, his hand flexes with the movements; I feel the shift of each tendon and bone.

We are still looking at each other. I can't find the will to pull away.

With my other hand, I play the melody a third time. As I do so, I feel the notes press themselves into my memory, and I feel David Mendes joining them. I think, *Oh, I will never see him again—never,* and I feel a sudden ache within myself, grief for a possibility dead before it could be born. *Don't,* I want to say, but don't . . . what? Don't leave? Don't stay?

"Lovely," he says quietly. "The melody, I mean."

"I . . . I'm glad you like it."

Mendes steps back from the spinet. My arm falls to my side.

"My thanks," he says, his voice somewhat strained. "For the demonstration."

"It was no trouble."

He clears his throat. "I'd like to pray, if you would permit it."

"What?"

He rubs the back of his neck with his hand. "I would like to pray for your recovery, your continuing health. With some of my patients . . . it is a tradition, I suppose."

"Oh. Of course. Do I need to do something?"

"Pardon," he says. "I shouldn't have— No matter. Could I take your hand again?"

Confused, I nod, stepping forward to offer him my palm. He cups it in his own. He is careful to keep the contact chaste, his skin barely brushing mine. But I can still feel the warmth of him, and the faint rasp of the calluses on his fingertips. His sleeve rides up, revealing his forearm: it is thatched with dark hair, interrupted by a trio of moles near his wrist. His hands are broad, and they swallow mine entirely. Something treacherous and wanting curls around the base of my stomach.

Mendes murmurs to himself in Hebrew, a half-sung whisper that holds no more meaning to me than the tone of the spinet keys. It is beautiful, all the same.

Once he is finished, he says, "Farewell, Cecilia. May you be blessed. May you be restored, in soul and in body."

He releases me.

"Farewell, Master Mendes," I reply.

Then he bows, turns away, and leaves my life just as he entered it: on a summer day in the Eden townhouse, in a house that is not my own, in a city I cannot forgive.

CHAPTER SIX

David

The night after my last appointment with Cecilia Thorowgood, I go with Jan to an alehouse. It is packed, and Jan soons falls into a spirited debate with a pair of gentlemen upon the worthiness of public libraries. I watch them and allow the noise and the crowd to distract me. We consume several hours there, and several more mugs of sack. I return home very late, still stumbling.

The house is quiet and dark. My father and Elizabeth Askwith must be asleep. I go to the kitchen, where I pour myself some water, using the moonlight from the window to see by. My reflection in the cup is haggard and frowning. I feel a sudden and sincere hatred for my face, ghoulish in the harsh shadows. I tip the rest of the water down my throat, tossing the cup aside.

In the garden, the air is cool now that the sun is hidden, and I find myself shivering. I go to inspect the glass beads hanging from the wall hooks. In the darkness there is no light to reflect upon them. They are clear and colorless against the brick, like frozen tears, each scarred with the reflection of the white feathers between them. I lift a strand and drop it, listening to it clatter against the wall. I remember Manuel gifting them to me, bashful as he pressed the pouch into my hands. *It isn't much,* he'd said—he'd always denied his kindnesses as he performed them. When I pulled the glass out, it was still warm from his grip. The feathers were dyed colors then; the sunlight has since bleached them. In Portuguese, *pena* means feather, but it also means pity, punishment, pain. An unfortunate omen.

I suddenly feel very foolish. It is clear that I am sulking. Drinking always puts me in a foul mood, and I shouldn't have indulged this evening. Leaving the beads be, I take a final gulp of the air before returning to the kitchen. Aware of my impending hangover, I guzzle two more glasses of water and take a swallow of a milk-thistle decoction.

I remind myself that I must sleep, so I ascend the steps to my bedroom. Untying my breeches and my sleeves, I go to remove my doublet, and then realize—with no more reminder than the press of my fingers against ivory buttons—that I gave Cecilia Thorowgood my favorite jacket, my soft green wool jacket, which I bought one week after arriving in London, and which has withstood a decade of English weather. I have left it with her, and the only way I can get it back is to return to the Eden townhouse and request its return.

But I cannot go back. I was too much of a coward to tell her what her sister planned for her, and perhaps I owed that to her, perhaps I still do, despite our mutual powerlessness. Still, I remember the fear in her eyes hours ago as I told her goodbye. I cannot bear to witness it another time. I remember her fingers sprawled across the keys of the spinet, her slow smile as she played her song. I remember the feeling of her hand in mine, the bird wing fragility of her bones and tendons, contracting in automatic response to my touch—her cold fingertips brushing over my palm. I remember the tremor in her voice as she said, *Farewell, Master Mendes.*

She still has my jacket.

It is hers now.

I spend my morning crushing rose hips with a mortar and pestle for a batch order of poultices. They stain my hands red as ripe apples, and the air in the kitchen fills with the summer scent of dying flowers and dry earth. My father sits at the table, reading.

The poultice is jarred and stored in the cupboard. As I start to wash the pot, someone knocks soundly upon the front door. I go to answer, precluding Elizabeth Askwith, who reaches halfway down the steps and then turns away, huffing, as she sees me approach. She often complains I do not give her enough work to do. We are similar in that regard: We both are best kept occupied.

"Sara," I say, surprised when I see the woman on the doorstep. She is in her best dress, a deep purple brocade. Her hair has been pinned back, twisted elaborately above her ears. She wears amber earrings, and she holds the basket I used to bring her tarts while she was sitting shiva.

Sara presents the basket to me. "I thought to return this," she says.

"You needn't have."

"It was just an excuse to visit. May I come in?"

"Yes, of course."

I stare at her back as she makes her way inside. She looks as beautiful as she always has, her dress slipping down her shoul-

ders like dark wine as she walks along the hallway. With her hair
up, I can see the baby hairs on the back of her neck, the soft,
dark, peach-skin blur of them shadowing her hairline. Manuel
had the same. The Cardozo siblings had always looked so very
alike, more so than Cecilia and her twin, despite not being twins
themselves.

It has been a long time since Sara was last here, but she re-
members where the kitchen is. She strides through the door and
places the basket on the counter. Her entry delights my father,
who cries, "Sara, welcome!" He cannot stand from his chair, but
he makes a sweeping gesture of greeting. Sara approaches to kiss
his cheek.

"Gaspar, hello," she says.

"Lovely Sara, I am glad you are here," he replies. "It has been
so long. I am sorry I could not visit you."

"Oh, please, don't be sorry," Sara says in Portuguese. We usually speak Spanish with each other; I suppose she wishes to im-
press him. "I've had many visitors," she continues, "and enough
food to drown in."

"David brought tarts!"

"Yes, he did. They were very good."

As they talk, I finish washing the pot. Sara sits opposite my
father to speak with him. She unwraps her shawl and drapes it
across the back of the chair with an easy familiarity, one I can't
help but find grating. She hasn't been here since Manuel died.

". . . Elizabeth Askwith's recipe," Father is saying. "She bakes
very well."

"Is she your new maid?"

"Yes, she is," he tells her. "And she has David in utter terror.
He will not look her in the eye, he is so afraid of her."

"Not so," I say.

"Ach, it is."

Sara clears her throat. "Perhaps, David, we ought to go to the parlor now. I have something to discuss with you."

"Will you have tea? Coffee?"

"No, thank you."

"Biscuits?"

"Go!" Father barks.

Sara laughs at this as I lead her to the parlor. I open the door for her. As she passes me, I can smell the sweet oils she uses on her hair. Feeling disquieted, I go to open the glass-fronted cabinet, where I keep our collection of porcelain. I fiddle with a jar as if I have some intention of rearranging things, but I do not.

"Sit with me," she says.

Reluctantly, I close the cabinet doors and turn to find Sara already on the couch. I sit beside her. She is staring at the window, biting her lip.

"Are you well?" I ask her.

She turns to look at me. "Well enough," she says. "And you?"

"Yes, fine," I reply.

"Are you certain?" she asks. "You seem . . ."

I shake my head. "I am tired, that is all. Is something the matter?"

"Well—I . . ."

She stares at her lap. A cloud outside shifts, casting a pane of sunlight over her hands, clasped tightly over her skirts.

"I have something to tell you," Sara says.

"What is it?"

"I have been made an offer of marriage."

I blink at her. I do not know how to react. She stares searchingly at me, awaiting a response. I look to the table, seeking a cup to hold, something to sip, to delay speech, but there is nothing. Weakly, I say, "Oh. So soon after . . ."

"The proposal came months ago, before Papa passed. I told him I needed time to think about it."

"Who?"

"Joseph Alvarez."

I frown. Alvarez is near twice her age. "The spice merchant?"

She laughs. "His son," she says. "He has been traveling the past few years, as an apprentice, and I don't know him very well. But we have met sometimes, to trade, and he has grown fond of me. He is younger than I am, but he is kind, and handsome, and he will help the business. I like him."

"So, you will accept?"

She says nothing. She draws her finger across the edge of the armrest, in a gesture of uncharacteristic anxiety.

"Sara," I say. "Why have you come?"

"I don't know."

With dawning dread, I ask, "To ask me permission? Is that it?"

She replies, "No, of course not. I suppose I am here only to—to make sure you won't care."

"I . . . I do care about you."

"But not in the way I would like."

I cannot respond. I shuffle on the seat. The rasp of my clothing against the cushion feels deafeningly loud.

I say, "After the funeral . . ."

"It was too soon, I know. You weren't ready."

She says it as if it is inevitable; as if someday, all the pieces of the world will pick themselves up as if they had never shattered, and I will be the man she imagines me to be. I wish I could believe that, also.

"I would marry you if you asked, David," she says. "Surely you know that?"

I do know that. I have known for years now.

Sara smiles encouragingly at me, but yet again I do not know what to say. Awfully, I almost want to laugh. This all feels so unexpected, so incomprehensible, that I cannot understand it as anything but a cruel joke.

Sara says, "I think we could be good for each other."

"What about Joseph Alvarez?"

"I don't know him very well," she replies. "I know you—at least, I have tried to know you, David. You are so withdrawn, so—so *mild*, and I thought . . . I thought if I waited, eventually you would take the initiative."

"But I didn't," I say.

"No, you didn't."

"I am sorry."

"Why?"

"This isn't what you wanted."

"Perhaps I should have given up long ago," she murmurs. "You had so little interest in me when we first met. I was only Manuel's little sister. But when he was unwell, and we spent so much time together, treating him—grieving him . . ." She folds her arms around her chest, and she drops her chin. Her eyes grow wet. "I thought perhaps your feelings would eventually match mine," she says, voice thick. "Since there is no one else. Is there?"

I shake my head.

"Then why?" she asks. "Why haven't we tried?"

"I couldn't say," I reply. "You are a wonderful woman, Sara. My heart—I haven't made space inside it for anyone, I think, in a very long time."

She stares at me. I stare back.

Her mouth goes rigid in determination. "Then marry me," she says, wiping away a tear.

"Sara—"

"Wait. Let me explain. I know you do not love me in the same way as I do you—certainly not *now*—but perhaps, someday, you could. Don't you think you could?"

My throat has gone very dry. I swallow, and it feels like a blade is sinking into my stomach. "Perhaps."

"We are both . . . I mean, there are so few of us here, in London."

"Yes."

"And we are well suited. Do you not think so? We were friends, the two of us, before we drifted apart."

"We were."

She leans forward and takes my hand in hers. "I admit that I do not understand you, David, not really; perhaps I never have. But I want to. I want to try."

"I . . ."

"So let me try," she says. "Please. Marry me. We could be happy."

She gives me a small, hopeful smile, pressing dimples into the hollows of her cheeks. And I know as she digs her fingers into my palm, pleading and insistent, that there is almost no reason to refuse. My father would be overjoyed at the match, and Sara is right—there are so few Jews in London. If not her, then who? The entire community would come to our ceremony; it would be a joyous occasion, an act of defiance, screaming to the city, *we are here to stay*. We could be wed beneath a canopy made of Manuel's silks. It would have made him so happy to see it. We could pray for him there and keep his memory alive.

Married by the fall, just like Cecilia Thorowgood.

Remembering her, I feel suffused with shame. I abandoned

Cecilia to her fate, and now—presented with an offer infinitely kinder than the one she will be forced into—I remain too much of a coward to agree.

"I—I don't know," I say to Sara. "This is very unexpected. I am sorry. You deserve an answer, but . . ."

She shakes her head. "I knew this would be a shock. Take time, please, to think upon it. I want you to be sure."

I bow over in embarrassment, resting my forearm on my knees. "I fear I will never be sure."

"You will," she says. "And it is me who ought to be apologizing, David. I should have been honest with you from the beginning. No matter how you answer me, I will accept it."

We sit in silence, Sara's hands in mine, her thumbs rubbing circles against my wrists. I feel a terrible disappointment in myself, but envy, also, toward her. I wish I knew my own desires as well as she knows hers. I wish I knew myself enough to know what I wanted.

"I will think upon it," I tell her. And I hate how relieved she looks in response.

We stay there, hands clasped, for a few moments longer. Then, in quiet agreement, we stand to leave. I bring her to the front door. At the steps, Sara touches the mezuzah lightly, pressing her fingers to her lips.

"Come see me," she says quietly. "When you know."

"I will. I swear it."

She kisses my cheek. "Farewell, David."

"Farewell."

She leaves. I look at the mezuzah, but I do not acknowledge it. Instead, I close the door very gently, to prevent my father from hearing. I cannot stand an interrogation, not now.

Returning to the parlor, I sit down and stare at the rug.

I still remember the day Manuel died. After the cart took him away, I went to Jan's house. There I ground coffee beans, bag after bag, until my arm ached, until I could heap great mounds of it like dirt across his counters. I heard the crack of them beneath the pestle and imagined that they were the bones of my chest; that I was crushing myself flat, so I could remake myself into something better. It hadn't worked, clearly. I am the same man I have always been.

And Sara wants me still. I don't understand why.

"David Mendes," comes a voice. Elizabeth Askwith is at the doorway. She is carrying a tray with tea and biscuits, frowning at the room. "Your guest is gone?"

"Yes, she is."

"I came to offer refreshment. You said, David Mendes, that I ought to offer refreshment when your guests come."

"Thank you," I say. "But she left."

She nods in some vestige of sympathy, although her face maintains its typical mixture of blankness and disdain. She puts the tray down in front of me. "It is brewed," she says, "so you ought to drink it."

"I don't want any."

"You ought to," she repeats, and leaves the room.

I stare at the tea set without touching it, and then I notice that one of the pillows upon the couch was pushed out of place by Sara as she sat. I rearrange it, and everything is as it was before she arrived. It is as if she was never here at all.

Eventually, Elizabeth Askwith returns with a tray bearing two letters, both sealed with the Eden crest.

"Delivered while your guest was present," she informs me. Once she is gone, I break the seal of the larger letter. In Lady Eden's meticulous hand, it reads:

Master Mendes,

Enclosed—a bonus for your endeavors. My sister's appetite
seems to have improved.

My thanks, sir, for your aid, and your discretion.

Sincerely,
Lady Margaret Eden

The envelope contains a check for an extraordinary sum;
enough to pay for my father's medicines for the year. I stare at it
in my hands with a heady mixture of elation and guilt.

The other envelope is sealed rather badly, and I expect that it
was done by someone in a hurry. Inside, the writing is so hastily
scrawled it takes me several minutes to decipher it:

Mendes,

I realized I never directly thanked you for your help. Your
decoctions are effective—if disgusting—but you listened,
too. Very few people have bothered to listen to me. I am
grateful.

The tune we played: Froberger's Second Toccata. You
should be able to find a performance of a higher standard
somewhere in this city; I've never managed to get it quite
right. Froberger is greatly admired for his dances, but his
early toccatas are truly flawless. Good music is a little
like medicine, I think: everything in perfect balance. Both
hands and heart required. Perhaps you might play again,
someday.

Regards,
Cecilia Thorowgood

The ink is smudged; she didn't bother to wait for it to dry.

I return the letter to the tray, and I find myself imagining a wedding: not mine and Sara's, but another entirely, one taking place beneath the vaulted ceilings of a Christian church. I see the wooden pews, courtiers in their finery, priests and posies of blue flowers. A faceless man at the altar takes Cecilia's pale hand in his, looping his fingers around her wrist. She looks at him with eyes hardened by resentment and resignation, then turns to me in the pews, where I am sitting as complicit and silent as the rest of the audience.

No man is a prisoner, she tells me, *if he can escape.*

CHAPTER SEVEN

Cecilia

I am accustomed to solitude. After all, in the months after Will died, I was entirely isolated. At first, I did have visitors; they were patient with me, as I was with them. My grief was as much surprise as anything else. I had a silence and a wide-eyed gaze that prompted earnest sympathy. They would take my hand and say, "Dear, dear, Cecilia." They would bring me gifts and brush my hair. They swaddled me in kindness.

Then the shock passed, and I became difficult. First came the crying fits, interspersed with a dullness, a strange detachment. As weeks became months, I became both cruel and vacant, a bitter shell. My visitors were discomfited by it—*offended* by it. I couldn't answer their questions; when my replies were forced, they were too harsh, too resentful. I had become unworthy of the effort my presence required.

So I was alone, even more than I am now. And when the letter came from Margaret, it felt like providence. I had so efficiently pushed people away; but now my sister claimed that she missed me. The plague was over, she was returning to London, and she *wanted* me to be with her. It was miraculous. I had ruined all that was good about my life in the country. I had pushed away my friends with my temper and my cruelty, and I had turned that house into a grave. If I had stayed longer, the dirt would have piled over me, and I would have died in a coffin of my own creation. Instead, I left. Will's brother has taken ownership of the house, and I can never go back there. I am glad of that. It was once a happy place for me, and the dregs of that happiness might still be there, under the floorboards, like dying flames. If I return, I might stamp them out.

So I must live in London with Margaret. I must rely on her charity and kindness. And now that my physician is gone, all is as it was.

I am alone again.

A week has passed since I played the spinet with David Mendes. Since then, the days have stacked themselves upon me, each heavier than the last. I stitch, and I read, and I take my decoctions. The tedium wears me away. The monotony of my life, the repetition of it, is ceaseless.

Today, of course, is no different: I stitch, I read, I take my decoctions. Once noon comes, I read a pamphlet about the war with the republic, and I draw a flower on the back of it. Then I sit at the desk, fiddling with an embroidery needle.

Eventually, someone knocks on my door. It is Margaret. She enters with a great profusion of fabric draped over one arm. It is an emerald silk, a gown I haven't worn in months.

"Good afternoon, Cecilia," Margaret says. I suppose it is afternoon now; I hadn't noticed it had grown so late. "Are you well?" she asks.

"Yes." I raise the needle in my fingers, as if to defend myself with it.

She casts a critical eye over me. "Your hair isn't curled," she says. "That's a shame. I've brought you a change of clothes. We have a visitor, and I'd like you to look presentable."

"I don't understand," I say.

Margaret sighs, exasperated, and then she approaches me, taking me by the hand. "Cecilia, listen," she says. "Sir Samuel Grey is here to call on you."

"Who?"

"Of the Kent Greys. He owns the townhouse opposite ours. He is a very wealthy man, and newly arrived at court. Unmarried."

"Unmarried," I echo. "Oh. I see."

"You must be respectful to him, do you understand? None of your usual nonsense."

I have no idea why a very wealthy man, newly arrived at court, would have any interest in *me*, a widow without prospects. Still, I don't care to find out. The thought of simpering to a foppish rake so my sister can sell me to him—it is unconscionable. I won't do it.

"I can't," I say. "I am indisposed today. I should like to rest. Perhaps Sir Grey might return tomorrow."

Margaret narrows her eyes in suspicion. "Come, Cecilia, don't be difficult. This is an extraordinary opportunity, surely you must realize that."

It is clear she will remain unmoved. I stand from the chair. My dress is only half laced, and the bodice gapes away from my middle. As I fiddle with the strands at my back, I say, "It's only that . . . I don't feel well. Shall we, perhaps, another time . . ."

"He is *very handsome*, Cecilia, and eager to meet you."

"I need the pot," I blurt.

"The pot?"

"Yes. My gut rumbles. Perhaps a mild dysentery. It kept me awake through the night, and I'd rather it didn't trouble me in front of Sir Grey . . ."

Margaret grimaces, but she says, resolute, "Then I'll wait outside the door."

"But—I might—"

"I'll wait outside the door," she repeats.

There's little I can do to protest. Margaret lays the dress upon the desk, making it a promise of her return. Then she walks out of the room, shutting the door behind her.

Unmarried, I think. *Unmarried, unmarried.* Who knows how old this man is; he's likely a widower himself, to be willing to court me after Will's death. My mind conjures images of a grizzled gentleman with a gold-tipped cane and wooden teeth, the sort of relic so often installed in earldoms these days, eager for a young bride to put on display: leering and wealthy and domineering. Another set of shackles, and yet my sister expects me to offer my wrists eagerly, to smile at my jailer as he turns the key.

I spin around. The sensation of panic has reached a sort of icy threshold, where suddenly all is very cold and slow and quiet. I stare at the window. There seems little communication between the frantic terror of my thoughts and the slow, deliberate movements of my hand, which reaches forward to press its palm flat against the glass. Outside, the weather is perfectly fair. The sun hangs low in the sky. A songbird rests on the windowsill of the floor below, chirping. Perhaps a maid has left it crumbs.

It feels as if I am watching my gallows being built. In a matter of minutes, I have measured every decision I have ever made, and found all of them wanting. My sister no longer wants me here, clearly. But I have nowhere to go except to the arms of a stranger—to be kept in his townhouse, to play bridge with courtiers and make babies and scrub all memory of my past away from me, to forget Will and kill him again.

I push against the window with greater strength. It swings open. The afternoon air is warm and muggy. The noise of the hinges scares the bird below, which speeds like musket shot into the sky. I swing myself sideways to sit upon the windowsill, my legs dangling against the outside wall.

I am only on the first floor; the fall would hardly kill me, but it is a decent enough drop. Below lies a patch of blackthorn. It grows a fine halo of frothy white flowers that look almost welcoming. Beyond it, there is a short section of lawn, and then the iron fence that surrounds the townhouse. The street is quiet. The gate lies waiting.

Once I discover the possibility of the jump, it feels like cowardice not to accomplish it. I stare downward at my feet in their fine silk slippers, floating above the clouds of blackthorn. My blush-colored petticoat blooms outward in the wind. The air stinks of the summer, dung and humanity, but also of dry grass and something brackish from the river. Mendes came all the way here from Portugal; there must be *something* in this city to cause him to make such a journey. Something worth wanting. Something worth seeing, beyond the glass panes of a window, and an empty road I have never walked.

I push myself off the windowsill. I had imagined the fall would occur slowly, but instead it is so quick that I don't experience it: I am at the window, and then I hit the ground. I keel forward in a tangled knot of limbs, silk, and hair, rebounding off the blackthorn. The sharp twigs beneath the flowers score lines across my palms, and the jarring impact causes a sharp stab in my abdomen, which is aching from lack of food. My knees slam against the ground, but they are saved from shattering by my skirts. The most painful result of the fall is my scratched hands, which sting terribly. When I stand, I wipe them on the wall. They leave thin trails of blood behind them.

Despite my wounds, I giggle in the triumph of my unsupervised escape. Then my stomach cramps painfully with hunger, as if to humble me. Wincing, I look down at my bloodied palms and my dirtied skirts. My body seems so pitiful I wish I could shuck it off of me, like shelling a pea.

No matter: I am committed now. My sister will be furious once I am found. I might as well use my freedom while I have it. I rush away from the blackthorn, heading directly toward the gate and the setting sun. The footman at the fence notices me— he cries out in alarm—but he is prevented from seizing me by propriety, and the gate has been left open just enough that I can inch my way through. He watches me, horrified, as I take off down the road. As I reach the main street, to hear the trundle of carriages and the cries of voices, I realize that—after months of captivity—I have left the townhouse entirely.

I will have to return eventually. I have nothing with me. I am directionless, without coin nor purpose, and even the exertion of running down the street has left me light-headed. But, for the moment, I am unfettered, remade. I stand by the side of the main road and greet the world with wide eyes.

London is madness, even here, in a well-to-do neighborhood. The road is teeming with people and animals. I see one man driving a pair of pigs down an alleyway; three boys are rolling barrels past me—they turn to stare—and in the middle of the road, directly in the way of the horses and carriages, there is a man and woman shrieking at each other in argument. She smacks him with her glove. He stomps the cobblestone with a mud-worn boot.

There is a flower stall on the other side of the street. The girl in charge of the stall has a tangle of red-brown hair and large, dark eyes. She can't be older than fifteen. As she rearranges posies, she sings in a loud, clear voice: *Sweet peas for your sweet, roses for your rose,* over and over, hitting a piercing high note on *rose* without fail each round.

I want to cross, but I dally so long in fear of stumbling into a horse that some passersby laugh at me. Eventually, I muster the courage, and I approach the stall, marveling at the variety of the blooms.

The girl pauses in her singing to smile at me. "Summer flowers, mistress?" she asks.

"I have no money," I reply. "Forgive me."

She glances at my gown, seeming surprised by the response; it is brocade, as are the slippers now suffering in the muck of the road. I must look quite wealthy. That is an irony, I suppose, as every penny to my name is in the charge of my sister. "Very well," she says. "'Haps another time."

She turns back to the bouquet she is arranging. "Perhaps," I agree, charmed by her, and her turnip-shaped nose, and her utter lack of interest in me. "What is your name?"

"Katherine, mistress."

"I must request your advice, Katherine," I say. "If you had one day in London, before you were gone forever, what would you do?"

"Goodness." Invigorated by the puzzle, she pauses in her work, furrowing her brow in concentration. "Without any money?"

"Yes."

"Sometimes you can sneak into a play without the beadles

noticing." She shrugs. "And the park is nearby. The king opened it recently. They have a canal there now."

"A canal? In a *park*?"

"Yes. It's pretty."

I open my mouth to respond, and then I hear cries from farther down the street, alongside a parade of stomping boots. Catching a glimpse of red livery, I realize that it is the Eden footmen—sent out, no doubt, to bring me back. I gasp, say to Katherine, "Forgive me," and duck behind her stall.

Katherine squawks in consternation, but I don't have time to explain. I am crouched on the filthy pavement, skirts gathered up in my hands, desperately trying not to keel over. Meanwhile, I hear footsteps approaching from the other side of the wooden boards concealing me from view.

"Pardon, mistress," comes a man's voice. "We are searching for a gentlewoman—blond, slight, dressed in a pink gown. Have you caught sight of her?"

My heart is beating like a war drum, my breaths short; it's absurd, but I feel as if I might never leave the townhouse again if I am discovered.

Katherine sniffs and rearranges one of her bouquets. "A gentlewoman," she says. "There's plenty of ladies 'round 'ere, sir; I couldn't rightly say which ones are blond or not."

The footman mutters something to himself, and then there's the clink of a coin hitting wood. My stomach sinks. "Has your memory improved now?"

Katherine pauses. She reaches over, presumably for the money.

"She went up Swallow Street," she says. "In a right hurry about it, too."

The footman thanks her and leaves. I crouch there for a good while before Katherine pokes at my shoulder.

"They're gone," she says.

I stand up, dust off my skirts. "Swallow Street?"

"Opposite direction of the park." She points south, toward the river. "You'll be wanting that way, mistress. And better be quick about it."

"Thank you, Katherine. Sincerely."

She shrugs and returns to her flowers. As I leave, she begins to sing again.

It is a short walk, but it takes me far longer than it should, as I become confused and turn myself around several times. Every time I see a man in red, my heart near stops, and I duck into an alley. By the time I reach the entrance of the park, the sun is low in the sky.

I stop by the gate and stare inside. It is vast, far larger than I'd imagined, a chessboard of grass, paths, and square-cut hedges. There is a square pool laid in its center: Its surface is almost perfectly still, reflecting the pink-red glow of the nascent evening. People promenade around its edges, some carrying lanterns. They are like fireflies, floating over the water. Strands of white gravel wind between them, and willow trees stoop above, making a canopy of green.

I didn't know London could be like this, not really. When Will and I were here, we were always in townhouses and parlors. What little I saw of the city was from a carriage window, with the stench of horse dung rising from the cobbles below. But this is like a scene from a painting, or an engraving in a book. It is wonderful.

I enter the park and stroll slowly down the path. I am unaccompanied, and I earn some concerned looks, but no one stops me and calls me an imposter, despite my sense of displacement. The people here are quite extraordinary. Many wear foreign fashions I don't recognize, oriental silks and blouses ruffled with French lace. I hear a dozen languages spoken, and I pass by a busker with a mandolin. He plays a capriccio I know for harpsichord. I wish I could toss him a coin, but I have nothing to give.

Pausing at the canal, I watch a pair of young boys folding an old pamphlet into a paper boat. They lay it gently on the water. It catches the breeze and surges forward. The journey is not a long one—the canal is only fifty feet or so wide—and soon the boat successfully reaches the other side, the prow bumping into the pavement. It tips over. The boys cheer, unbowed by its capsizing.

Someone bends down and rights the boat before pushing it back toward us. The boys call thanks and crouch to reach for it. I glance across the canal, then look again, astonished.

The rescuer is David Mendes.

His hair is down, he wears no jacket, but it is him, of that I am certain—he is not the sort of man easily mistaken for someone else. And I am not one to believe in Providence, but what else can this be?

I had sincerely believed we would never meet again, and I am surprised at how thankful I am that I was wrong.

He stands, smiling, and then he notices me, also. The smile falls from his face, to be replaced by shock. Our gazes meet across the water. I wave, but his expression becomes guarded.

His reflection ripples, stretching toward me, in defiance of the hesitation in his face. It seems likely he will walk away; why wouldn't he? We both know I shouldn't be here unsupervised, and that he would court trouble by acknowledging me at all. But I don't want him to leave. It is a comfort to see someone familiar in a city of strangers. I would call out to him if I could, but he is distant enough that I fear he won't hear me.

I turn to the boys. "May I try?" I ask, gesturing to the boat.

They are wary, but I give them a pleading look, and they hand it to me. I bend down to the water. I wish I had a stick of graphite, or something else to write with, to communicate more clearly. Instead, I settle for plucking a daisy from the grass, tucking it into the paper, hoping it will express my good intentions.

I don't trust myself to aim it properly. "If one of you could send it back to that man, I'd be very grateful," I say. The boys are sniggering now—they have noticed the flower—but they oblige.

The boat bobs over to Mendes. He has been watching us with a suspicious expression, eyes narrowed, but he still crouches to retrieve the boat. Pulling the daisy out from under the sail, he pinches it between thumb and forefinger. I can't see his expression.

He pushes the boat back toward us, and he walks away. I sigh. Better for both of us, I suppose; we could both be punished for fraternizing without my sister's permission.

"Bad luck, mistress," one of the boys comments. Before I can reply to him, he snatches up his boat. Grabbing the other boy's hand, he leads him away.

I watch them go, crestfallen, my solitude renewed. Unwilling to move, I stand there for a little longer, pressing the sole of my slipper against the water. The ripple expands outward like a firework, lanterns glittering in the shattered reflection.

A hand extends into my vision, a daisy in its palm. I look up to see Mendes's frowning face.

"Good evening," I say.

"Good evening, Cecilia."

I gesture to the daisy. "That was for you."

"Why?" he asks, still clearly confused. When I fail to answer—I am not certain, myself—he closes his hand and drops it to his side. "I . . . What are you doing here?"

"A flower seller told me to visit the park. I am glad she did; it is very beautiful."

"Is your sister with you?"

"No. I am alone."

"Alone," he repeats, and his frown deepens. "Why?"

"I jumped out of a window."

"What?"

"A suitor came to call. Margaret wants me to marry him, but I'd rather not, so I jumped out of the window. I landed in some blackthorn." I show him my hands, still bloody from the fall. "See?"

His expression goes through a number of complicated movements, torn between concern and confusion.

"Look," I say. "It's been done now, and I can't undo it, so . . . We both ought to accept that, I suppose."

He sighs, scrubbing his hand over his face. I expect him to pivot and leave—he is clearly wary of speaking to me, rightfully so—but instead he says, defeated, "Does it sting?"

"Pardon?"

"Your hand. Does it still sting?"

"Yes. It was a good fall."

He turns away. "Follow me."

Mystified, I trail after him as he walks farther down the canal. We reach a section of path bordered by tall, woolly plants, crowned with purple flowers. With practiced efficiency, Mendes strips one of the plants of its leaves, then bends to dampen them in the water.

He puts his hand out questioningly. Hesitantly, I offer him my bloodied palms. He pauses for a moment, bringing them closer to his face to inspect. In a foolish fancy, I briefly wonder if he will kiss my wrist—but he doesn't, of course. He lowers my hands and begins to clean away the blood with the wet leaf. I am surprised by its softness; it feels like felt against my skin. "What is that?" I ask.

"Lamb's ears," he replies. "It'll do. But you must have it bound properly when you return."

"Why are you here? In the park, I mean?"

"Meeting a friend. He is late, as is typical of him." Mendes finishes his work, letting go of my hand, and his gaze meets mine. "All this to escape your suitor?"

"Yes, I suppose so."

"Was he truly that terrible?"

"I don't know," I say. "I haven't met him."

Mendes smiles, but there seems to be something melancholy behind it. "My father has often said a brief acquaintance makes for a happy wedding, but that certainly seems too brief to me."

I laugh a little at that, then ask, "Your father? Did he come with you to England?"

"He did. We arrived nine years ago."

"I never asked you why you left Lisbon."

Mendes seems reluctant to reply, glancing nervously beyond my shoulder. I consider telling him it doesn't matter, but then he says, "By law, Jews are not permitted to live in Portugal."

"Oh," I say, confused. "Then how . . ."

"My family was forced to convert during the Inquisition," he replies. "But we continued to practice in secret for many generations."

"Surely that was very dangerous. Why didn't they leave?"

"They had many reasons. They had lives there, family, a community. To leave would mean incredible uncertainty. But . . ."

"But?"

He sighs. "I also often wonder why they stayed. I left when I could, as have many others. Perhaps I simply lacked the courage to remain. I don't know."

"It doesn't seem a matter of courage at all," I say. "You *chose* London. I think that is brave. It is a frightening place. I am quite terrified of it."

His expression softens at that. "You have been brave, also," he says. "If foolhardy. Have you no money?"

"None."

"Where do you intend to go?"

"Well, back to the townhouse, eventually. I have no other choice."

His nose wrinkles. "Where you must meet your suitor."

"Yes."

The bloodied leaves of lamb's ears are still clutched in his fist. He drops them. They float slowly to the ground, the breeze scattering them across the path; one falls into the water and spins in a pirouette.

"I wish I could do more to help you," he says. "Forgive me."

"There's nothing to be forgiven."

"I'm not certain of that. In truth, I already knew—"

A voice calls "David!" from behind us, and I turn around to see a man approaching us. He is tall and ginger-haired, walking with a loping stride that is somehow both elegant and ungainly. He stops in front of us, frowning at Mendes. "I have been looking everywhere for you," he says. His accent is foreign, perhaps northern European—markedly different, at least, from David's. "I thought we were to meet by the fountain."

"Pardon, Jan."

The man notices me then. He gives me an assessing look. "Oh, I *see*." He grins and bows to me. "Good evening, mistress. My apologies for the interruption. I am Johannes van Essen."

"Cecilia Thorowgood," I reply, curtsying.

"Cecilia is an . . . ex-patient," Mendes explains. He has gone a little pink.

"You are Master Mendes's friend?" I ask Van Essen.

He nods eagerly. "You know, David and I were to head to Temple Bar soon. You are welcome to join us."

"Temple Bar?"

"There is a coffeehouse there. It is quite marvelous. In the evenings there is lively debate, and music, also."

Mendes makes a sound of aggravation. "Jan—"

Interrupting him, I say, "Are women permitted there?"

"Indeed. There are all sorts at Temple Bar. Jews and Dutchmen, too." He grins again. "Well, Mistress Thorowgood? What say you?"

Had I been asked before I saw the park, when my vision of London was solely filth and fear, I would have likely declined. But now I find myself gripped by curiosity. I have never had coffee before, and I would like to try it at least once.

"I am grateful for the invitation, Master van Essen," I say. "I'd be glad to come, if Master Mendes will permit it."

"Call me Jan, please. David, she *can* come, can't she?"

"Your sister will be looking for you," Mendes says to me.

"I know," I reply. "But if this is my only evening of freedom, I intend to use it well."

"Ignore him. He is always dour." Jan offers me his arm, and I loop my hand through his elbow. "We are both delighted to have your company."

He leads me down the path. Mendes trails behind us. I turn my head to look at him, and our gazes meet. His black eyes reflect the pink of the sunset and the green of the grass. I realize that they are not colorless, as I once had thought, but rather every color at once: like mirrors, reflecting all else. I feel a flush of pleasure at his attention, and then shame for it immediately after. This newfound attraction is unwelcome. It will never be reciprocated, and it will lead me to nothing but further grief. I must forget it. There is nothing else to be done.

One evening of freedom: the cure Mendes prescribed to me, albeit far smaller a dose. Then back to the townhouse, I suppose. Back to my sister and my suitor. Back to my embroidery needle and my emerald silk and the endless tedium of my confinement.

One evening of freedom. I will make it count.

CHAPTER EIGHT

David

I came to this coffeehouse with Manuel once, a little over a year ago. I had just lost a patient, a young woman. She'd had a tumor in the stomach; by the time I discovered the true cause of her pain, it had been too late. I'd been in the room as she'd passed.

Manuel had always been able to tell when I needed distraction. He'd bought drinks for us, and sweet biscuits. We sat across from each other. He did not ask me what was wrong; he knew better than to press me. The coffeehouse was mostly empty that evening, but there was a storm outside—the last of the spring rains—and it did enough to fill the silence. The steady patter of the water against the roof was some measure of distraction from my thoughts. Not enough, but some.

He knew I didn't want to speak of it, and that if I eventually did, I would do so without his prompting. Instead, he fetched a pamphlet for himself, and one for me also. We sat and read until the biscuits were gone and the coffee no longer steamed.

Our eyes met over the top of the page. He smiled.

I thought, *If only we could stay here always, you and I, and pretend the earth is no longer turning.*

I never did tell him about the patient in the end. But I felt better for having him there. That afternoon will remain with me always, and for good reason: It was one of the last times I saw Manuel before the plague came. It was a time when he was most himself, when the qualities that endeared him to me were most evident.

No matter. I have become skilled at putting such thoughts away. Whenever I return to this place, and I recall that day, I file the past down, soften and reshape it into something I can hide. Each time I do so, the memory gets smaller. Perhaps, eventually, it will disappear entirely, and I will lose Manuel for good. I don't want that to happen, but I have no choice; it feels like the only way to cope with his loss.

"David," Jan says, snapping his fingers in front of my face. "Return to the living, I beg of you. We need to find seats."

The room is a crush of noise and color. Someone has had the foolish notion to bring up war reparations as the topic of the evening's debate, and the argument is already near a brawl, screams and insults being hurled across the room. We stand in the doorway, and Cecilia—astonished, clutching her hands to her chest—says, "Will there be a fight?"

"Perhaps," I reply. She needn't look so excited about it. "Jan, is there any possibility of a table?"

Jan, who has a better vantage point than either of us, peers over the top of the crowd. "Ah, there," he says. "A booth's just been cleared."

He surges forward. Cecilia goes behind him, elbowing her way through the horde, parting them like Moses. I am left following in their wake.

Cecilia and I slide into the booth. It is quieter here, the light dimmer. Jan remains standing; I give him a desperate look, but he smirks at me and says, "I must go hawk some beans. I will return later."

Before I can stop him, he turns and leaves. Cecilia watches him go. "Hawk beans?" she asks.

"He is a roaster. He sells to the brewer here."

"Oh. How do we order?"

I lean over the side of the booth and hold two fingers up to the serving girl. She nods.

"Like that," I say.

"I suppose that makes sense, considering the noise." She peers over the crowd. "There are so many people here! How extraordinary. I must admit that you were correct, Master Mendes. I feel much better to be out of the townhouse and doing something different."

I don't reply. The imprint of her fingers on my knuckles as we played the spinet has been a phantom presence, lingering for days after we last touched; I felt her hand on mine as I picked herbs in the garden, as I poured wine and lit candles for Shabbat, as Sara smiled at me in my parlor.

Now she is here again, when I thought she would only ever be a memory, and anything I can think to say seems inadequate.

The serving girl comes and deposits a tray on the table, laden with a pair of coffee bowls, a kettle, and twin dishes of sugar and salt.

Cecilia reaches for the kettle. "You should wait," I tell her. "It is still brewing."

"Oh. How long?"

"Only a short while."

"Like tea," she says.

"A little. The difference is that we drink the grounds."

"Like chocolate?"

"Yes."

An awkward silence settles over us. Then Cecilia asks, "Are *you* married?" and I splutter in shock. "Pardon," she says. "Was that too abrupt?"

"Somewhat," I reply.

"I—I have forgotten how to talk to people, I suppose. It has been some time since I went out."

"How long have you been shut in that house?"

"I came to London in February."

"Five months," I say, appalled. "Five months, and you didn't leave once?" She doesn't respond, staring down at her hands, gripping the edge of the table. I feel a fleeting moment of guilt; I hadn't meant to sound accusatory. I clear my throat. "I am not married," I say.

"Why?"

I think of Sara. What would she think of me now—if she could see Cecilia and me together, huddled like conspirators over a dish of coffee, pretending there is no more significance to this meeting than sugar and salt and roasting beans?

Would she be angry? Amused? Betrayed?

I say, "I have never had the inclination to."

"No inclination to marry," Cecilia repeats, clearly confounded by the sentiment.

"My life is busy enough as it is." I open the lid of the kettle to check on the coffee; it seems strong enough, so I pour it into the dishes.

Cecilia sniffs hers cautiously. Then she takes a small, hesitant sip, and immediately begins to cough. "It is bitter!" The dish slops dangerously in her hands. "It is one of your decoctions, disguised."

Her face is scrunched up in disgust, cheeks red, eyes flaring with righteous indignation. It is desperately endearing. I take the dish back from her. "I swear to you, it is not," I say. "I will sugar it. And a little salt will also help."

I do so and pass her the dish again. She takes another sip. "Better," she mumbles.

We drink in silence. Eventually, I drain my dish. When I look back at her, Cecilia's is also empty, and she is reaching for the kettle.

I pull it away from her. "I think not."

"Why is that?"

"You will be overstimulated."

"I won't," she replies, miffed. She bounces her foot against the floor. "May I ask you something?"

"Yes?"

"Why is it that you wear a beard, when it marks you so clearly as foreign?"

"It is preferred that Jews remain unshaven, when possible. I couldn't wear one in Lisbon. Still, I am obvious enough a Jew, even without it. It is a wonder that my family ever passed for gentiles at all." I pause. "I suppose, in a way, we did not. We were only ever conversos."

"Conversos? As in, converts?"

"Yes."

She sighs. "Your life is so different from my own. I can't imagine living under such permanent suspicions."

"We are not so different as you might think."

"We are as similar as an oak and a dandelion."

I chuckle. "How so?"

"You have roots here," she replies. "You are steady. But I don't belong anywhere; I seem constantly near to blowing away."

"Both an oak and a dandelion have roots."

"One is easier to fell than the other."

"But both are deserving of standing," I say. "Life has value, regardless of who lives it."

She smiles at me with disarming warmth, and I feel my cheeks heat. Jan chooses that moment to return, which is something of a relief. "Three sacks, with two more for next week," he says triumphantly. He slides into the booth to sit next to me, gesturing to the serving girl for another coffee. Then he sees the embarrassment on my face. "Ah. Am I interrupting something? Shall I leave you two be?"

"No, of course not," Cecilia responds, clearing her throat. "Mendes said you are a coffee roaster, Jan?"

"I suppose you ought to call me David," I tell her, resigned. Hearing her say Mendes seems wrong now. It makes me feel as if she is still my patient.

Cecilia smiles again. I pour myself another dish of coffee and take a gulp.

Jan launches into an anecdote in which he describes attempting to pay a bailiff with a single unroasted coffee bean, which he claimed would yield a tree when planted and make its owner great returns. The scheme had not worked, of course—frankly, I doubt the incident ever occurred—but the story sends Cecilia into a fit of giggles all the same.

It is wonderful to see her laugh again. It transforms her entirely from the wraithlike woman I had last seen at the townhouse. In the light of the wall sconces, she looks far less severe: The warmth of the room has made her skin blush red at her cheeks and collarbone, and her hair glows like spun sugar. She has a small scattering of freckles on her cheeks, which I hadn't noticed before; her mouth is slightly uneven, dipping subtly to the left. There is a tiny scar drawn across her lower lip, like a stitch of silver thread. A childhood injury, perhaps.

Jan says my name. "Pardon?" I reply. I haven't been following the conversation.

"It grows late," he says. "I fear I must leave. Supper at mine Wednesday, remember."

"I know." It is growing late; I can only imagine the panic Lady Eden must be in. I fear we will be found by the constables soon enough. I give Cecilia a significant look, and she sighs.

"I suppose I ought to leave, also," she says.

We exit the coffeehouse and walk to the main intersection. It is a warm night, with a light breeze. There is a peddler standing across the road with an impressive collection of broadsides to sell, paper fluttering in the wind. Cecilia notices him and seems delighted. "Look at that!" she says. "What does he do if it rains? Doesn't it ruin them all?"

"I shall say farewell to you here, Cecilia," Jan says, smiling. "It was an honor to meet you."

"And you, sir. David, how much does a broadside cost?"

I sigh and retrieve a penny from my purse. She snatches it from me and rushes across the street.

Jan watches her go with a wistful expression. "Poor thing," he says.

"I doubt she wants your pity, Jan."

He laughs. "No fear of that, David," he replies, patting my shoulder. "I meant you."

Then he leaves as I scowl at his back. I understand what he is implying, of course, but it can't even be considered. Anything between Cecilia and me would be utter madness, and there the thought must end.

Soon enough, Cecilia returns. She has bought a lascivious ballad entitled "The Lusty Coachman of Westminster," which she seems far too pleased by. My embarrassment clearly amuses her. I instruct her to hide it before we return to the townhouse.

"It isn't yet midnight," she tells me. "Can we see the river?"

"The river?"

"The Thames, David. I have heard it passes through London, although perhaps that was mere rumor?"

I sigh. "If we see the river," I say, "we must be quick. And then we ought to return. If your sister calls the constables . . ."

"I know. We will be quick, I swear."

I surrender. I lead her south, until we reach the Thames. At this time of night, the riverbanks are largely deserted, but boats still pass through, sporadic points of light dancing across the horizon like fireflies. Cecilia turns so the breeze catches her hair, and she tips her head toward the stars. Dimly illuminated by a streetlamp, light pooling on her cheeks, she looks like a painting by a Dutch master.

Bringing her back to the townhouse will feel like imprisoning her. But what other choice do I have? She is Lord Eden's sister-in-law. She has no money nor prospects. The constables will come for her, and if I am found complicit in her disappearance, I could see the noose. I have no choice but to ensure her return.

"The moon is full," she says. "Like a pearl."

I glance up. It does look something like a pearl, stars stranded at either side: a brooch pinned to the night. "I treated a pearl merchant last year," I say. "He does trade in Virginia. He said there are so many pearls there men pluck them from rivers like grapes from a vine."

"What was wrong with him?"

"Cramping of the stomach."

"How did you treat it?"

"Foxglove."

"Foxglove? I thought that was poisonous."

I reply, "It is, in certain doses. Brewed correctly, it can stop a man's heart in one swallow."

"A dangerous cure," she says.

"For both doctor and patient. No doubt some physicians have administered too much and made themselves a poisoner."

"Does that happen often? Treatments causing more harm than the sickness itself?"

"It is a constant risk," I say. I don't wish to explain further. There are some medicines I prescribe only out of desperation, knowing that death is already a certainty. I gave Manuel foxglove, also. And henbane, eventually, to lessen the pain.

Cecilia inches slightly closer, her arm pressing against mine. "What sort of pearls did he trade, your patient?" she asks. "Did he show you any?"

"He had many *barrocos*. Pardon, I don't know the English name. Pearls that are not round, but irregularly shaped. He said that they often sell for more than those that are perfect. He showed me a little chest full of them."

"Were they beautiful?"

"Yes. They were tiny, like seeds to be planted, in a thousand different colors."

"Barrocos," Cecilia murmurs. Her pronunciation is atrocious; I resist the urge to laugh. Still, she knows I am amused, because her eyes meet mine, and her lips twitch. The backs of our hands brush.

If only we could stay here always, you and I, and pretend the earth is no longer turning.

Cecilia glances to the sky, then turns to look at me directly. "I apologize, David," she says, "if I have forced you to keep me company today."

"I wanted to."

She glances down at the water in a movement that might have seemed bashful, if bashfulness weren't so contrary to her nature. "Would you see me again, if I wished it?"

"As your doctor, you mean?"

She doesn't reply for some time, staring at me with a faint frown, as if considering something. Then she says, "No. I don't want you to be my doctor. I want to see you again as I have today, without expectation nor objective."

"I . . ." Shocked, I look back to the Thames, uncertain how to respond. "Why?"

"I enjoy your company. I would like us to be friends."

"But—even if . . ." I shake my head. "It doesn't matter. Your sister would never allow it."

Cecilia doesn't bother to deny this, and we both fall quiet. The moon watches us impassively. On the water, a barge floats by, stuffed full of raucous gentry. They cast paint spills of light and color across the water, their laughter a dissonant chord against the patient rhythm of the tides. Neither of us speak until the noise fades away.

"We could meet in secret," Cecilia says. "Tomorrow night. Why not? I could sneak out again—through the door this time, late, when Margaret is asleep, and then we could find each other."

"I can't do that."

"Why? You don't want to see me?"

"If we are found out . . ."

"I will take the blame if we are discovered, I swear. I only want . . ." She sighs, covering her face with her hands. "I know it is selfish to ask," she says into her palms. "I don't want to put you in harm's way; I could go alone, but . . ."

"Don't go alone," I say, alarmed. Cecilia would be in great danger, out after dark in London, with neither money nor chaperone.

She drops her hands. "Does that mean you'll come?"

"I . . ."

"Please come," she says. She takes hold of my forearm, leaning forward to look at me, pleading. "We could meet at midnight. The intersection by the townhouses. Say you'll be there."

There is no sensible response but refusal, and yet the words cling to my throat. The way she is staring at me—through her eyelashes, desperate, luminous—is utterly overwhelming. I feel as if any reply will be inadequate, as meaningless as silence.

"Please, David," she says. "I beg of you. We hardly know each other, it is absurd, but . . . I feel better when you are with me. I don't know why, but I do."

"My company can't provide you a cure, Cecilia," I tell her. "I can't restore you to the way you once were."

"I don't expect to be as I once was; I don't think that's possible. But I'd like to be someone I can recognize as myself. I despise this hollow stranger I've become."

"You will always be yourself. No one can take that from you."

"Then prove that to me," she says. She lifts her chin, and the breeze sends her hair sprawling around her shoulders. "I need you to prove it. I need someone else to help me prove it, someone who is not Margaret, who is not myself. I see that now. And even if you can't provide a cure, even if you can't treat me—you must see me again. Promise that you will."

In the planes of her face, hope overlines desperation like oil upon water. Rejection and acceptance seem cruel in equal measure.

I say, "Only once. It can't be more than that."

"I know."

"Very well," I tell her. "Tomorrow at midnight. I will meet you then."

She is so pleased she laughs, a sound clean and bright, and I release my reservations. When we met, I saw myself in the mirror of her grief; since then, I have been unable to separate reality from reflection. If I left her now—if I never saw her again—I would leave some part of me with her, trapped behind the glass.

So I must see her again. Even if only once.

Even if I know that it may lead us both to ruin.

When we return to the townhouse, Lady Eden runs down the stairs to greet us, skirts in hands, eyes welling with tears. She flings herself at her sister, embracing her. Cecilia remains stiff and pale within the shackle of her arms.

"I am so glad you are safe," Lady Eden says. "I was sick with worry."

Cecilia replies, "I didn't go far. Only to the park."

"Without chaperone—and through the *window*. Were you hurt?"

"Master Mendes found me." Cecilia detaches herself from Lady Eden. "He treated my wounds, and he insisted on returning me here immediately."

This is far from the truth. But I understand why she has lied when Lady Eden turns to look at me; for the first time, her expression is entirely free of contempt. She clasps her hands together and says, "I am so grateful, sir," with disarming earnestness.

I bow so my face is obscured, hoping to hide my shame at the deception. "Of course, my lady."

When I straighten again, I notice a small, fuzzy shape emerging at the top of the steps, and it barrels down them with great speed. It is only when a wet nose presses against my calf that I realize I am being accosted by a small, doe-eyed spaniel. It scrabbles at my leg with great vigor, yapping plaintively.

"Duchess!" someone calls as a person comes in chase of the dog, he himself almost falling down the steps in his eagerness. "Duchess, down! Oh, pardon, sir!"

The newcomer is vaguely familiar: I realize, with some surprise, that he is the handsome green-eyed man I bumped into the first time I went to Saint James's Park.

He recognizes me at the same moment I do him. "What luck!" he says, delighted, as he scoops the dog up into his arms. "It must be Providence, sir, that we meet again."

"Yes," I say, confused. "Good evening."

"Good evening." He sweeps me an extravagant bow. His clothing is as ridiculous as it had been when last I saw him, ribbons traded for a great waterfall of lavender lace, shoes extravagantly high heeled. His luxuriant brown wig is so long it hits his elbows, which is entirely unaccountable to me. It must become stuck in closing doors very often. "I am Sir Samuel Grey," he says, "of the Kent Greys."

"David Mendes."

"A pleasure, Master Mendes." Grey turns the full force of his formidable smile on Cecilia; she smiles back reflexively, although there is also some shock in her expression. "And you must be Mistress Thorowgood. I am glad to meet you at last."

Pale faced—clearly she had envisioned this meeting going very differently—Lady Eden says, "Sir Grey, I thought you had already left."

"Ah, yes, pardon. I went to bid Uncle Robert farewell, but on my way out, I stumbled upon your library and found myself waylaid. And then the pantry. And the music room, also. Duchess loves the sound of the harpsichord." He kisses the dog's nose. "She has the ear of a virtuoso, if not the fingers of one."

"Uncle Robert," Cecilia says, her eyes narrowing.

Sir Grey blinks at her, surprised. "He didn't tell you?"

"Tell me what?"

Lady Eden clears her throat and addresses me. "My thanks again, Master Mendes," she says, "for returning my sister safely."

A clear dismissal. I bow to her, and then glance at Cecilia; she is still staring at Sir Grey, confounded.

"And a pleasure as always, Sir Grey," Lady Eden continues, giving him a meaningful look.

"Ah—right," Grey replies. "I shall return tomorrow?"

"Please do," Lady Eden replies.

There is, of course, no such invitation extended to me.

Grey and I repeat our farewell to Cecilia. Her expression is wary and hopeful as she curtsies to me, and I feel a pang of guilt. I wish I could offer her something more to help—there must be some words of comfort, or some reassurance, that would be superior to what I have already said—but I have no choice except to turn and leave.

As we walk out of the front gate, Grey deems it somehow appropriate to initiate conversation. He stops and turns to me. "Forgive me, sir," he says. "But I must ask—how do you know Mistress Thorowgood?"

"I was her doctor."

"But no longer?"

"No longer," I echo.

"Providence, then, for you to have found her. I fear I must have somehow made a bad impression upon her, if she would rather leap out the window than meet me!"

"Perhaps," I reply in as mild a tone as I can manage.

Sir Grey begins tapping his foot against the ground in an odd, syncopated rhythm. His right arm swings back and forth in a careless, meaningless gesture, and his spaniel—tucked beneath his armpit like a roll of linens—squirms in consternation, yapping loudly. He makes a distressed noise. "Pardon, Duchess. I forgot you were there!"

I watch him as he attempts to placate the dog, and I find myself further aggravated. The day has been long, and I am exhausted. My head feels like a cannonball upon my neck. Small, floating dots impugn on my vision and swirl in an ill-timed dance. Sir Grey suddenly has the character of an actor in a comedy, awaiting my reply so we can continue through the script.

I clear my throat. "I must . . ." I say, and then I don't know how to continue. I gesture weakly to the road.

"Oh, yes, of course." Grey bows to me. "I shall return home, then. Farewell, Master Mendes."

"Farewell."

He crosses the street with the dog cradled in his arms like a baby, turning to give me another smile before disappearing into his home. I am left alone on the pavement, staring at the gilded crest on his door.

I look back to the Eden townhouse. I recall the promise I made to Cecilia to meet with her tomorrow, and my chest tightens with anxiety and anticipation. I wonder if she doesn't want to see me, not really—if all she wants from me is an excuse to leave this place for another night, and taste freedom again.

I stand by the railing, frozen in thought, wondering if I ought to return and tell her I have changed my mind.

And then, unbidden, I recall our hands over the spinet keys. I envision her fingers against mine again, now scratched with wounds I tended; our eyes meeting; the warmth of her skin; and I am undone.

I turn away from the townhouse and walk back the way I came.

CHAPTER NINE

Cecilia

The door shuts behind David. I hear a snatch of Sir Grey's voice, chattering from ahead, but I can't tell what he is saying, and I am given no opportunity to decipher it. The moment we are alone, the relieved smile falls from Margaret's face. She grips my arm so tightly it hurts, and she pulls me up the stairs.

"Maggie," I say as she drags me through the corridor. And then, once we are in my room, I repeat, "Maggie." I don't know how to continue. She doesn't look at me. She flings me over to the bed and goes to stand by the window.

"Are you hurt, Cecilia?" she says to the glass.

"No. Not really."

"Where did you go?"

"To the park."

"Why?"

"Because it was away from here," I reply truthfully. "And I didn't know where else to go."

Margaret nods. She takes hold of the windowsill and grips it tightly, as if the wall is in danger of detaching from the rest of the manor and it is her obligation to keep it in place.

"Have I been so cruel to you?" she asks. "Are you so truly desperate to leave?"

"It wasn't that," I reply weakly. "I swear, Maggie, I only . . ."

"You only what?"

"I . . ."

"Answer me, Cecilia."

"I—If—" There is a pang of nausea in my stomach, and I find myself hunching over. "The thought of meeting a suitor . . . it frightened me, and—"

"You were reckless," Margaret snarls. "I have never known you to act with such stupidity. You are not stupid. So I must conclude that you were reckless on purpose. That you wanted to hurt yourself."

"I am sorry," I respond through gritted teeth, trying to breathe through the sudden tightness in my chest.

"You don't understand," she says, her voice growing steadily colder. "You have never understood, I realize that now. Mother told me to keep you safe, and everything I have ever done has been to that end. Our entire lives, I have done all in my power to ensure you were secure and content. Was it wrong to ask, this once—to ask you to be *reasonable,* just this once—!" She gives a shriek of anger and claws at the windowsill, her nails wailing against the wood. "I told you when you came here that I wanted you to be happy."

"And yet you would have me marry a man I have never met," I reply, temper fraying. "I heard what Sir Grey said—*Uncle* Robert. What is this, Maggie? Why am I here?"

She scowls. "You are here because you are my sister, and I care for you."

"I used to think that, but now I'm not so certain."

"Sir Grey's mother was Robert's sister, may she rest in peace. And now he is Robert's heir," she says. "Until—until we have a child of our own."

Margaret bites her lip, turns away from me. Her lashes lower, her shoulders hunch. Perhaps she expects me to interrupt her now, to twist her vulnerability into a knot to bind her—as she would me—but I cannot. I recall instead the last time I saw her this way, when she first showed me the house, years ago, after she had moved in: a small room not far from my own, the door usually kept locked. It contained a large wooden cot, with a mother-of-pearl inlay in the headboard; a large chair for a wet nurse to sit upon; a small, almost childlike rug, with an oversized and insistent pattern of rose vines; and Margaret herself, lashes trembling, as she told me, *Perhaps someday*.

"Cecilia," Margaret says. "Sir Grey is in need of a wife."

"And if I were to marry him, and Robert were to die, you would become our ward." She flinches; I know I have struck home. "You would have your title and your status maintained," I say, "because your little sister would become your guarantor."

"Am I so wrong for wanting security?" she demands. "To prevent myself from living reliant on another's charity, alone and unwanted?"

"Like me?" I ask her darkly, and she draws in a sharp breath, shrinking back slightly.

"Robert was the one who suggested it," she says, voice shaking. "He thought— Sir Grey has struggled to find a match. It seemed a good idea."

"And yet you failed to suggest it before I arrived here. Because you knew, perhaps, that I would refuse?"

"Cecilia, you are a widow!" Margaret cries. "A widow, and an impoverished one, at that. Here is a man our age, handsome, wealthy, willing to consider you—and yet you leaped out of a window rather than meet him. It feels as if you would rather die than accept the help I have offered. Why? Do I not love you enough? Have I not given you enough?"

"When you invited me here," I say, "I thought it was because you cared for me. But it was because of this, wasn't it? Your marriage scheme."

She says, "I do care for you."

But she doesn't deny it, either.

My chest tightens, and my ears roar. I hunch over and curl my arms around myself. My breaths have quickened, but my lungs feel slow; they push the air away before it is inside, like overeager bellows, putting the fire out.

"You are not in your right mind," Margaret says quietly. "That much is clear. Once you have calmed down, you will understand that I have your best interests at heart. You frightened me today. I can no longer trust you to keep yourself safe."

"Maggie—"

"You are not permitted to leave the townhouse again," she says. "Accompanied, or otherwise."

"Until when?" I exclaim. "You can't keep me prisoner here."

"You are not a prisoner. You are a patient, and you require treatment. I will ensure you are safe until you are well. You will take your medicines, and you will be polite and apologetic to Sir Grey, once he returns."

"But—"

"I will have the windows locked. You can't leave again. You could hurt yourself. And this time, to have to rely upon a *Jew* for ensuring your safety—I can't countenance it."

I bristle. "Mendes is—"

"I don't care what Mendes is. He is irrelevant now. You must stay here, where I know you are safe. I can't risk you disappearing. I was so *frightened*."

I begin to protest once more—opening my mouth to say her name—but then she makes a choked sound, and I realize she is crying. My complaints die in my throat. I haven't seen Margaret cry since we were children. She wipes a tear from her cheek with the heel of her hand, then she steps toward me, crouches down, and gathers me into an embrace.

I could struggle, but what would be the use? Instead, I go limp in her arms. It feels as if I am the paper boat in Saint James's Park, bobbing in the water, sent sprawling by the wind. It may be that Margaret is correct: I am a risk, a burden. I am capable of hurting myself, of making decisions contrary to my own well-being. I have never been much for temperance, nor self-control. That was how it was with Will; they call it falling, but with him it was a slide, a slip—a gentle slope, only realized once I reached its end. I never had a choice but to love him, even when he was engaged to someone else. And now David—

And now David. Whatever I feel for him—nascent as it is, uncertain and breathless as it is—it heralds danger, for both of us.

Perhaps if I am not imprisoned, I will take myself to the gallows.

Margaret continues to cry. Her hands press against my back like brands. I close my eyes, and I pretend I am beside the Thames once more. Night sky, summer breeze. David beside me, and the moon a pearl above us.

The next morning, I beg permission to go to the courtyard. Margaret doesn't allow it until she has seen me eat every bite of the pottage I have been brought for breakfast. I do so far too quickly, stuffing my mouth full of it. I take my decoctions, all of them, even the one for melancholy, as I promised David I would. And then—once I am outside—I hide behind the linden to cough most of it up.

Margaret doesn't notice my sickness. She waits in the doorway, reading a book of sermons clutched between whitened fingers.

My wounds from the fall are already well healed. The leaves David used worked as well as any bandage. The scratches are now only thin lines, like strands of pink thread laid across my palm. As I walk my loops around the tree, I trail my hand across the bark, feeling the sting of the coarse trunk against the itching skin. It is painful, but the pain is welcome. It grounds me. I feel light-headed today, as if I might fade into nothingness.

David promised he would see me again tonight. Will he come?

Will I go?

Margaret calls my name. When I turn to her, I see there is a manservant standing with her in the doorway.

"Sir Grey has returned," she says to me.

She marches me to my room and has me change into my primrose dress, which we must pin tighter, as its bodice is now too large. As she dusts my cheeks with rouge, she mutters to herself, "There. Much better."

I ignore her. In the mirror, the woman who returns my gaze remains plain and uninspiring. My cheeks are hollow, and the yellow of the dress makes my skin look sallow. No amount of rouge will help.

After she deems me presentable, Margaret leads me to the parlor. I so rarely visit this room: it is cavernous, smelling faintly of tea and wallpaper paste. Sir Grey is sitting in one of the chairs, conversing with Sir Robert. He stands to greet us. He is wearing a chintz coat in orange and pink, so bright it hurts the eyes. I have a better impression of him in the daytime: he is pretty, boyish, with an impressive waterfall of a wig, and his smile is so wide and eager it seems to split his face in half. I realize he is likely younger than I am.

He bows. "Good morning," he says.

"Good morning," I reply, voice faint. Margaret jabs me in the waist with her elbow, and I fall into a stuttering curtsy.

We all sit together beside the tea service. Robert—who addresses Sir Grey with a coolness better befitting a schoolmaster than an uncle—inquires as to the health of his sister, and this somehow leads Sir Grey into an anecdote about crashing his barge into a wharf. He speaks without pause nor consideration, but he has a pleasant, high-pitched voice. It is airy, almost musical. It is easy to ignore the meaning of his words, hearing only the tones beneath them.

I fiddle with my skirts at Margaret's side, saying nothing at all. Eventually, Robert stands, and with a pointed look offers Margaret his arm; I realize they intend to leave Sir Grey and me alone together—not quite an impropriety, considering we are technically family, but near enough.

"Maggie—" I say, pleading, but she shakes her head.

"We have an appointment at court, Cecilia. The servants are here if you need anything."

"But—"

"Farewell, Sister," Robert says to me gruffly; then he gives Sir Grey a somewhat pointed stare. Sir Grey blanches in response.

They leave, and we are alone. Grey smiles at me, folding a foot over the opposite leg, displaying the pristine sole of his shoe: an open-backed mule, high heeled and square toed. He doesn't know what to do with his hands, and he picks absentmindedly at his nails, rolling his fingers together as if he is weaving.

"Mistress Thorowgood, I am aware that this is rather odd," he says.

I raise my brows, disarmed by his candor. "Yes, it is."

"I know we are strangers, but . . . We have seen each other many times through the window. Do you remember?"

"Oh! That was you?"

"It was!" He gives me a little wave, in the manner of the silhouette I had seen across the road. "You see?"

"I see, yes. I . . ." Sighing, I continue. "Forgive me, Sir Grey, for disappearing yesterday."

"Oh, it's no matter. And you must call me Samuel. Actually, no—call me Sam. That seems much friendlier. May I call you Cecilia? Is that too forward? At court there is a great fashion for first names. Thomas—as in Sir Thomas Clifford—says it is reflective of the king's egalitarian spirit—"

I have the sense he will chatter endlessly unless I stop him. "Cecilia is fine," I say.

"Excellent. But regardless!" He leans forward in his seat, coat gaping open. It is lined with purple silk. He smells strongly of perfume. "What say you, Cecilia?"

"I . . . to what?"

"Uncle Robert thinks I ought to court you," he says. "I know we hardly know each other. But I *must* take a wife, as Uncle Robert has insisted, and your sister has told me many wonderful things about you."

I blink at him, quite in shock. After a long pause, his expression becomes pleading, and I realize he has taken my silence as refusal.

"In all honesty," he rushes to say, "I know I am quite ill-suited to marriage. I am not a particularly enticing prospect, I accept that. But I hope you might consider it still."

"Ill-suited to marriage?"

"The physicians I have spoken with say I am afflicted with a permanent restlessness," he tells me. "My thoughts are like bees, swarming in my skull. Sometimes they fly out of my mouth without warning, and sometimes they buzz so loudly I can't hear anything else at all. I fear afflicting someone with such madness without warning would be cruel."

"It is not madness, surely," I say with a flash of sympathy. I understand what it is to fear your own mind. "Only . . . difference."

He smiles at me. "I should hope so. Regardless, I hope my offer might be amenable to you."

I open my mouth, then close it. I know what my sister would tell me in this moment: *Patience, Cecilia. Affection comes with time. This is the best that you can hope for.*

He seems sweet enough, handsome enough. And despite all the pressure placed upon us by our relatives, I have the sense he would accept my refusal.

But what other choice do I have? My widow's pension is small, and I am reliant on my sister's charity. If I cast myself upon Will's family, beg them for refuge, they would take me in—but for how long? How long until I meet a similar fate, to be handed to another gentleman as a consolation prize?

"I cannot make any promises," I tell Samuel Grey. "But I promise to consider it."

Grey blinks at me. He unfolds his legs. Then he refolds them in the same position as before; unfolds them again. "Really?"

I smile quizzically. "Yes, really."

"Goodness!" he says. "Did you know, I have asked two women this month already. I poured tea on the last one. Accidentally, of course, although she maintains otherwise."

This is so oddly tragic, so patently absurd, that I bend over and begin laughing into my skirt. Grey also laughs, albeit with some confusion, and for some time we don't speak at all.

"Sir Grey—Sam—" I say once I am recovered, and I offer him

my hand across the coffee table. He takes it in both of his as if to kiss it, but then he has a crisis of confidence, and he stares at my knuckles instead. I pry one of his hands away, shaking the other. "I have the sense," I tell him, "that we are each other's last resort. Considering this, we really ought to be friends before anything else, and see what may proceed from that."

"Friends," he says. "What an excellent idea! Are you certain?"

"Quite."

"I shall call upon you again, then. Do you know how to play whist?"

"I don't."

"Nor do I. We shall learn it together."

"I would be happy to," I reply. I pause, and then add, "May I ask you something?"

"Of course."

"You said your thoughts are like bees. Do they ever sting you?"

He cocks his head, eyes wide. He looks very much like his spaniel. "Why do you ask? Do yours sting you?"

"Yes. Quite often."

"Hm." He frowns in thought. "There is something my father once told me when I was young."

"What was that?"

"Bees sting because they are afraid, not because they are angry."

"That makes sense," I say. "I am often afraid."

He smiles at me. "So, then, you must be brave. That is the only solution. Not an absence of anger, but an absence of fear."

"An absence of fear? That is impossible, surely."

"Oh, yes," he says. "Of course it is. But it is worth trying, isn't it? Impossible things happen all the time. They killed King Charles, and now Charles is king again."

I laugh. "They are different men, I think."

"I know that. But it is amusing to consider, isn't it? Even from death, we can be restored."

Impossible things.

I think of David and myself by the Thames; Will and me in the church; the well whose edge I sat upon years ago, as I stared into the hungry dark. I could have fallen, I could have pushed myself down—but I didn't. I walked away.

David walked away, also, from Portugal and his past. He chose this city, chose life, and perhaps I can, too. He has lit within me an ember of something indefinable. It is stubborn and small, but it is present. I don't yet know what it is. Hope, desire, affection; it doesn't matter. Perhaps I should douse it, before I catch fire.

But I would rather burn than start drowning again.

That night, Margaret comes to my room far earlier than normal. She shuts the curtains and tells me to prepare for bed.

I do so sullenly, and then am left alone without so much as a candle to facilitate distraction. I am supposed to meet David in a half hour, but I can hardly lie here staring at the ceiling for all that time. So I prepare to leave, redressing, putting my sturdiest boots on, pinning up my hair. At the threshold of my bedroom I pause, recalling Margaret's fury the last time I ran away. But I am committed now. I can only pray that David keeps his word, and we remain undiscovered.

The window to my bedroom is locked, but my door is not. I sneak downstairs; I am not brave enough to attempt the front door, so I go toward the kitchens, thinking to leave through the back, as I did last time. I have my hand on the doorknob before I realize I can hear voices inside.

"—came back up," a woman says. It is Margaret. "Isn't there something a little . . . gentler?"

"If I dilute it, my lady, it will be less effective," comes the reply—another woman, whose voice I don't recognize.

"Very well, then."

There is a long pause. Through the door, I can hear water bubbling in a pot, the slow swish of the liquid being stirred.

"What's that?" Margaret asks.

"The poppy extract. It's nearly finished, my lady—one moment. I must speak the charms."

The unknown woman begins murmuring to herself, in a language I can't recognize, and my eyebrows raise. Margaret, consorting with pagans? Poppy extract? What on earth are they making?

"There," says the woman, and I can hear something being poured. "Finished. Now, as always, there may be nausea, confusion, a desperation to sleep. But it should do what you require. It has a bitter flavor, so mask it with food—something rich, ideally."

Margaret replies, "I always do."

My breath catches in my throat. My fingers curl against the door.

She wouldn't—she *wouldn't*—

I remember us as girls, her bringing me milk and honey, smoothing my hair down. It doesn't make sense. None of it makes any sense.

I don't have time to consider it. There are footsteps coming toward the door, and I don't have anywhere to hide. I could rush back down the hallway, but it is too long, I don't have time; instead I look quickly at the door, the hinges, and I step sideways and press myself against the wall, praying.

The door opens. Heavy as it is, the women leaving the kitchen do not bother to open it fully. It swings toward the wall, stops a hair's breadth from the tips of my shoes as I huddle behind it. I see nothing of my sister or her wise woman leaving, my vision blocked by the door, but I hear the rustle of their skirts. As the door swings shut, I catch a glimpse of them disappearing into the foyer.

I release a breath and try to slow my thrumming heart.

Once I have composed myself, I enter the kitchen. The keys to the back gate are on a hook on the wall. Now is not the time to agonize over what I have heard; freedom is in reach.

I leave the townhouse for the second time in two days. It feels just as illicit as it did before, even though I am leaving via a door this time, rather than a window. The back gate brings me to an alley behind the house, which stinks of urine and seethes with shadows. I cover my face with my sleeve and scuttle like a spider into the main road, which is still busy, despite the lateness of the hour.

There are a good number of people here, more than I had expected, all milling around the pavement as if waiting for something. Lanterns line the street, dotting the area with warm pinpricks of light. The flower seller—Katherine—is packing up her stall; I wave to her, and she waves back.

Once I am near, she gives me a small, hesitant curtsy. "Good evening, mistress."

"Good evening, Katherine," I reply. "It's quite busy tonight, isn't it?"

"There's a pageant coming by." She gestures to the crowd. "They're all hoping to catch some coins."

"A pageant?"

"Yes. My Lady Carlisle was married this afternoon. They should be here soon."

A pageant to celebrate a marriage sounds extraordinarily extravagant, but I suppose such things are common in London. With little better to do, I stand with Katherine by her stall, waiting alongside everyone else.

She gives me a curious look. "Might I ask, mistress, why you are always here without company?"

"Two times is not always," I huff. "I should have company soon."

"Oh? A gentleman, perhaps?"

I flush, seeing the corners of her mouth twitch in amusement. "Not that sort of company. Or—well, he is a gentleman, but . . ."

Then I hear a distant drumbeat, and I trail off. For a moment, I believe I have imagined the noise—Katherine is still looking at me quizzically—but soon the beat sounds again, and the crowd begins to whoop and separate, crowding to the edges of the cobbles to clear a space.

The beat is soon punctuated by a trumpet call, and then another. I gasp, for sheer shock at the sudden cacophony—with it comes the clash of a cymbal, and the round begins again. Once my surprise fades, I find myself tapping my fingers on my skirts to match the rhythm.

"Here they come," Katherine says in hushed excitement. A glowing light has emerged at the end of the street, slowly approaching us: lantern bearers in scarlet livery, their burdens swinging trails of fire through the air like shooting stars. Behind them come the drummers and the trumpeters. Gold ribbons protrude from the open mouths of the instruments, dancing in the expulsions of air. The drummers shout between each beat— "the Lord and Lady Carlisle are married!"—and the crowd watching roars in answer: "A marriage! A marriage!"

"Are there more musicians?" I ask Katherine once the shouting ends, and she laughs in response. Because then, quite suddenly, all the rest come, in a great horde that turns the corner of the street and swallows it whole: lutenists on donkeys wearing gold tassels around their ears; children in togas and animal masks shaking tambourines; poets declaiming verse from gilded wagons pulled by teams of strongmen wearing velvet capes; a wisp of a girl in a flower coronet, sitting on the shoulders of another woman, both singing a madrigal; dancers in silks, young and old, male and female; and dozens upon dozens of drunken revelers, who—having been subsumed within the mass of the pageant like wine poured into a barrel—pull others near them into the fray, so that the procession grows larger and larger with each step it takes, louder and louder, more and more joyful.

The noise is too great for Katherine to speak, so instead she simply jabs my arm and points at something. The target of her attention is clear: the bride and groom themselves, at the center of the crowd. They are young, likely younger than I, flushed with excitement and laughing with delight. They ride white horses with silver saddles and reins adorned with tiny bells; the bride's hair is down, falling in a russet veil to her midback, with white blooms and sparkling gems threaded into each lock. Her dress is a palest white, near translucent, and she wears a crown that frames her head in glowing spears of gold. Her husband beside her wears white, also, and a similar crown of silver. With one hand, he clutches her palm, and with the other, he throws coins to the crowd—but he never looks away from his wife. He is the moon to her sun.

I don't bother to chase the coins, but Katherine does. I soon lose sight of her as she plunges into the melee. I don't care. The pageant, its noise and color and joy, has made me a part of it already—as much a part of it as the trumpeters or the poets or the bride and groom. And when a group of dancing girls in emerald dresses spins by, offering hands to me so I can join them, I follow them gladly. We all clap and laugh as we twirl around the

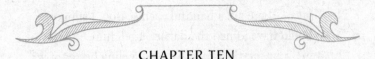

CHAPTER TEN

Cecilia

It takes some effort to recover fully from the ordeal of the pageant, and I bow over by the wall for several minutes. Eventually, I hear someone saying something behind me; I am too overwhelmed to decipher it. Then a hand lays very lightly on my back, and I flinch, turning around. It is David. He is in his work clothes: a dark jacket, his hair tied back, beard newly trimmed. Perhaps he came from an appointment. In the warm light of the lanterns, he seems to glow and flicker like a candle flame.

"Hello," I say, smiling. "You're here." Then I stumble a little. He seizes my forearms to prevent me from falling over.

"Are you all right?" he asks.

"Yes," I say. "More than all right. But I am a little dizzy. They were spinning me."

He chuckles. "I saw. Are you able to stand on your own?"

I lean a little further into his grip. "Not yet," I lie. "I feel as if I have been in a windstorm."

"It was an impressive pageant. They clearly spared no expense."

"Are those common here?"

He shrugs. "There are a handful each season, I suppose."

"You should have joined the dance," I tell him.

"I haven't your mettle, I fear. Are you feeling better now?"

"Yes."

He releases me. "I was worried," he tells me, "when I couldn't see you through the crowd."

"Did you think I hadn't come?"

"I . . . yes, I suppose I did. I assumed that your sister would be displeased at your disappearance."

"She will be, if she discovers it. But I managed to escape undetected."

"Was your suitor angry with you yesterday?" he asks.

"You mean Sir Grey?"

"Yes."

"I . . . no, he wasn't angry. I'm not certain he *can* be angry. He is sweet natured, if a little strange."

"The meeting went well, then?" he says.

"What do you mean, went well? I haven't agreed to marry him, if that's what you're asking."

His lips thin. "But you haven't refused, either."

He seems aggravated. I smile. "Does that upset you?"

"Why would it upset me?"

"I wouldn't know," I say. "You tell me."

"Cecilia . . ."

I shouldn't be provoking him like this; it is like poking at an aching tooth with my tongue, hoping for some outcome other than pain. I turn away from him and start walking down the street. "Wait," David says, chasing after me. "Where are you going?"

I stop. "I suppose I don't know. I thought we could follow the pageant."

"It's long gone by now, I fear. You want to dance again?"

"To hear the music, more than anything. It has been so long since I heard a performance like that."

He gives me a considering look. "Come with me."

I take his arm as he offers it, and we walk together toward the heart of the city.

"It is only a short way," he tells me. "But you must say if you want to stop and rest."

"Where are we going?"

He smiles, but he doesn't respond. Instead, he says, "You seem happy, you know. I mean—you *seemed* happy when you were dancing. Much happier than I've ever seen you before."

"How long were you watching me?" I ask.

He rubs at the back of his neck with his free hand, clearly embarrassed. "Not for long. It was difficult not to. Well— I mean—"

"I *am* happy," I say, interrupting him. "Perhaps it was your epithymum. Does it really cure melancholy? I didn't believe it could, until now."

"In truth? I don't know. Perhaps being willing to take it means a patient is already bound to recover; perhaps it really does ease sorrow. There's no way to tell."

"Have you ever taken it?"

He seems startled by the question. "No," he says. "I haven't."

We continue for a few minutes more, and then we reach an opening in the road. Beyond it, there is a large square, where there are dozens of fashionably dressed people milling about and sitting on benches, all drinking and smoking and laughing. Abandoned stalls and signs indicate that during the day, this is a market—but for now, it has become a playground for the jubilant souls spilling out of the theater at the square's other end. A performance has clearly just finished. Its audience, now released, tumbles over one another like pebbles in a stream, eager to gulp the fresh air and join the others in their amusements.

I give David a curious look. "Covent Garden," he says. He points to an elderly man who is clearly apart from the rest of the crowd, sitting on a stool at the corner of the square. He is dressed in austere, old-fashioned clothing, and he doesn't seem much interested in anyone around him. "He will begin soon. We should take a seat."

Mystified, I follow David to an unoccupied bench. We watch as the elderly man pulls a case from beside him onto his lap and undoes the clasps. He puts his hat down in front of him. Then he pulls an instrument from the case: a silver flute, tarnished with age, which he handles with the careful delicacy of an artisan.

I laugh, delighted. "Did we come to hear the flautist?"

"He is very good. He always plays after the Wednesday performance."

I hum and shuffle closer to him. "Do *you* play anything, David? I never asked."

"No, I don't. I sang sometimes when I was a boy. But my father is a much better singer than I. He was *hazan*—a singer—at our synagogue for a few years, when we came here."

I filed away the word *hazan*, alongside *converso, baroccos, decoction*. His English is threaded with so many extraordinary words, the vast pattern of things he has encountered; my language feels so plain by comparison.

The flautist begins. David is correct; he is very good. His playing reminds me of a songbird trilling, light and fast, fingers flying across the instrument. A number of people stop to toss coins into his cap. He doesn't acknowledge them.

The flautist finishes a song, and we clap alongside the others in the square.

"I used to dream of that," I say as the flautist pauses to count his coins. "Playing for a crowd, I mean. I imagined performing at court with the king watching."

It is only as I say this that I realize I have moved closer still to David, and our hands are brushing against each other on the bench; he doesn't move away. He watches me with dark eyes half lidded, a hint of a smile at the corner of his mouth. "Do you dream of it still?" he asks me.

"I'm not certain. It feels so impossible."

"There are many things far more impossible than that," he says. "When I was a child, I dreamed of making a golem that would do my work for me."

"A golem?"

"It's a . . . sort of servant, I suppose. You make it out of clay and use magic to make it do your bidding. I thought I could build one, and it could learn how to be a physician in my stead. Then I could live in the garden forever and spend all my time climbing the pomegranate trees."

I laugh at this. Then—in a foolish moment of impulse— I place my hand over his. "A shame you never managed it."

"Yes," he says, and his fingers curl beneath mine.

I feel like a girl again, pining after the village boys who grinned at me when I walked into church: giddy with attraction, ecstatic at the slightest brush of skin. It has been so long since I last felt like this. Not since the earliest days with Will, not since we danced around the roses at our wedding. The thrill of that relationship had been brief, before we became comfortable and contented. We'd fallen so easily into domesticity, the two of us; we had no barriers in our way.

But this, David and me—it is not easy. It never can be. That is evident enough, in the agonized movement of David's eyes toward our hands, the war I can sense in his thoughts. And with war comes wounds: It hurts us both that we have to be afraid; that the eyes of everyone around us feel as sharp as knives; that we cannot fall into this as two other people would, without faith and fear and obligation to prevent them. It hurts that every touch must threaten such a heavy price.

But it hurts more, I think, when David pulls his hand away.

The flautist begins to play again. I find I don't have the patience to listen, and I stand up.

David follows me as I exit the square. "Shall we return to the townhouse?" he asks me.

"I don't want to go back yet, we've hardly been out at all. Let's go somewhere else. What's open this time of night?"

"Nearby? Alehouses." He seems little enthused by the idea.

"What about the park?"

"It is closed."

"I don't see how they could close it, really," I say. "It is so enormous, and the fence is so low. It must be quite pretty after dark, with the sky reflected in the water. I'd like to see it."

He pinches the bridge of his nose. "You want to break into Saint James's Park?"

"Yes, why not?"

"Why not," he mutters. "Why not. *Por que não, a esta hora—*"

He *is* tiresome sometimes. Ignoring him, I take his arm, dragging him in the correct direction.

As we approach the park, the scent of the air changes from city stink to grass and summer blooms. I take a deep breath and sigh in pleasure. David seems less impressed. He fiddles with his hair tie, saying, "We ought to return soon."

"It isn't *that* late yet. Earlier than we stayed out last time."

"Even so," he replies. "It will be dark in the park. Perhaps we should find a lantern."

"Oh, hush. The moon is enough."

I regret this claim, however, when we reach the park itself. It is almost pitch black inside. The view of the path is obscured by the looming shadows of the trees, and the gate is closed.

"See," David says. "Locked."

"We could still go inside," I say. He looks positively queasy at the suggestion, and I can't help but laugh at him. "You would make a terrible criminal, you know."

"I shall take that as a compliment," he replies.

"It wasn't one. Did you never sneak out as a child?"

"No. I took a cake once from my mother's pantry, after she told me not to. I ate some of it, then cried for shame and put it back."

"What, half eaten?"

"Yes."

I snort. "That is worse than if you finished it."

Then I hike up my skirts and prepare myself to vault the fence. Alarmed, David reaches for me, but I slip out of his grasp. "Cecilia, listen—if we were to go in there, it is likely we would be mugged, or else—oh, wait—*don't*—"

I tumble down the other side of the fence, onto the grass, falling flat on my back. "Cecilia?" David says. There is a rustle of fabric, a curse, and then he is standing beside me. It is so dark I can't see his face, only a vague silhouette. "Are you injured?"

"No."

He offers me his hand, pulling me up. "I suppose we're committed now. If we follow the path, we will reach the canal. It should be brighter there."

He begins to walk, and I follow, gripping his sleeve so I don't lose him. It takes barely a minute before we break through the cover of the trees and reach the center of the park.

Saint James's is different at night. The darkness obscures reality: the grass looks like a puddle of ink, the fountain in the distance a sweeping skeleton of stone. The moon makes the sky a curtain, a half sphere of light parting the darkness and peering through the gap. I almost gasp to see it, pausing at a tree to stare.

Beside me, David comments, "It is cold tonight. Did you bring a jacket? I believe you still have one of mine, somewhere, which I left with you."

I turn to look at him. He is barely visible in the moonlight, but unlike the park itself, the darkness hasn't changed him. He is as much David Mendes as he has ever been, earnest and concerned and kind. When I don't reply, he says my name in question, and his voice feels as familiar as one of my harpsichord pieces. He is luminous. The moon cannot compare.

I whip around so he can't see my expression. "I'm fine," I say, and march toward the canal. He sighs and follows me.

It is certainly as beautiful as I had imagined: The stars are reflected so faithfully in the water that the sky seems endless, wrapping around us like a shroud. I point at the canal. "See?" I say. "Isn't it lovely?"

"You could have looked at the sky from *anywhere* in the city and seen the same thing."

"Perhaps you ought to see a fellow physician, David. You are so dull I fear you will soon bore yourself to death."

David throws his head back and laughs. He has an ugly laugh, unreserved and overloud. It is quite wonderful. "Perhaps so," he agrees.

We continue a meandering path along the canal. I walk along the edge of the water, at the raised area of the pavement, lifting my arms to balance myself. After I stumble and nearly fall, I use one hand to hold on to David's shoulder. He doesn't protest.

We reach the end of the canal. Instead of rounding the corner, I step down and turn to him, expression grim.

"Is something the matter?" he asks.

"What if I *do* marry Sir Grey?" I say.

His expression shutters. "I don't know," he replies. "What if you do?"

"He seems sweet enough."

"Yes."

"He would allow me my freedoms, I think. Give me security. We would likely spend half the year in London, too; I'd be near my sister."

"I thought you didn't like London."

"I think I could come to like it," I admit. "If I had the time to learn it properly. Tonight has taught me that. But I have never lived in a city before, not really. I don't know if I can."

"You can, if you wish to," he says. "I felt the same once. When I first chose to move here, I wondered constantly if I was making a mistake. I feared this city would be cruel, but it was not. Or rather—even though it *has* been cruel sometimes, I have never regretted coming here."

"But you are brave," I tell him, my throat tightening as I speak. "And I am not."

"You are brave, also."

"I am not. When Will—" My stomach turns, and I stop speaking. I breathe shakily. David waits without prompting me. I continue. "When Will passed, I was asked if I wished to see him—to see the body—before they took him away. To say goodbye. And I couldn't. I couldn't stomach it. I couldn't even *look* at him. I wasn't brave enough."

"Will didn't need you to look at him," David replies. "To look would have been for your sake, not his. It was your right to refuse." I shake my head, breaths speeding to gasps. He reaches toward me, offering his hands, and I take them. "Cecilia, I think you have more courage than I do. More courage than anyone else I know."

"That can't be true. If I had courage, I would have told Samuel

Grey to leave me alone. I would have refused my sister and refused the world, and . . ."

I trail off. David smiles encouragingly at me. "And?"

And I would have told you how I felt about you—how I have felt about you, I think, since you took my hand in yours and showed me I was still alive.

I don't say it. I look into his eyes, and he stares back at me, unwavering. He is as steady as the ground beneath my feet, fingers warm against my skin, patient, accepting; and if Will was a slip, a slide, *this* threatens a plunge. *This* is why they call it falling. I must step away from him, or soon I will be lost entirely.

I don't step away. His hands loosen—releasing me—but I clutch on to him, keeping him there. Our fingers interlace.

"What are you doing?" David asks me. But he lets me cling to him, all the same.

"I don't know," I reply. "Will you pull away again?"

He doesn't say anything in response. His hands remain in mine, and the silence grows expectant.

I can hear my pulse thudding in my ears. "Why is it," I ask him, "that the heart sometimes speeds or slows?"

His grip on my palms tightens, and I take a step closer to him. He says, voice strained, "For many reasons."

"Such as?"

"Well—it is affected by stress, for example, or exertion, or fear. Different responses mean different things."

I raise one of his hands, pressing his fingers to my neck, so he can feel my pulse. It is thrumming like a songbird's wings.

"What does this mean?" I ask him.

He breathes in shakily. I expect him to step back, but he doesn't. "I . . ."

"What does it mean, David?"

"We can't," he says.

"We could pretend we can. Just for a moment. Please?"

"We can't," he repeats. "Tell me you don't mean it, Cecilia. I won't know what to do if you mean it."

"Can a heartbeat lie?"

"No."

"Then how could I not mean it?"

He shakes his head. "A delusion, merely. A temporary madness."

"Then I am mad," I say. "What does it matter? I am tired of others telling me what to think, what to believe. I know I want you, David, and I think you want me, too."

David is silent. I step closer to him—closer—he doesn't move. He doesn't speak. He just watches me, and his hand around mine closes tighter, his thumbnail pressing into my wrist.

I take the final step needed, and I kiss him.

He is so shocked that he doesn't respond. My lips press against his; he remains unmoving, then I pull away. His expression is stricken and confused. Regret comes swiftly. I almost clap my free hand to my mouth, as if to prevent myself from doing it again. "I—I— Pardon," I stutter, panicked. "That was *very* impulsive—I shouldn't have—"

"*Merda*," he says. Then he wraps his arms around me, pulls me in, and kisses me back.

It is desperate, a little clumsy. His hands roam across my back and shoulders and hair. We struggle to find a rhythm at first, but then, suddenly, we are moving together, and I feel fire at the edges of my fingers and my throat, and his breath is my breath, my heartbeat is his. When I press my tongue against his lower lip, he gasps and leans closer; we almost fall into the water, which we avoid only by virtue of David grasping my waist and spinning me around, leading me into the patch of lamb's ears he once used to treat my palm. The soft, cloudlike fuzz of the leaves ghosts across my elbow. I pull away from him to giggle.

"Um," he says, looking quite winded.

"Pardon. It tickles."

"Oh."

"Not you. The plant." I pull him in again. "No matter. Kiss me more now."

"Well—I—we should—" Our mouths meet, and he groans in surrender, protests forgotten. He smells like grass and night air, tastes a little of coffee, and his hair is soft as I weave it between my fingers. He is only a little taller than I am, so I needn't crane my neck for our lips to touch; it is perfect. If this is to be my last night of freedom, I can think of no better way to spend it. I would rather this than an alehouse, or Temple Bar, or a theater. I think I would rather this than anything.

Eventually, David pulls away. "Cecilia, listen," he says. Despite his grave tone, his arms are still around my waist, and he seems reluctant to release me. "This is— I shouldn't have— Look, we shouldn't be doing this."

"Why?"

"There are numerous reasons. You are all but betrothed; we met only weeks ago; I am your doctor—"

"You *were* my doctor. No longer."

"I am still taking advantage of you."

"Do it more."

I lean forward again. He veers back. "Cecilia," he repeats. "What will happen once we leave this park? Where could this possibly lead?"

"I don't know," I reply. "I don't want to think about it. I don't want to think about widows or doctors or Jews or anything else.

I am sick of all of it. I want to be here, as Cecilia, and I want you to be here, as David. Nothing more than that."

"But—we can't *possibly*—"

"Do you want me?" I ask him.

He looks at me as he would the sun without clouds, as if I am blinding. "Yes," he says. "I do."

"And I you," I reply. "Here, in this place, in this darkness, we need nothing but that. Nothing but wanting. We can make it so."

He cups my cheek, searching my face for hesitation. I kiss his wrist.

"*Querida,* forgive me," he says, and then he brings his mouth back to mine.

I close my eyes and lean into him. All is well again. I will make this evening perfect: there is no past or future here. Nothing matters but this, the touch of his lips against mine, the soft leaves of the lamb's ears brushing my skirts.

Behind us, the moon and its reflection in the water glow like twin lanterns, strung from earth to sky. The darkness here allows for impossible things: two moons, two sets of stars, and the two of us, together.

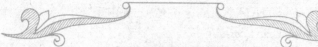

CHAPTER ELEVEN

David

We walk back toward the fence and I help Cecilia clamber over it. I do the same, then turn to her to see her face stricken with terror. I understand why: She must return to the townhouse. I will go home. We may never have another moment alone together.

We both stand by the fence, illuminated dimly by a streetlamp, staring at each other in mutual horror.

"What are we going to do?" she asks me. "We could meet like this again? In secret?"

I scrub my hand across my face. "I don't know," I say. "How long before we are discovered?"

"If I could convince my sister to hire you—"

I gawp at her. "*Hire* me—I can't be your physician *now*!"

"If you are not, then how will I see you?"

"I don't know," I repeat.

"I want to see you," she says, pleading, and my chest tightens at the desperation on her face.

"This can't continue," I reply. "You know that it can't. You are to be married."

"Not necessarily. I haven't agreed—"

"I am a *Jew*, Cecilia!" I cry, too loud, and she flinches. "Your heart shouldn't beat like that for a Jew."

"But it does."

"And if I could prevent it from doing so, I would. If I could prevent my own from doing the same . . . But I can't. It does not matter whether you are betrothed, whether what you feel for me is real, how we met or how we will meet again—we can only ever be a fantasy. A brief dalliance we must forget."

My voice is strained and shaking. I should be calmer than I am. I owe it to her to maintain my composure; I am only upsetting her further. But I am frustrated and grieving and *wanting*, even now, and I cannot control myself. I want her as a river wants the ocean, as night wants the dawn, and it feels as if I will waste away for want of her if I leave her here like this.

But I must leave her.

Her eyes well with tears. I reach for her, unable to prevent myself from doing so, but she turns away. "Everything I do is wrong," she says. "I grieve wrongly, I love wrongly."

"There is nothing wrong with you."

She laughs harshly. "We both know that is a lie."

"I am not lying."

Cecilia veers back toward me, sneering—she is itching for an argument—but then I hear a gasp from behind us. I turn around to see a group of people at the end of the road, watching us from afar.

For a moment, I almost wonder if the pageant has returned— there are men carrying lanterns, swinging wildly from their sticks. But it is not the pageant. It is Lady Eden and her servants. She wears a nightgown and robe, shawl clutched tightly around her, slippers muddied with city dirt. Her expression is desperate and wild.

"*You*," she snarls, approaching us. At first I can't tell if she is addressing her sister or me; but there is no disdain in her features, only fury. Cecilia, then. "You left—I was so worried—and you were with *him*?"

Cecilia takes a faltering step forward. "Maggie, I—"

"With *him*," she snaps once more.

"We went for a walk in the park—"

"A walk! I discovered you were gone, and I thought you might be here, since you came here last time; in that I was clearly correct. But if I had known you were with Mendes—Lord, I have been a fool. I have been so naïve."

"Maggie," Cecilia says. "Listen to me—"

But Lady Eden is not looking at her anymore. She has turned to me, her expression warped with disgust and anger.

"Master Mendes," she says. Her voice is colder and darker than I have ever heard before. Lady Eden has a light voice, a singer's voice, like a silver bell; it is strange to hear it pitched this low. "Did you arrange this meeting with my sister?"

I have no recourse but honesty. "I did," I reply.

"What were your intentions?"

I give a small, bitter laugh. "To go for a walk."

Her hands flex at her sides. Her focus is now entirely upon me; Cecilia is forgotten, and I have the sudden, absurd urge to tell her to run away. But there is nowhere for her to go. There is nowhere for either of us to go.

Lady Eden takes a step toward me, and her posture threatens violence.

"Well?" she says. "Tell me, sir. What excuse can you give for your actions?"

"My Lady Eden, you can't treat Cecilia as a prisoner. I know you care for her, but it is wrong to keep her locked away."

"Oh, I see. You think yourself her rescuer."

I shake my head. "I only—"

"You are her doctor. *Were* her doctor. That is all. Nothing more."

"I—I know."

"Do you?" she asks. "Perhaps she has convinced you otherwise. But tell me, Master Mendes: If William Thorowgood were still alive, do you think that she would even glance in your direction? Do you think she would allow you to take the liberties that you have?"

I flinch at that, betrayed by how much the comment hurts, how true it rings.

Cecilia interjects, horrified. "Please, stop this. It isn't his fault."

She turns to me, her gaze apologetic and pleading; it is as if she expects me to protest, also, to reassert my honor, but I can't. This is my fault, in part if not entirely, and I must accept that.

"I am ashamed of you, Cecilia," Lady Eden tells her. "Thank the *Lord* Sir Grey and my husband don't know about this. We are returning to the townhouse. Master Mendes will go back to wherever he came from, and, God willing, you will never see him again."

Cecilia's eyes flash with anger. When she speaks, her voice is sharp as a scalpel. "Maggie, be reasonable."

"Reasonable!" she cries. "What right do *you* have to speak of reason? This is my fault, I suppose. I should have known. You lose all sense at a man's attention, and it takes very little before you are sweet on him. It was the same with Will, was it not? One smile, and you decided he was yours. An engaged man, and now this. You ought to be ashamed."

"Ashamed!" Cecilia snarls. She is so angry that her pulse is jumping at her throat, and her hands have tightened into fists at her sides. "When you are the one who has been *poisoning* me?"

"What?" Lady Eden and I both say simultaneously, and Cecilia bares her teeth in some parody of laughter.

"I overheard you, Margaret," she says. "In the kitchens."

"In the . . ." Realization dawns on Lady Eden's face. Her expression twists, grief and embarrassment and fury, all at once: "Cecilia, that potion was for me. To . . . it's for fertility."

The blood drains from Cecilia's face. Her lips part, but she doesn't speak.

Lady Eden shakes her head. "You are not in your right mind," she says. "These false accusations, this bizarre infatuation— Cecilia, he is a *Jew*, for God's sake, and a scavenger besides. He picks at you while you are weak, and you know no better. He knew you were to be married while he treated you, and he pursued you still."

Cecilia's eyes meet mine. All the anger in her expression has gone, replaced entirely by dread.

"You knew?" she asks me.

I swallow, throat tight. "Cecilia, I . . ."

But I cannot continue.

"You knew," she repeats. It is not a question this time.

Margaret smiles, triumphant. "Master Mendes, you are dismissed," she says to me. "If I ever see you near my sister again, I shall go to the constables."

Cecilia hangs her head. Lady Eden surges forward and digs her hand into Cecilia's arm; it is a cruel movement, clearly painful. She tugs Cecilia away from me and throws her behind her as if she is a sack of flour.

I could stop her, but to what end? There is nothing more to be done or said.

It was always going to end like this.

"It was all my doing, I assure you," I tell Lady Eden. "Not Cecilia's. She shouldn't be blamed."

She makes a disdainful sound and turns away from me. "Come," she snaps at Cecilia, laying a hand on her shoulder. As she shoves her backward, my gaze crosses Cecilia's. I ought to turn away, to say something, but I don't. I am paralyzed by my own cowardice.

"I am sorry," I say.

"Yes, you ought to be," Lady Eden replies—but I am not speaking to her. I am apologizing to Cecilia for all that I have done. I have made the physician's greatest error, and I have given her a cure worse than the illness. I have made myself a foxglove, in too great a dose; and now I have broken her heart.

Afterward, I return home. I do not sleep. I spend all night mixing medicines and labeling jars, and by the morning I am so exhausted I start making mistakes. When I finish a peppermint oil electuary for a patient with an irritable bowel, I realize that I have measured the licorice root wrong, and the entire thing must be poured out onto the garden gravel.

I go to fetch my father from his room, carrying him down the stairs so he can breakfast with me in the kitchen. As he eats his pottage, I stew a new tisane recipe, angelica and marigold for his heart. It must be sweetened, or it will be undrinkable. I search the shelves for sugar.

"Did you sleep well last night?" Father asks from his seat at the table.

I lie. "Yes."

"You did not," Father says.

"I did."

"Are you eating?"

"Yes." I spoon in the sugar.

"You look thin."

"I am eating," I repeat more forcefully.

Removing the pot from the flame, I sieve the liquid into a copper bowl. Our kitchen faces east, and a square of sunlight brightens the concoction to a molten gold: a temporary alchemy. When I pour it into the cup, it returns to a pale and unappetizing yellow. I pass it to him. He wrinkles his nose as he sips.

"Honey is better than sugar," he says.

"Then I will use honey when I brew it next."

He makes a spiteful noise, but he makes no further complaint. He knows as well as I that the physic is needed, for his chest pains have worsened recently. We have devised a rigorous routine of tisanes, decoctions, and exercises; it does something, but not enough.

Father takes another sip from the cup, grimacing. Then he inspects me with narrowed eyes. "You are upset," he says. "That much is clear. What is it, Davi?"

"Nothing I am willing to speak of."

He says, "Come here."

I cross over to him. He takes my hand in his.

"I am proud of you," he says. "You work very hard. You know that, no?"

"I do," I reply, feeling my eyes prickle. "Thank you."

"You must forget your troubles. Whoever thinks too much will never reach Jerusalem." He pauses. "Certainly, something has happened to upset you so. Is it a woman?" I splutter, and he grins in triumph. "Oh? Sara? I always thought you would eventually see sense."

Sara. I haven't thought of her in days; the sudden guilt is crushing. I bow my head. "I already said I'd rather not speak of it."

"Not Sara?" he asks, bewildered. "Who?"

"A gentile," I say in a vindictive moment of self-sabotage. "An old patient."

He goes silent with horror, staring at me with his eyes widened. I feel immediately remorseful for upsetting him; my mistakes are not his burden to bear.

He says, "Davi, you *can't*."

"I know. It is finished now. I will never see her again." At this, he looks so relieved that it pains me. I feel like the marigold crushed beneath my pestle. Pulling my hand out of his, I say, "I will go buy us some pasties for dinner."

It is a peace offering, but Father will not permit me peace. "What of Sara?" he asks. "She is a wonderful woman, Davi. Surely, this gentile is not preventing you . . . ?"

"It isn't *that*," I snap, my temper finally fraying. "Not only that. It— I don't love her. Sara, I mean."

"What? What is this really about? You have been acting so strangely recently, and this concerns me. You have not gone to synagogue in months."

"I . . ."

"You lie sometimes, and say that you have, but I know it is not true. Why? What is the reason? Surely it is not laziness."

"I have been busy," I reply.

"Too busy for Hashem?"

"No, of course not—I just—"

"You what? What could possibly be a suitable excuse?"

"Do you ever feel as if we are not Jews, not truly?" I ask him, and he looks utterly astonished. I regret the question immediately, but frustration pried it loose.

"What do you mean?" he says.

"When we were in Portugal, we did not practice. We did not go to synagogue. We couldn't hang a mezuzah."

"Because we had to hide. We were still Jews, of course."

"Yes, but—but we were not Jews as we are here. As you have become."

"We wore a mask; we had to," he says.

"But I was born a Jew beneath it," I say. "I was raised wearing it. Now I can't take it off. I don't know how."

He sighs. My father's sighs have the character of a gale; it seems as if they should gust around the room and topple things over. "It will take time," he says. "Time to adjust."

"It has been years."

"You must be patient."

"I am finished with patience," I say. "I despise the chimera I have become. If I marry Sara, will I become a real Jew, finally? We make sacrifices for this, for the sake of our blood, our faith, but will they ever be worth it? If I marry her, if we have a family, will it be worth it then?"

"David . . ."

He reaches for me once more. I shake my head.

"Listen to me," he says. "You cannot seize happiness by fleeing sorrow. They often lie in the same direction. Sara is a good woman; and you are lonely, I think, for all your friends and amusements. You have a big heart, with more than enough space to share. Consider it."

"I . . ."

"Consider it, Davi," he repeats stoutly. He sits back in the chair, takes another sip of the tisane, grimacing. "You cannot spend your entire life running away."

Father's hand trembles, and he nearly drops the cup. I hear his breath catch, and I reach forward to take the cup from him, alarmed. His face is pale.

"Are you well?" I ask him. "Your heart?"

He presses a hand to his chest. "Only a stutter," he says.

By the midafternoon, I am so exhausted that I can no longer stay awake. I nap on the couch, and in my fitful, half-woken sleep, I dream of Portugal. I dream of myself at nineteen, just graduated from the academy, when my father and I had already decided we were leaving Lisbon. We had friends who had gone to England—the petition to live there openly was in its final stages—and they told us there was a shortage of able physicians. We were both restless men, travelers; over the course of my youth, we had gone on numerous trips across the country, even to Spain, where my father's fame as a doctor had brought him work in Andalusia. This seemed an extraordinary opportunity for adventure. *London,* a city larger than life itself, was opening its doors to us.

But I don't dream of adventure. I dream of the moment my mother says, "I will not go with you."

We are at the breakfast table. My father drops his apple. He is less in shock at the meaning of the words than at the timing of them. My mother loves Lisbon, and we both knew she would resist leaving. But to say it like *this,* before our sincerest plans have been made, before any discussion has even been had—it is not characteristic of soft-spoken, sweet, plaintive Ana. She usually asks advice even on the slicing of bread.

"Ana," my father says. "Querida—"

"I will not," she repeats.

The dream changes. I am no longer in the kitchen. I am younger, a child sitting on the bottom step of the staircase, staring at the crucifix my mother has hung above the front door. It is there to remind us, each time we leave the house, what face we ought to be wearing. *Keep it secret, Davi. Keep us safe.*

I am nineteen again. I stand in front of my mother as she

presses a packet of lettuce seeds into my hand. The coach is behind us; we are leaving. But she is only being stubborn. She won't stay here and live as a *gentile* without us. Father says she will come eventually. I know that she will come eventually.

"Tell Gaspar to plant them," she says. "He will know the best place."

But Father doesn't plant them. I am planting them, in our garden in London. I am watching them grow, and the days are passing and the years are passing, and I wear a mask and grow a beak as the plague comes. I leave our house and watch Manuel driving a plague cart down the street, smiling and waving at me. The cart is empty of bodies, and he is healthy and whole. I have succeeded this time. All is well.

I take off my bird mask and my oiled coat. I go back into the house and return to my bedroom. Cecilia is in the bed; she is waiting for me to examine her. Her skirts are rucked up to her chest, a sheet draped over her hips. I press my fingers to her abdomen, drawing them down to the tops of her thighs, feeling her shiver beneath my touch. I watch her face as I do so. Then she kicks the sheet away and threads her hands in my hair, pushing me down. I bend to kiss her stomach. Her legs part, and my lips move lower, lower still. She sighs and widens her stance, welcoming me. She tastes of salt and sweet and linden flowers, wet and wanting. And I shouldn't—I *shouldn't*—but I am lost to her; lost to the way she gasps and whimpers, the way she bucks against my mouth, the way she breathes my name. The sounds she makes are like the music she once played for me; they seem to make a song just as the spinet did. And soon she is close, she is reaching, hands scrabbling at my shoulders, trembling beneath me, begging me to continue, my name falling from her lips each time a chord, another note—

David, she says, *I want you, I want you, I always will—*

I awaken, disoriented. The afternoon sun reaches through the gap in the curtains. For a moment, I forget the dream was a dream, and I reach out beside me, expecting Cecilia to be there.

She is not there. She never was.

CHAPTER TWELVE

Cecilia

Margaret is not speaking to me. I am not speaking to Margaret.

Two days have passed since she discovered David and me. Since then, I haven't left my bedroom. She always locks my door now. It doesn't matter, really; all my resistance has been bled from me, as if I have been leeched. Perhaps I shall never do anything again. Instead, I shall sit in this bed and grow bitter, bitter like dandelion greens, sprouting from the mattress and sitting stubborn until they are plucked.

Time passes. I look out the window, staring at the summer sky. I blink, and the sun has made half its journey. The breakfast plates go untouched, but my treacherous stomach growls in hunger. David's treatments have left me the ability to eat, but not the will to do so. I could cease eating altogether and grow ill again out of spite. Starving Cecilia is gone, but I could bring her back, if I wished to. It would be a pointless and miserable achievement.

He knew, all this time, what my sister intended for me, and he kept it hidden. He knew, and he wanted me still.

I don't know whether to be angry or grateful.

I am awoken late one night by a hand on my shoulder, a hushed voice whispering my name.

"Maggie?" I mumble drowsily, and I peel open my eyes to look at her.

She hasn't a candle with her, and her figure is indistinct in the black: the vague lines of a nightgown, the loose coils of her hair. I wonder a moment if I am dreaming.

"Come with me," she says, wrapping a hand around my wrist.

I am so confused by her presence, so disoriented by my sudden waking, that I make no protest. I stumble out of the bed, bare feet on the floorboards, and she tugs me toward the door.

We go through corridors, down steps. Margaret says nothing to me except to warn me of a threshold, her grip around my wrist loosening gradually as we progress, as if her fear of my escape is easing. As the veil of sleep begins to fall, I wonder if I *should* escape—but it isn't as if I have anywhere to go. I am in my nightgown just as she is, eyes still gummy. She is my only anchor in the darkness.

We reach a familiar door and spill out onto the courtyard. This summer is warm enough that the air is the same temperature outside and in, and the stones beneath my feet still linger with the heat of the sun.

There is another figure standing by the tree: a woman, with a large metal cauldron at her feet. The moonlight illuminates her, but I don't recognize her.

She gives us a small curtsy as we approach. "Good tidings,"

she says, and I know her voice—it is the wise woman whom my sister was speaking to in the kitchen, the last night I saw David.

"Cecilia," Margaret says, "Alice is going to help you."

"Help me?" I say, voice still thin with sleep. "What do you mean, help?"

The women trade a significant glance.

Margaret tells me, "You may have been bewitched."

"Be—" I cut myself off to bark a laugh, the sound scraping my dry throat like sand. "Bewitched? Surely, you can't be serious."

"It isn't your fault," Margaret replies. "If anything, it is mine. And we can't be certain, but if it is so—"

"David didn't bewitch me, Margaret. No need to blame him for my folly."

Margaret shakes her head. "The sister I know is reckless, but she would never debase herself to—"

"The only one debasing herself here is you."

"Mistress Thorowgood," Alice says gently. "It is often difficult to tell . . ."

"I . . ." *know my own mind,* I am going to say, but then I realize that often, I *don't* know my own mind—that is the issue—and so I am reduced to glaring.

"I won't force you to undergo the treatment," Margaret says, crossing her arms. "But at least consider how odd this all seems, Cecilia. To run off like that, out of nowhere, with a . . ."

"A Jew? Is that what you were going to say, Maggie?"

"Yes."

"He is a better man than any you'll ever meet," I reply. "Honest and intelligent and *good,* and if you cannot see that—if you refuse to—then you are even more ignorant than I thought."

She doesn't respond; she just frowns at me, hands curled tightly around her elbows.

I turn to Alice. "What is your treatment?" I ask her.

She points to the buckets. "Blessed and boiled with vervain," she says.

"Am I to wash my hands in it?"

She pauses, and then replies meekly, "If my mistress desires. But for the greatest efficiency—"

"You should be sluiced with it," Margaret says. "I had it warmed before we came here, so it shouldn't be too onerous."

"How thoughtful," I reply drily.

"As I said, you needn't—"

"No, I must." I stand in front of Alice so I am between her and the linden tree, spreading my arms in invitation. "It is the only way to disabuse you of this ridiculous idea, and spare David from further accusation."

Margaret's shoulders slump. I can't tell if she is relieved or dejected.

Alice directs me to stand between the roots of the linden, in a patch of summer moonlight, the trunk of the tree solid as a stone column behind me. She hangs a silver cross around my neck, dabs the same symbol in charcoal across the backs of my hands, mutters incantations to herself. Meanwhile, I watch Margaret's unmoving figure, and I wonder when she began to dabble with cunning folk. She's always been prone to superstition, but this seems one step from popery, or even paganism.

Alice steps back and hefts the cauldron into her arms. She hesitates.

"Go on," I say.

The water hits me with a force nearer to a slap than a rainfall, smacking me in the face and chest. It is hot enough still that it is steaming—it doesn't burn, but it feels like a brand somehow. It stinks like one of David's decoctions, bitter and citrus and the iron tang of the pot. My hair sticks to my brow, my nightshift clings to me like a second skin. As the water drips from my chin, I begin to tremble—but it is with anger, not cold.

"Is that all of it?" I ask Alice.

"There's still more in the pot," Margaret replies.

"Well," I say to her, "I am still in love with him, so I suppose you should use the rest of it, too."

She recoils as if I have hit her. Meanwhile, Alice shakes her head. "I don't think—"

"Do it," I tell her.

"Do it," Margaret echoes.

The second sluice comes, less a shock than the first, but no less intense. I keep my eyes open the entire time, despite the stinging caused by the herbs in the water, and I stare directly at Margaret. She stares back at me. We are two girls again, twins splashing in the river by our childhood home, each daring the other to dive in; or perhaps I have already dived in, and she is trying to pull me out. I'm sure that's how she sees it. I'll have to disappoint her.

"Enough," Margaret says sharply when Alice prepares herself for another swing of the cauldron.

I push my sodden hair back, wringing water from it. "By all means, keep going if necessary."

"Enough," Margaret repeats. Alice puts down the pot. "Clearly, it isn't working."

I sigh. "You knew it wouldn't work, Maggie. You can't really have thought I was *bewitched*."

"I don't know what I thought. I suppose I hoped, foolishly, that this might help you somehow."

"I don't want your help." I shake the water from my fingers, step away from the tree. "I'm going back to bed."

I walk back toward the door, ignoring the way the hem of my

dress is dripping, the goose pimples on my damp skin. Then Margaret calls after me and I pause, despite myself—although I don't turn to look at her.

"You need my help," she says. "As I need yours. You need to stop living in this fantasy you've created. You can find happiness again, Cecilia, but it can't be with him. You know that in your heart. I'm certain you do."

I can't respond. My throat tightens; a trail of water runs down my cheek. Without acknowledging her, I go back into the house.

The next day, Margaret comes in the morning, acting as if nothing has happened. She has my peach-colored gown draped over her arm.

"Sir Grey has come for a visit," she tells me.

What choice do I have? I stand, stiff and doll-like, as she and one of the maids dress me. Our eyes meet in the mirror; gray meets blue, storm against sea, and I feel the icy sensation of Margaret's disdain crawl down my neck. We have never resented each other like this before. It is my fault as much as hers, I suppose. But I can't bring myself to regret it.

Once I am deemed presentable, she sits me in my desk chair and puts my embroidery hoop in my lap.

"Stay there," she tells me, "and I will bring him up."

She leaves with the maid. Sullenly, I stitch three stitches of my embroidery. It is a posy, and it looks like child's work. Unthreading the needle, I hold it in the light of the setting sun; it glints like a rapier. I turn it back and forth, watching the blade flash. I drop it. It skids away to slip underneath the bed.

Groaning, I go to retrieve it, crouching to the floor to reach for it. Instead of the needle, my fingers brush fabric. I tug the object out to see that it is David's green jacket, the one he lent me the second time we met. I suppose this explains where it has been these past few weeks. It is soft and heavy, with wool the shade of the underside of a leaf. I should throw it away, but instead I clutch it to myself and stare blankly at the wall, taking several ragged breaths that feel as if they have been torn out of me.

Someone knocks on the door. Then there is the sound of a key turning, and it opens. Still kneeling on the floor by the bed, I raise the jacket to shield myself from view. It doesn't work, of course.

"Hello, Cecilia!" Samuel Grey says. "Awfully sorry to come into your room like this—I know it's not proper—but, well, your sister was insistent you could not leave it, and that I ought to see you anyway. But perhaps you do not want me here all the same. Should I leave?"

I put the jacket down and look at him. He has his dog, Duchess, with him, tucked beneath his arm; he is wearing a lavender silk jacket the same color as my bedspread. There must be something utterly woeful in my expression, despite my efforts to affect a smile, because he flutters his hands and says, "Oh dear, oh dear, oh dear."

He brings Duchess over to me, and she shoves her cold nose against my elbow. Sam pats my shoulder awkwardly, squatting beside the bed. "Is something the matter?"

"Pardon," I tell Sam, mortified.

"There is no need to apologize. What's happened? You needn't tell me if you don't wish to, but . . ."

"It is rather complicated, I'm afraid."

He sighs. "I am quite terrible with complicated things, I must admit. But I shall do my best to understand."

I shake my head. Duchess circles around David's jacket and

sniffs at it before flopping down to curl up within the lining. I watch her, eyes stinging.

Sam offers me his arm to help me up, and I take it. We both sit on the edge of the bed. It is terribly forward of us to do so, but I don't think either of us much mind.

Sam watches me in silence for a moment, teeth worrying at his lower lip.

"The thing is," Sam says, "I don't particularly want to get married, either. No offense."

"None taken."

"But it is obligatory, you see. I am Sir Grey and heir to the Eden titles, too, at least until Robert has a baby. And if I die those lines go extinct—my sisters are married themselves, you know, so they aren't candidates. Oh, it's awful." He rubs his cheek with his hand, smearing the rouge he has used down toward his chin.

"I'm sorry," I reply, which is a pointless comment, but he still smiles at me as if I have said something terribly kind.

He says, "You know, I used to have a little bird—a parrot—from very far away. It was bright green and it talked."

This segue seems so abrupt that I can't think of a response. Thankfully, he doesn't seem to need one. "It didn't talk in English," he continues, "because it had spent most of its time with Spanish sailors. It only ever said one word, which was *saltamontes,* over and over. I'd wake up to it in the middle of the night, hearing it scream, *Saltamontes, saltamontes,* driving me half mad."

"What does that mean?"

"Grasshopper," he says. "Isn't that curious? What sailor was saying the word *grasshopper* enough to teach it to a parrot?"

I snort. "Is that all?"

"What?"

"Well . . . I just thought . . . Is there a point to the story? It isn't a metaphor?"

"A metaphor? Oh no. I thought you'd find it amusing."

At that I laugh properly. He laughs, too.

Below us, Duchess huffs. I look down at her, cocooned in David's jacket, and the smile slips from my face.

Sam follows my gaze. "That is a man's jacket," he says.

"Yes."

"Was it your husband's?"

"No."

"Ah," he says. And then, after a long pause: "I see."

I twist my hands in my lap, press my nails into my palm. "It—it doesn't matter. It's finished now."

"I'm sorry," he tells me in an echo of my own platitudes.

"My sister is insistent we marry, and I . . ." Breathing shakily, I hunch over. Sam's hand flutters awkwardly over my back, then withdraws. "There isn't much to be done, Sam. I am her ward. I have no money of my own."

"You have no widow's pension?"

"None. My husband's family is not as wealthy as the Edens, and the heir was a minor when he died."

"But that is terrible," Sam says. "There must be some other resolution. I shall ponder it. I am not a man of great wit, I must admit, but for a dear friend, perhaps I might find a flash of genius."

I give him a small smile. "Thank you. I appreciate the effort."

"Will your sister permit you to go into the courtyard, do you think, if I accompany you?"

"I do not know."

"I will ask her," he says, standing. "I shall say I intend to propose, if necessary."

He leaves me alone with Duchess. She rises from David's

jacket and paws at the side of the mattress until I lift her up. Once in my lap, she curls against my chest, snuffling at the fabric of my gown. I rub at her velvet ears. Sam has put a purple bow around her neck, to match the jacket he is wearing today. She seems somehow to sense my sorrow, and she leans her head into my palm.

Sam returns eventually, looking triumphant. "I am permitted to accompany you to the courtyard," he says, and so he leads me with my hand in the crook of his elbow, like a grandmother down a church aisle, out into the corridor. Duchess follows at our heels, yapping.

After two days in bed, my knees are weak; I almost stumble down the steps. In the courtyard, the air is warm and still. I glance to the window of the first floor and see Margaret's figure, watching us from behind a curtain. I suppose it would have been too much to ask for privacy.

We sit on the edge of the fountain. Sam laughs at Duchess, who is snapping at one of the streams of water as if she might catch fish from it. I watch him laugh and think he is beautiful, and kindhearted, and that he would be as good a husband as any gentlewoman could wish for. This revelation is more bitter than any decoction I have ever taken.

Sam tells me a story of court, something about laxatives and a bear and a gauche comedy that no one enjoyed. I listen only half present, watching the wind pass its hand over the linden. In the fading light of the sunset, its white blooms glow like clusters of stars. They are now mostly shed; soon the tree shall be entirely green.

I think of David. I think of Will. I think of Margaret. Partway through his story, Sam seems to realize I am not listening, and his voice falters and stops. He reaches over to take my hand.

"All will be well, Cecilia," he says.

I do not believe him. I look down at his hand folded over mine, skin pale as my own, nails bitten short.

And there is nothing in particular that does it: nothing new happens to cause my sudden realization. It is rather that I become aware of the sameness of things, how everything is just as it has ever been. I am sitting here, in the house I have been sitting in since I came to London in the first place. If I had not found his jacket beneath my bed today, it would be as if David Mendes had never been in my life at all. I went to sleep sodden and exhausted last night, stinking of vervain, for a memory I might never regain.

This place exemplifies my life. It is not even a prison; it is a portrait frame I have been painted within, as the world passes by outside.

How did it come to this? How could I permit it?

I owe Will more than this. I owe myself more than this, owe David more than this, after all he did to show the city to me. I must leave this place and start anew. There is only one path before me now, and so that is the path I must take. No matter where it leads, it is better than standing still.

You can find happiness again, Cecilia—but it can't be with him.

"Sam," I say.

"Yes, Cecilia?"

"I will marry you," I tell him, and his grip on my hand loosens. "If you will have me, I will be your bride."

My sister doesn't weep to hear the news, but she pulls me into an embrace, fierce and thankful, and I know that this surrender has forgiven me the war.

Sir Eden voices no pleasure except a long, satisfied puff on his cigar. Sam hovers at the door of the parlor wearing an awkward smile. He had asked me, *Are you certain,* until it seemed his throat was hoarse; but I am certain. I have made up my mind, and I will marry again. I hope that this husband will bring me less grief than my last, even though I know he cannot bring me even an ounce of the joy.

Later that afternoon—once Sam has left—Margaret sits me down to discuss wedding arrangements. The Edens are paying, of course, and so it is their decision; no need to put it off, she tells me, as a month is all that is needed to procure the license.

"I doubt the ceremony will be at Whitehall," she says. "But you must meet some of the court beforehand, regardless. They at least ought to know who you are."

The words *meet the court* fill me with an odd mixture of anxiety and giddiness. Margaret pushes the plate of biscuits toward me, perhaps mistaking my expression for nausea.

"The tailor will come tomorrow, to measure you for your dress," she says as I nibble nervously at a biscuit. "And for jewels—"

"I don't need a new dress, surely? I still have my gown."

"You will be dressed in style, Cecilia," she says firmly. "It won't do to have the Edens appear stingy."

I recall the husband and wife on the streets of London, the dancers, the music. "Will we have a pageant, then?" I ask her, and she laughs.

"You are a genteel widow remarrying," she replies. "Not the countess bride of a duke. But there will be a banquet, very grand, and that will be more than enough."

The next morning, I find myself at the mercy of a horde of tailors, who poke at me with needles and take my measurements as physicians once did; I am to be remade entirely. New stays, new bust, new shoes, new life. As well as a new deportment for court, I am to be made a wedding dress: a gown of watered silk, pale blue, trimmed with gold lace and a thread of pea-sized pearls. I will be permitted to wear my old wedding pearls in my ears, to match the dress, but the necklace is to be a gift from Sam. It is a collar of sapphires and diamonds, once his mother's. Sam gives it to me on a velvet pillow, and it is so heavy I can hardly lift it up.

And there is the ring, too, of course. Sam brings that along-side the necklace. It is gold with no less than seven diamonds, the centerpiece rose-cut and clearer than water. It is a little too small, but he assures me we will have it resized. When I take it off, it leaves a red ring like a brand below my knuckle—the ghost of the ring still around my finger.

Once the tailors leave, it is on to the florists for my bridal garland. We are told it is an awkward time for flowers, too late in the season for many of the usual choices. I ask if I might have linden, then, and the florist is alarmed. Best avoided, he informs us, as it was the choice for pagan marriages, in those barbaric days before Christ. Margaret crosses herself.

My sister and the florist settle on larkspur for purity, and as-ters for faithfulness. Once he is gone, I ask who will be invited to the banquet. Margaret is vague in her response, stating only that there will be "many guests of consequence."

"Will we invite anyone *I* know?" I ask her. "Or only your friends at court?"

She gives me a pitying look. "Who would you *like* to invite, Cecilia?"

I pause at that. I could invite Will's sisters, but we were never close, and they associate me too strongly with his loss. My friends in Suffolk are all married now—we haven't spoken since I was widowed—and I am suddenly struck with the totality of my isolation.

My silence is response enough. Margaret pats my arm.

"You will like the ladies at court," she tells me. "Many of them read as much as you do, and they enjoy music."

There is to be a salon next week that the *king* is attending; she insists that we will all go, her and Robert and me and Sam. The thought makes me feel sick. I was raised on stories of Charles and his brave flight from the Roundhead forces—hiding in the boughs of an oak tree to avoid detection, passing himself off as a servant, sleeping in a farmer's hut. My mother had the king's portrait above the mantelpiece, spent the years of the commonwealth hosting secret Royalist meetings in the wine cellar. When I was a child, it was a constant fancy of mine that I would meet His Majesty someday and play harpsichord for him. Sometimes I'd ask Margaret to pretend to be him, and she'd put on a footman's wig and a paper crown. Once the piece was finished, she would cry, *Brava, brava!* while stamping her foot. Now she speaks of him as if he is a casual acquaintance. It feels utterly extraordinary.

That night, I cannot sleep. I rise from my bed and consider going to the music room, but I cannot wake the rest of the household with music. Instead, I go to the library. It is an impressive space, far more extravagant than any other such room I have seen: books stretch from floor to ceiling in soldier-like rows, austere and awaiting orders. Between each bookcase, there are plinths displaying illuminated manuscripts, interrupted by the occasional marble bust. Their morose, stony expressions make them appear like reluctant invaders in a room otherwise populated by pages.

On the back wall, a large mirror reflects my silhouette back to me, and a set of opulent red chairs sits huddled by the unlit fireplace. The air smells of paper and tea. I wander past the shelves, trailing my fingers over the books' leather spines. Catullus, Hobbes, Aquinas; so many men, so many words, and yet the thin layer of dust on each volume proves they are forgotten. When I die, there won't be any books with my name in them—only a gravestone. *Here lies Cecilia Grey.*

I pull out a random book to find a discourse on coffee drinking, then I notice the volume shelved beside it: *The Present State of the Jews, Wherein Is Contained an Exact Account of Their Customs, Secular and Religious.* I take that book instead, and when I see the table of contents, I can't help myself—I turn to the section on weddings.

There is a form of marriage contract, it reads, *in present use among all the Jews, whereof we have a Copy translated by Cornelius Bertram out of the Babylon Talmud. And these contracts being signed, the Woman from that time forward becomes the man's Wife. To this form of honoring and worshiping the marriage, the contract alludes to the Song of Solomon, reading: I am my beloved's, and my beloved is mine.*

I imagine Sam and me at the altar, his mother's sapphires like an oxen's yoke around my neck, the priest imploring my future obedience. *I am my beloved's, and my beloved is mine.*

I remember Will and me in the same position, years ago, him smiling at me; the dappled sunlight through the window of the country church; the whoops and hollers of our families as he bowed down to kiss me. *I am my beloved's, and my beloved is mine.*

And then, inevitably, I think of David. I think of how the stars cast pinpricks of light in his dark eyes that night, and the way his mouth felt on mine, his hand curling around my waist, the heat of his breath, the smell of the grass and the darkness. I feel the ache of wanting him to travel from my heart to my hips. I lean against the bookcase and close my eyes.

I am my beloved's, and my beloved is mine.

CHAPTER THIRTEEN

David

After the third night of alehouses in a row, Jan can tell something is wrong. As we stumble out onto the street, he takes my hand.

"Do you remember the night we met, David?" he asks.

I remember, of course. It was a summer evening much like this one, three years ago. I had drunk too much wine at a seder, and afterward I went to a molly house named Mother Tiffin's. There I met a beautiful man who had promised me comfort, and I had acted on desires I had long acknowledged but thought controlled. Once I'd sobered enough to understand what I had done, I'd stumbled outside the door and slumped down to the curb, burying my face in my knees. Jan had followed me out, concerned about the stranger who had fled the place with tears in his eyes. The initial introductions had been uncertain, uncomfortable, but then he'd asked me, "Do you like coffee?" and I had replied that I did. We went to his house, and he kissed me by the front door, mostly to get it out of the way; it felt so unnatural and awkward that we fell about laughing immediately after. I spent the day with him roasting coffee beans. He told me absurd stories about his life that were mostly fiction. I told him about my work, and my father, and my life in Lisbon.

"I have known you for years now," Jan continues. "And I— I just . . . I am concerned for you."

"It's nothing"

He says, "It isn't nothing. It clearly isn't. Let's meet tomorrow morning at the coffeehouse, when our heads are clearer. Then we can speak of it, yes?"

Concern is so deeply etched into his brow, in the insistence of his grip, that I can do nothing except nod.

"Good," he says. "Surely there is nothing that cannot be fixed with the ear of an old friend."

The next day, I have my morning appointment, and then I go to Temple Bar, running a little late. When I arrive, Jan is not there.

I presume irritably that he is late because he is hungover—as I am—or because he spent the entire night at Mother Tiffin's, as I know he went back there after we parted ways. I spend a good forty minutes sitting by myself in the booth, scowling, before the serving girl comes and demands I buy something or get out.

I leave the coffeehouse, going for a walk around the neighborhood. Once I return it is over an hour past the time we are supposed to meet. I walk again. He is still not there. I am now concerned.

His house is nearby, so I go there first. No one answers my knocks. The only other solution I can think of is Mother Tiffin's, so I pay for a cabbie to take me there. I walk down the narrow street with a growing sense of foreboding, and I stop to find the place with its windows smashed, door broken on its hinges.

I stare at it, horror slowly filling my belly. There is a candle seller in the store opposite, so I turn around and enter cautiously into the shop, the bell above the door announcing my arrival. The room smells strongly of tallow and oil. A portly, red-faced man stands by a counter in the corner, snipping at old wicks. He growls a greeting, but he seems more interested in his task than me.

"Pardon," I say, and he glances up. "Do you know what happened to the alehouse across from here?"

He raises his brows. "The molly house, you mean? 'Twere raided in the night by the constables. They all got dragged to the bailey."

I groan. "Jan, *burro*," I say to myself.

"Good luck you weren't there, then," the man says. "Nasty business, if you ask me. I knew Ma myself. Nice lass. The fellers, too. They weren't harming no one."

I thank him and leave, swearing softly under my breath. This has happened before. Never when I was at Tiffin's, but at least twice when Jan was; the charges had amounted to nothing— a slap on the wrist and a small fine—but there is always the risk of a particularly zealous bailiff and a quick march to the noose.

Beginning the short walk to the bailey, I press my fingers against my money pouch, wondering if I have enough on me for a bribe; I imagine not. I would pray now, if I felt as if it would do anything. I know, intellectually, that Jan is likely to be fine—but my imagination is often cruel. I see gallows in my mind, the jeering of a crowd. My grip on the pouch tightens.

When I reach the monolithic edifice of the bailey, the outside is heaving with people waiting to petition. It is as representative a group of Londoners as I have ever seen: distraught mothers, sozzled gentlemen, bedraggled children weaving between legs. The highest and the lowest of the city, all united in the need for complaint.

If Jan was arrested the previous night, he will have had his trial by now. There is nothing for me to do except wait by the gate and hope I can see him as he is led out of the courtroom. I lean against the brick wall and measure my breathing, trying to tamp down my anxiety.

The last time I was here, waiting for Jan, Manuel had been with me.

It was the spring before the summer he'd died. We'd been walking together, discussing the Royal Society's most recent lecture, when we'd passed Tiffin's and I noticed it had been cleared out. The panic I'd felt then—Manuel had seen it in my face immediately. He'd said, "David, please, it'll be all right," as I gasped for breath. In Portugal, such an arrest would have invariably led to an execution. I'd known that Jan had been there; I'd been certain he'd die for it.

There is an irony to that now, standing beside Manuel on that April day, weeping in terror that *Jan* would be lost to me.

Manuel had come with me to the bailey. We stood in this very spot, him watching me with his amber-brown eyes, lids half lowered. He knew what the molly house was; he had inferred, as anyone would, that I had a friend there because I sometimes frequented it myself. I kept waiting for judgment or disgust, but he waited with me in the same, silent placidity he always did, soothing me occasionally with soft smiles and platitudes.

It made it worse, somehow, that he wasn't disgusted, that he wasn't shocked. If he had been, it would have justified my cowardice. If he had been, then I would have been certain he'd never caught on, he'd never realized what I felt.

But even then, I didn't tell him. We stood together in front of the bailey, and everything I'd left unsaid curled like smoke between us, disappearing into the breeze. And when Jan came out—exhausted, shaking, but well enough—I had been so relieved I'd laughed, and Manuel had laughed with me.

There is no one here to laugh with me now.

I press my back more firmly against the wall, cross my arms, close my eyes. Even here in the shade, it is mercilessly hot. I can almost pretend I am in Lisbon, imagine cicadas chirruping from the trees edging our home, the ripe-sweet scent of the pomegranates.

There is a loud, creaking sound—the gate swinging—and my eyes fly open. A dozen men in various states of disorder are pouring out of the bailey, their clothes covered in mud, blood, or both. Laughing in joy at their escape, many of them embrace as they limp or scurry away. Among the crowd is Jan, who appears uninjured; when he spots me, he gives a great cry of pleasure before loping toward me.

"David!" he says, sweeping me into a hug. "You are here! How?"

"We were supposed to meet this morning, remember? I heard what happened at Mother Tiffin's. I came to find you."

He takes a step back and shakes his head. "Yes, of course. I . . . Terrible," he says. "It was terrible. A few managed to flee, but the rest of us were taken. The constables were rough, too."

"Are any of your friends in need of a doctor? Are you?"

"Good of you to ask, but no. We have been fortunate—only scratches. And released, also, albeit several sovereigns lighter."

My breath catches in my throat, and I turn away from him. My memories of Manuel, the strain of the morning—the everlingering thought of *Cecilia, Cecilia, Cecilia,* like a drumbeat beneath all else—these things have affected me more than I thought they would.

"I thought I'd lost you," I say roughly. "I was terrified."

"Ah, *schatje*," he replies, using the Dutch term for *dearest*, and he embraces me. "Courage, David. It would take more than this to fell me."

"I am not brave, Jan. I have no courage to draw upon."

He releases me and gives me a chiding look. "Nonsense. Who came to a city he had never seen before, merely in the search for something better? Who went into plague houses without care for his own survival?"

"Many people have done such things," I say.

"And they are brave, also," he replies. "We all are: you and I and all the rest. London is a city of lion hearts, David. It has survived centuries of war and death, and it will survive a thousand more. Don't forget that."

Then he strides away from the bailey, and I have no choice but to follow him.

I return home that night to discover a pamphlet that has been left on our doorstep. I pick it up. It is entitled, *A Historical and Law Treatise against the Jews and Judaism*.

Such things are not uncommon for me to find, unfortunately, and better it be used as kindling than left for another to see. I glance over it and see that the author has listed the supposed "crimes" that merited our expulsion from England in the first place, hundreds of years ago:

First, for blaspheming the name of Jesus Christ.

Second, for stealing, crucifying, and mangling Christian children.

Thirdly, for cohabiting with and debauching of Christian women.

At this, my stomach turns, and I crumple the pamphlet in my fist. Once I am inside, I throw it into the scrap basket.

I go upstairs to give my father his medicine. When I enter his room, he is fast asleep, and I must shake him awake.

He props himself up with pillows as he drinks the decoction, grimacing. I watch him.

He puts the cup down on the bedside table. Then he looks at me, frowns, and says, "David."

"What is it?"

"You are crying."

I lift my fingers to my cheek. When I draw them away, they are wet.

We look at each other with twin expressions of astonishment. I rarely cry, and certainly, I cannot remember the last time I did so in front of him.

"What is the matter?" he demands. "Explain."

His tone brokers no argument. I sit on the bed. "It really is nothing," I say, wearily. "I am tired. Confused."

He waits expectantly for me to continue. I prepare an inane elaboration—another denial, another deflection—but when I look at his face, and I am met with the intensity of his concern, I cannot bear to lie. I haven't the energy for it anymore. I am so tired.

"I think I have fallen in love," I say. "Fool that I am for it."

His frown deepens. "I see. It cannot be Sara, I think, since she would never bring you such grief. So, then, it is this gentile you spoke of. Am I correct?"

I do not reply, which is more incriminating than if I had. Father says, "David."

"I know."

"What would you do with this girl, hm? Where could it go?

You cannot marry her." He shakes his head. "I want grandchildren. I want you to find a wife, and to have the life of a happy man."

"I wouldn't be happy to live that life," I reply. "The wedding, the children—I do not want those things. I never have."

"But . . ."

"Is it not enough simply to be?" I demand. "Not enough to live as I wish, and be thankful for it?"

"Not as a Jew. I wish we were permitted such things, but we are not."

I turn my head away, swiping another tear from my cheek with my palm. I look at the collection of badly whittled figurines on his bedside: a horse, a dolphin, a bird with its beak open.

"I know," I say. "You needn't worry. I won't see her again. She is likely to be married soon. She is a gentile, and even if those things didn't matter, eventually, it would end. She would tire of me. I would fail to keep her happy."

"What? Why do you think that?"

"Because I always fail," I say. "Everything I have ever done has ended in ruin. I abandon people. I give them useless cures. I watch them die, or I leave them to rot, or I do not love them as much as I should; and I call myself a physician still, a man still—"

"David—"

I stand up. I am trembling and dissolving, pulling apart at the seams, and I cannot stand to see him sitting there, perfect and pleasant and whole.

Father says, "You must calm down."

"I am calm."

"You are not," he says. "Listen to me."

"I—"

"Breathe and listen."

I breathe in deeply, but it does little; my chest still feels tight, my pulse pounding. Still, my father takes my silence as leave to continue speaking.

"I still believe you ought to marry Sara," he says. I open my mouth to protest, and he raises his hand. "It is your choice, I know. But either way—I want you to make that choice for the right reasons. If you want that life, seize it. Otherwise . . . you are not a failure, Davi. You are more than worthy of any woman you might wish to pursue. I will fear for you, if you choose this gentile—of course, I shall. I will fear it will make you unhappy. But you are not happy now, either." He shrugs. "I want you to be happy, above all else. You do know this? That this is all I want?"

"I know." I sit beside him again and take his hands in mine. We have the same gardeners' calluses, the same short, clean nails. These four hands carry generations of knowledge, centuries of Mendes physicians. Just us two now. Perhaps never another.

"You have not been well," he says. "For some years. Ana was the same: prone to melancholy. I should have pressed you more. Our work can be a burden, as much as a blessing."

"Will I ever stop feeling responsible? For those I haven't helped? For those I have lost?"

He says, "Perhaps not. But you must forgive yourself for it, either way."

"I do not know if I can."

"Try, Davi." He pats my hand. "For me. For your love. I think you ought to try."

I feel tears welling again, and I turn to hide them. I rearrange the figurines on the table and take up the cup so I can wash it in the kitchen.

Father makes a choked noise. When I turn to him, his face is pale. His breaths are short. "I think—" he says, hand coming to his chest, and then, "I feel—"

I lurch forward. "What is it?" I ask him, clutching at his arm. "Your heart?"

He pauses—opens his mouth, then closes it—and shakes his head, wincing. "No. Only my joints," he says. "Or a cramp, perhaps. My shoulder. A hot cloth would help."

I breathe a sigh of relief and stand. "I shall fetch you one," I say. "Wait there."

"Of course. Soak it well. I am sweating, also."

"I will."

"Make certain the water boils."

"I will," I repeat, smiling.

As I reach the door, he says—voice tight with pain—"Davi."

"What is it?"

"I am grateful for you."

"It is only a cloth, Papa," I reply.

"Close the door behind you. There is a draft."

I do so, and I head down the steps.

In the kitchen, I heat the water, listening in case my father calls. I hear nothing. The water bubbles. I soak the cloth and wring it out. As I watch the dark patch fade, I recall his shuddering, the paleness of his face, the quickness of his breaths. A sudden terror grips me. I push it down. He is a doctor himself; if it was something more than a cramp, he would have known.

I remember him saying, *I am grateful for you.*

He would have known.

I drop the cloth to the counter and run back up the stairs. When I reach his room, the door is closed. I knock.

"Papa," I say. "Papa. Are you well?"

I knock more.

"May I come in? Papa?"

There is no response, and in the empty space where his words should be, there is instead only the stuttered rap of my knuckles against the door, over and over, slower and slower.

"Papa?" I say again, quieter now.

But I know—as a bird knows to sing, or a heart to beat—that he will not respond.

Each year during the days of repentance, we recite the Avinu Malkeinu. In that prayer, we sing our failings to God: *Avinu Malkeinu. Our Father, our King. We have sinned before You.*

Avinu Malkeinu, my Father, my King: Perhaps the moment I abandoned You was two years ago, when the plague was at its worst. Most of the community had left the city. Our street was empty but for me and the Cardozos, who had remained only because Manuel was already sick. I went to see him wearing my plague mask, offering him what little relief I could. He was so feverish he called me Father. He could not see my face behind the crow's beak. I was glad of that, because it hid my tears, and prevented my panic from spreading to his family. I was in love with him, and I didn't tell him. Now, I never will.

Avinu Malkeinu: the next morning, You were not there, either. No one was there. The synagogue was empty and I had taken the mezuzah from the doorframe. I had sent my father to the countryside to avoid sickness, and I was alone in the house. In the garden, I pruned the lilac. The birds seemed louder than they usually were. London was emptying, and they were celebratory in their newfound solitude. My mask remained hung on the stand, next to my oiled coat. When I went on house visits later that day, I stuffed the beak with fresh herbs, to protect myself from the miasma that spreads the disease. Other physicians often refused to see Jews; those patients I saw were very grateful for my time, and they were relieved to see me in the trappings of a plague doctor. But I was no specialist in such illnesses, and these visits were merely a comfort, rather than a cure. I dispensed physics to limit their pain, to lower their fevers, to help them sleep. I could never be the difference between living or dying.

Avinu Malkeinu: Did You see the irony of it? Law requires that infected houses put red crosses upon their doors, like the slaves in Egypt, painting with lamb's blood. This is what the Cardozos did. But I could not pass over them. Instead, I knocked and was permitted within, a premonitory reaper, selling false hope, and sorry smiles.

Avinu Malkeinu: I have sinned before You. In the waning days of that accursed summer, I went to the cupboard to find the last of the henbane tincture. I found a note behind the bottle; my father had written it and hidden it there before he left for the countryside. *I am with you still, Davi*, it said. *God is with you. Remember: He who saves a life is as if he saved an entire world.*

But I could not save them. I could not save Manuel, and I could not save my father. All these people in my wake, whom I have failed—they trail after me.

Avinu Malkeinu: Forgive me. I cannot forget, no matter how much I might try.

CHAPTER FOURTEEN

Cecilia

Determined to introduce me to court, Margaret secures us an invitation to a salon. The event is being held by an heiress I do not know. Sam assures me she is a great friend of his, but this does little to assuage my nerves.

Margaret herself curls my hair tonight, tightens the laces of my emerald-colored bodice, dusts my face with powder. Her dress is very similar to my own, in an amethyst tone rather than green. I wonder if she thinks others will take pleasure in the novelty of a matching set of twins. Our mother had dressed us in similar clothing when we were small, but it has been long since we were presented as a pair.

She instructs me in etiquette in the carriage, while Robert reads a broadside in the opposite seat, and Sam fiddles with his ribbons. She says I must take great care with how I address people: *Her Grace, His Lordship, Your Majesty.* I must curtsy neither too low nor too high. I must laugh lightly and cover my mouth as I do so. Her words spill into one ear and dribble languidly out of the other. The back of my neck itches—she has fixed a few curls there with fish glue—and my dress is too heavy for the summer, leaving me flushed and sweating. My eyes meet Sam's, and he gives me a sympathetic look. He is in green, too. I wonder if that was intentional.

We arrive at a house identical in appearance to the one we left. In the foyer, the hostess is introduced to me as Mistress Myddleton: She has auburn hair and doe-like eyes and a soft chin, and she smiles at me with earnest warmth as she welcomes me inside her parlor, which is full of people. She deposits us beside a banquet table resplendent with sweetmeats and chalices of port. Robert wanders off to greet a group of men in pale wigs and old-fashioned stockings, and Margaret is quickly engaged in conversation with some court ladies. Sam, mercifully, stays by my side.

"Mistress Myddleton is one of the Windsor Beauties," Sam tells me as he passes me a glass of port. But I am not listening; I am staring, stricken, at the man on the other side of the parlor. He is at least a head taller than everyone else, and of the two dozen or so present, at least half are gathered around him. His hair is dark, and his face is not particularly handsome—thin-lipped and large-nosed—but it is so immediately recognizable that it doesn't matter. He laughs loudly at some turn in the conversation; the sound booms warm and bright, a log tumbling onto a fire.

"Oh! I shall introduce you," Sam says. He ignores my desperate refusals as he seizes my elbow and draws me toward the king.

It takes some struggle to part the crowd, but we reach him finally, and I drop into a shaky curtsy. Sam bows. The king says, "Samuel, we see now why you have been avoiding us!" which leads to guffaws from the room.

Sam, flushing a little, gestures to me. "Your Majesty, my betrothed, Mistress Cecilia Thorowgood."

"Charmed," he replies. "I hear you are the sister of Margaret Eden?"

I feel as if I shall faint. "I—I am, Your Majesty."

"Hm. You look very little alike. But you have made the better match, I should think, as Sir Eden is about as interesting as blanched gruel."

I glance over at Robert; if he heard the comment, he hasn't reacted to it, staring disinterested into his port glass. I ought to reply with something witty, but I am so nervous I can't think of anything. I manage a respectable, "I quite agree," which produces a ghost of a smile on the king's face, but then his eyes flit away, and I realize he is already losing interest. I can't tell if that is a relief or a disappointment.

"John," the king says, turning to another member of the crowd, "you and Lizzie, then . . ."

Sam draws me away from the group. Once we are beyond the reach of the king's eyes, I gasp as if I have been struggling for air. "Oh, I did make a fool of myself—"

"Nonsense. You were perfectly composed."

"I was not!"

Sam makes a dismissive gesture. "Everyone is like that the first time. You'll get used to it."

Margaret elbows through the crowd to find us. "You ought to have informed me," she snaps, frustrated. "I would have introduced you myself."

"Why shouldn't Sam have done it?" I reply. "He is my fiancé, after all."

Margaret opens her mouth, but then closes it; she knows she has no worthy response. We are left in an awkward silence. Sam, shuffling nervously from foot to foot, perks up when someone from the other side of the room calls his name. A gaggle of rakes are competing to pluck flaming, brandy-soaked raisins from a crystal dish without burning themselves; they want him to participate. Delighted, Sam gives me a pleading look, and I roll my eyes and gesture for him to go.

Once he is away, Margaret says, "You ought to stay with me for the rest of the evening. I will introduce you to the other ladies."

I glance over to the small group of court ladies by the tea table, Mistress Myddleton among them. They are giggling to themselves about something. As I look around the room—feeling the insistent press of the dark wood furnishings, the oriental rugs, the half-naked women in the portraits on the wall—I suddenly feel terribly out of place. This is my sister's habitat, not mine. I am a country widow with a broken heart, pretending sophistication. If I try to speak to anyone here, they will surely realize that. I suppose that is why my sister wants to speak for me. Why she wants to wear me at her side like a piece of jewelry, show me off, glittering and silent.

"I . . . will take another glass of port," I say, and lunge away toward the banqueting table, leaving Margaret behind. I pause there, stomach rolling—I couldn't drink another glass of port, even if I wanted to—and then I notice that there is a spinet in the corner. The lid is open; there will be musicians performing later on. I wander over to it and press a key lightly. No one seems to notice, and the sound is quickly disguised. The chatter in the room is raucous. The rakes shriek as they snatch at the burning raisins, the women laugh, the king and his cortege compete to speak the loudest. I am simply another piece of furniture.

I play a light fugue—I hear some murmurs of appreciation from the women nearby, which does something to improve my confidence—and so I continue to play. I find the fugue becoming a toccata: Froberger's Second, the same I played with David by my side. A lifelong rival, this piece, one I have never been able to conquer.

As I whittle away at it, I allow myself to imagine that instead of standing here, I have left the party entirely. I imagine that I am walking away from this Mayfair townhouse and its scrubbed-tile doorstep, and I continue walking away until I have pierced the heart of London. I walk with the Thames threading its needle beside me, by the banks with my skirts in hand, and the summer breeze pulls the pins from my hair while my silk slippers go dirty with dust. As I walk, I can hear the sounds of a wedding pageant, drums and dancers, laughter and light. I picture the coffeehouse at Temple Bar and the soaring cathedrals and Covent Garden with its flautist, and I imagine the street leading toward Saint James's Park, with its wattle-and-daub houses. I see the gate, the canal, and the lamb's ears, and then—inevitably—I imagine David standing on the other side of the water, his hair tied back as it was when we first met, and his case clutched in one hand: sturdy boots, sage-green jacket. He would see me, and for a moment he would be perturbed—his brow furrowing, his fingers clenching the handle of his bag—but then he would understand. He would drop his things.

Querida, he would say, and I would hear him, even with the canal between us.

The toccata flies away from me, too high, too quick, notes trilling like a bird, my fingers swooping upward on the keys.

Querida, he says again. *David,* I reply, and I walk toward him—he offers me his hand—I reach for him—

My little finger hits the highest key. I can go no further, and my hand skitters against the side of the harpsichord. The daydream fades and dissolves, my mind clears, the song stops. In the empty space the music has left, the room is entirely silent. The women are not laughing, and the rakes are not shrieking, and even the king himself has gone quiet. I look up from the spinet to find everyone watching me.

"Cecilia," Margaret sputters, horrified, from where she stands beside the tea table. Her face is pale. And for a moment, I share in her horror, and I truly believe I have done something terrible—that I have been horrifically rude by playing the spinet without asking. My stomach sinks, my hands begin to shake. Bile rises in my throat.

Then someone begins to clap. The remainder of the room joins them, and I am applauded for a performance for the first time in my life.

The king says, "Brava! Brava!" his voice booming through the crowd. And then, once the clapping finishes: "What a beautiful melody, madam."

"I . . . Thank you, Your Majesty."

"Froberger's Second, was it? A fascinating interpretation."

"It is imperfect still, Your Majesty, but I am grateful for the praise."

"Imperfect!" he repeats, astonished. "I can't fathom how it might be improved."

My eyes dart nervously around the room. Behind the king, Sam is smiling at me; Margaret, relieved, is smiling, too. *Everyone* is smiling at me, even the king. This moment is something I have always wanted. It is everything I aspired toward as a child playing make-believe with her sister, without the weight of her grief pinned to her shoulders. And all I can feel is disappointment: that I didn't play well enough; that I will never see David again; that—in all the distant years that stretch before me—I will never be able to remember this day without knowing my triumph was hollow.

I don't know what to say to the king. I can't thank him again, can't apologize. So I curtsy—not too low, not too high—and I bow my head to hide my tears.

The party soon grows raucous. Margaret and Robert decide to leave by midnight, and it is testament to her pleasure with my newfound popularity that my sister permits me to stay—leaving one carriage with me, sending for another. *Return with Sir Grey,* she tells me with an indulgent pat on my cheek.

I converse extensively with some of the ladies, who are fascinated by my music. Many of them play harpsichord or virginal, but in the reluctant manner of those forced to by education. They seem to enjoy my passionate defense of the art, made only more impassioned by the wine that seems to flow endlessly from the servants' pitchers. Eventually, however, the party proves too much for me, also, particularly when the men decide to go and approximate a game of tennis in the garden using apples as balls. Sam is delighted by this—he is always delighted by such things—but I am not. Red-cheeked and aggravated, in the impetuous manner that tipsiness sometimes causes, I decide to leave without him. It is hardly as if my sister will discover the lie, after all.

"I'll take the carriage and send it back to fetch you," I tell Sam, who is at least twice as drunk as I am, and is currently attempting to pick crushed apple out of the curls of his wig.

"You're certain you won't stay?" he asks me.

"I'm tired."

"I'm Sam." He giggles and presses the pad of his thumb to the tip of my nose.

I roll my eyes, squeeze his arm, and go toward the exit. At the front door, I hear someone call my name, and turn to see Mistress Myddleton coming toward me.

"Leaving so soon?" she asks, smiling dazzlingly at me.

"Forgive me."

She laughs. "No, I understand. The menfolk have started their nonsense again. Regardless, I adored your performance tonight. Would you return next Tuesday? I am hosting a dinner. You ought to come. And bring Sir Grey, of course."

"I—well—certainly," I say, and her smile widens. "Who will be attending?"

"His Majesty, I expect, and whoever he deigns to bring. My cousin, and my husband—he ought to be returned from the estate by then." She grimaces. "He was taken ill last year, and his recovery has been slow. I had hoped the country air would do him some good, but . . ."

"I know an excellent doctor," I blurt out before I can think better of it.

"Oh? I'd be most grateful; nothing we've done has worked. You must send me his details. And anything else that comes to mind—I am a great collector of letters, you know."

Someone calls her name then, so she gives me another smile and departs. I leave the house feeling giddy and exhausted in equal measure.

The coachman helps me to my seat without any reaction to my clear inebriation, rectifying my stumbling step with the practiced, unperturbed movements of a man who has seen and will see far worse. We set off at a blistering pace—or, at least, it feels blistering—with the wheels shuddering and jolting me back and forth like a bell clapper; ten minutes into the journey, I must rap on the ceiling to command him to stop driving.

I tumble out of the carriage and onto the dirt of a London road, pressing my hands against my thighs, resisting the urge to reacquaint myself with sweetmeats the hosts served this evening. Meanwhile, the coachman waits in patient silence.

As I measure my breathing, the sounds of the city surround

me. It is late, but not terribly so; the lamps are still lit, and I can hear yelling and laughter in the distance. The air is pleasantly cool and smells of river water. I drag it to my lungs in slow, grateful gulps, concentrating on the way the lace of my sleeves rubs against my elbows.

Once my nausea has passed, I stand up and glance around myself, taking better stock of our location. The coachman has stopped on a side road, but at its end I can see the main street. With pleasure, I realize that I know where we are.

"I'm going for a walk," I tell the coachman. "I'll be back soon."

At this, he finally looks somewhat alarmed. "Mistress, I must insist I accompany you—"

"I just want to go around the bend. There's a coffeehouse there that I once went to."

"A coffeehouse," he repeats skeptically, but I am already walking away. I fear he will follow me, but he does not, and soon I am on the main road of Temple Bar.

In a half jog, I make my way to the spot I recall the coffeehouse being, ignoring the stares of the others in the area, who are no doubt fascinated by the drunken aristocrat muddying her skirts in the dirt. It is nearly one o'clock in the morning, but it is open. Light spills in glowing puddles from the windows; the door is half ajar; inside, I hear a choir of laughter at a ribald joke. I cannot resist the temptation, and I go inside.

The air is heavy with the scent of rushes and fire and coffee beans, and the noise is inconceivable. I sidestep through the crowd toward the booths—I know who I am looking for there, although I refuse to admit it to myself—and a small gaggle of men in scarlet coats pause in their discussion to stare at me. I fear they will bother me, but they just smile, and one laughs a little to himself, then turns back to continue the conversation. It is as much as I could hope for, considering I am all in silks and pearls at a Temple Bar coffeehouse past midnight. My nurse-maid once warned my mother I was so curious I was likely to cast myself into the hearth, just to know what it felt like to be burned. Perhaps I never shook the habit.

I look at the people sitting in the booths. David is not there, and I release a breath of disappointment and relief—because if he *were* here, what on earth would I do? Fall to my knees and beg him to carry me away? Apologize? Pass him a wedding invitation with my and Sam's names on it, and say, *He is a good man, David, but sometimes I dream that he is you; sometimes I think that every kiss I have from now until I die will be only an echo of the ones we shared; and I think I am being cruel to Sam by pretending I can forget you, cruel to Will's memory by wanting you like this, but for the first time I understand why the poets liken love to fire and famine and war.*

Someone calls my name. I turn, whip fast, to see Johannes van Essen staring at me from a seat in one of the booths.

"Cecilia," he says, and he smiles, standing to greet me. "What Providence!"

He comes to me and bows, then shakes my hand for good measure. He remains as handsome as the last time I saw him, a few weeks ago, but his hair is a little longer, ginger curls just brushing his jaw. A thin film of stubble covers his cheeks, and there are dark bags under his eyes.

"Please, sit," he says, and we return to the booth. Once he has ordered coffee for both of us, he asks, "What brings you here?"

"Impulse, mostly," I say.

"Looking for David?" I must fail to hide my chagrin, because he chuckles. "You will not find him here for a while yet, I am afraid."

"Why is that?"

Jan's expression sobers. "His father passed," he says. "Near three weeks ago now. He has finished his period of mourning, but he is still keeping to himself."

My breath catches in my throat. I never knew Gaspar Mendes, of course, but David mentioned him, and I know they were close. I feel grief on David's behalf, in a helpless, self-resenting sort of way. While he has been mourning, I have been playing harpsichord at parties and drinking with the king; it all feels so frivolous when compared with something so terrible.

"I am sorry," I say.

"Why?" Jan asks. "It is not your fault, Cecilia."

"I think I have caused David far more harm than good. And now this—I fear I have merely added to his suffering."

Jan frowns and considers this as the server comes and sets up our coffee. He lifts the lid off the pot to inspect it, sniffing, then nods. "This is a good batch," he says.

"Look, I—"

"What has happened—no one could have prevented it," Jan tells me. "We cannot choose whom we love. If we could, my life would certainly be far easier. Neither of you is responsible, and yet you both seem determined to take the blame."

"I have made his life more difficult."

"And he yours, in some ways, surely? You are being fools, both of you." He pours us the coffee. "He is bereft without you. Anyone with eyes can see that."

"He told me we couldn't see each other again."

Jan rolls his eyes. "For a Jew, David would certainly make a good martyr."

I snort in amusement and take a sip from my dish. It is so strong it makes my toes curl. "Yes, he would."

"You could find him if you wanted," Jan says.

"I know."

"I think he would be glad to see you, for all he has pretended otherwise."

"My sister spoke unforgivably to him," I reply.

"You are not your sister."

"I am engaged to be married."

"Really?" Jan shrugs. "You have not said the vows."

I take another sip, and I shudder at the bitterness. "I—I *can't*, Jan."

"Why not? You came here tonight to see him, no?"

My gut squirms. "I wasn't thinking. I was flinging myself into the fire, as I always do."

"How so?"

"If I had seen him, nothing would have changed. He would have told me to leave, told me he didn't want me the way I want him."

"You can't be certain of that," Jan says.

"I don't need to be certain. I have already lost so many things. I lost my husband, and I lost David before I ever had him, and I cannot risk that loss again. There is only so much grief I can bear."

Jan frowns. "You sound like David when you speak like that."

I snap, "Perhaps that is because David is right."

Jan doesn't respond. He just stares at me, still frowning, hands curled around his coffee dish.

I sigh. "Forgive me, I know I can be . . . harsh."

"A little. I understand, though. I know it is difficult."

I give him a strained smile, then drain my dish. Standing up, I say, "I am tired, and drunk. I ought to return home. Thank you for the coffee, Jan."

He doesn't look insulted by the abrupt exit, thankfully, only saddened. "Cecilia," he says.

"Yes?"

"If you see David again," he says. "*When* you see David again. There is something you should bear in mind."

"What is it?" I ask.

"He has lost people, too. He has loved and he has grieved." Jan shrugs. "We all have empty rooms in our hearts. Better to fill them, surely, than to lock their doors and hope they are forgotten."

CHAPTER FIFTEEN

David

Time passes, as it always has and always will. No amount of tragedy has ever changed that.

Sara comes while I am sitting shiva, with a basket of cherry tarts. She sits beside me on the floor and puts her arm around me as I press my face into her shoulder.

Others come, too—everyone from the community—and they take my hand in theirs and offer me the traditional condolence: *May heaven comfort you.* Sometimes I forget to reply, and they squeeze my palm, and say it again: *May heaven comfort you.*

Once my shiva is done, Jan comes to help Elizabeth Askwith and me remove the cloth from the mirrors and clear the food we have not eaten. He asks me when I will move, and I tell him I intend to stay. He stares at me blankly, as if I have spoken to him in another language.

"This house is too big for you alone, David," he says.

He is correct; it was, in some ways, too big for me and my father, also. I ought to leave, find a smaller set of rooms with a smaller garden, let Elizabeth Askwith find work somewhere less enamored with its own past. Gaspar Mendes is still here, in the carvings on the bench and the flowers that grow from soil he tended. His room is still as it was, and most of his things are inside there—in the wardrobe, or in chests that I pushed under the bed. The wooden figurines he carved are the only things I cannot bring myself to conceal, and so I take them out and put them in my cabinet alongside the porcelain painted with flowers.

I eat three meals a day because I should, I wash and sleep because I should, because if I don't, then I have to admit that everything is different and that I am not the same. I double my appointments for the first week after my mourning is done, so I am away from the house from dawn until dusk. Despite the merciless heat of this year's summer, during the earliest hours of the morning, the air by the river is still bracing. I never wear a jacket, and when the cold reaches its fingers beneath the sleeves of my shirt, it is a relief.

My friends maneuver around me as if the floor is made of glass. Sara does not push me for an answer to her proposal; Jan is gentle and patient; Elizabeth Askwith continues her work without any question as to why a single bachelor requires a maid at all. And between it all, I ache with missing my father, and I ache—shamefully—with missing Cecilia, whose absence now somehow seems all the more bracing. When people ask me, *How are things,* I know that Cecilia would not ask the same; she wouldn't need to. She wouldn't be patient with me, she wouldn't send me sympathetic smiles and pat me on the arm. She wouldn't afford me the indulgence of self-pity, because I rarely afforded her such things. It is strange how you can know a person so briefly, and yet learn them so well you can conduct conversations with them in their absence. I imagine telling her, *It is difficult,* and she replies, *I know, David. I know.*

~

In August, I am hired for a new job: another court family. Another Saint James's townhouse, another suspiciously generous wage. I should know better than to accept, but the emptiness of my life in the past weeks has dulled the blade of my caution. What have I to lose?

Master Myddleton was afflicted last year with a fever of the glands, and as is the case with many such illnesses, it is taking him months to recover. He is beset by constant exhaustion. I suspect the issue is actually the quality of his sleep rather than some chronic condition. I see him on a Thursday, provide him with some medicines the next day, and consider the job done.

Then, the following Tuesday, I am awakened past midnight by a footman banging on my door, insistent I must come to the townhouse at once. I doze in the carriage on the way there.

Upon my arrival, I am informed by a distraught Mistress Myddleton that her husband fainted during a dinner party and is now unconscious in the parlor. On our way up the steps, I can hear the sounds of the party: Someone is playing the harpsichord quite exquisitely.

The décor of this townhouse is more modern than that of the Edens', and the corridor leading to the parlor has been tiled in black and white like a checkerboard, marble statues standing between each window in languid poses. The parlor itself is a confection of honey-yellow and scarlet, and Master Myddleton lies snoring on the chaise longue. When I go to inspect him, the scent of brandy immediately hits me. I sigh: It is already clear what the issue is. Illnesses can make people far less tolerant of their drink. After ensuring the affliction isn't anything more serious, I turn him so he is lying on his side, propping him up with pillows, and remove his wig so he doesn't overheat. I leave one of my milk thistle decoctions on the table with a note—it will help with the hangover—and I depart.

At the base of the staircase, I pause to jot down a message for Mistress Myddleton explaining the situation. I could seek her out, but she is entertaining her guests, and I don't imagine she'd want them to see me. As I write, I listen to the muffled cadence of the party, booming voices, clinking glasses. The distance makes their conversation a foreign language, perceptible but incomprehensible. A woman laughs brightly, and there is something about the sound that seems familiar—but the noise fades as quickly as it came, subsumed in the deluge of other speakers.

I hand the note to the footman, who places it delicately on a silver dish, then heads toward the dining room. I take my hat from the stand, shrug on my coat, stare at myself briefly in the mirror by the door—sighing at the frown lines marring my forehead—and then I realize I have forgotten my medicine case upstairs.

Back, then, to the checkerboard tiles and the marble statues and the grunting snores of Master Myddleton. I take my things, check his pulse once more—just in case—and then leave the room.

Cecilia is standing outside.

The door closes behind me. I hover at the threshold. I look at her, and she looks at me.

I have never seen her so beautiful. Her hair is curled and pinned up at her ears, eyes lined with kohl, skin flushed with wine and heat. It is warm in the gallery, and there is a thin film of sweat on her neck and forehead. Her dress is a little loose, slipping indecently low down her shoulders. I want to dip my fingers into the hollows of her collarbone. I want to press my mouth against the line of her jaw. I want to close my eyes, but I can't.

"Cecilia," I say, voice low and hoarse. "What are you doing here?"

"I . . . Mistress Myddleton invited me."

"Were you the one who commended me to her service?"

"Yes."

I release a breath, shoulders slumping. "Why did you do that?"

"She needed a doctor."

"Is that all?"

She takes a step toward me, from a black tile to white. I watch her, still and silent. We are chess pieces, and she is taking her turn.

"I missed you," she says. "That's why I did it."

"How do you want me to respond to that?"

"I want you to feel the same."

I take my own step forward—white to black—and reply, "Last time we saw each other— I thought you'd be angry at me."

"For knowing about the betrothal?" She sighs. "I was. I am. But I have missed you more than I have resented you."

Hearing that makes me ache with gratefulness, with relief, with want of her—but I must remain resolved. "There is nothing more to be said between us," I tell her, as firmly as I can. "We both know you ought to turn around and go back to the dining room, pretend this never happened. You never should have come up here in the first place."

There are only three tiles between us now. She moves forward. "You haven't missed me, then?" she asks. "You haven't thought of me, in the weeks since we last saw each other?"

"Of course, I have."

"Then—"

"Everywhere," I interrupt, temper rising, "You have been *everywhere* since we first met. I can't escape you. Everywhere I go, you are there, whether real or imagined. And now that you are standing in front of me, I still can't be certain whether you are truly here or instead some sort of waking dream. But—whatever you are—you ought to leave."

She looks crestfallen. "We could talk, at least. Just for a little while. I know things have been difficult for you. I saw Jan, and . . . Your father . . ."

"*Don't*," I snarl, and her eyes widen. "Cecilia, leave, *please*. I haven't the patience."

She shakes her head. She is wearing earrings, cherry-sized pearls, and they swing wildly with the movement. The color on her cheeks intensifies. I wonder how much she has drunk to-night; enough, at least, to make her dangerous. "You are intent on your own suffering," she says. "You know that? You and your martyr complex, your dramatic declarations—"

"*Martyr complex?*"

"You make everything so complicated, when it doesn't need to be!"

"*Life* is complicated—"

"Oh, shut up!" she snarls. "You are as bad as the rest some-times, you know. Stop talking to me as if I am your patient. Men see a woman having feelings and decide it is their job to remove them. Yes, I missed you, but I didn't know we would meet in this way. I thought you could aid Jane—Mistress Myddleton—and now here you are chiding me for *helping* you to get a new client. I know you have been grieving, but I don't think that excuses it. You don't think I know what grief looks like? You think you are permitted to treat me cruelly because of it?"

She steps forward another tile; I step back. A queen and a pawn.

"I should go," I say.

"Of course. Run away, as you always do."

My jaw clenches. "Cecilia, enough."

"Shall I handle you like porcelain? Shall I coo at you and say, *Yes, David, your life is so difficult, I pity you terribly*, so you can go home and be smug in the knowledge you have a gentlewoman pining for you?"

"What is it you want from me?" I demand. "You complain I treat you cruelly, and yet you won't let me leave. You want me to yell at you instead, is that it? You want me to rant and rave about the sins you have committed, that *I* have committed? Would that make you feel better?"

"Maybe!" she cries. "It would be preferable to your absence!"

I am very close to saying something unforgivable; I clamp my mouth shut, grit my teeth, hands fisted at my sides. She is breathing heavily, her flush trailing down her cheeks and neck, all the way below her collarbone. Her chest is heaving, dress falling, hair in disarray from the force of her movements, eyes bright with anger. She looks like every one of my most illicit imaginings, and it is shameful how much it affects me. But it *does* affect me, after weeks of misery and exhaustion, to stand before the woman who has haunted me and see her like this. I can no longer separate anger and desire.

Instinctive, unthinking, I find myself moving forward, ignoring the tiling entirely. I seize her by the waist, spinning her around, pressing against her so we stumble backward and butt up against the closed door. She gasps and loops one arm around my neck, raising her head in the expectation of a kiss; it takes all the temperance I have to bring my lips to her ear instead.

"You have such *infinite* trust in my self-control," I murmur to her. "I did once, too, but I am not myself recently, querida. I am fraying at the edges, and you continue to test me, and there is only so much more I can bear before I break."

She arches her back, pressing into me. I swallow a groan. "Break, then."

"There is a roomful of courtiers downstairs."

"I doubt they can hear." She laughs breathlessly. "You know the king is there, too?"

"What?"

"I don't care if he knows," she says, plaintive. "I don't care if any of them know. You have driven me to madness, David Mendes. I am yours entirely."

I look down at her, squirming in my arms, eyes glassy, mouth parted. Her lips are the color of rose hips, and it would be so easy to take them with my own and make them bloom, pretend we are any other two lovers having a tryst at a party. This close, the scent of her is almost dizzying, perfume and dessert wine and salt-sweet heat. I skim my mouth across her collarbone, the swell of her breast. She whimpers. Reason is impossible. I bring my face to hers, her hand lifts to press against my cheek—something glints on her finger—I turn my head to kiss her wrist—

And then I see the ring.

I release her. I step back. She frowns in confusion, says my name, her hand still raised. Then her eyes follow mine, and she realizes what I have seen. Her arm drops.

There is a lump in my throat, coal black, heavy. I swallow around it.

"David," she whispers. "I . . ."

"It is official, then."

"Yes."

"When will you . . . ?"

She fiddles with the ring, twists it on her finger. The diamonds glint in the light of the sconces. "Ten days."

It feels as if I have been punched. "Ten days," I echo.

"It isn't—he—we aren't like that," she says. "We are friends."

"He will be your *husband*, Cecilia."

"Yes, but . . . That doesn't mean anything."

"It does to me."

She flinches. "What would you have me *do*, David?" she asks, voice breaking. "It is my only choice. My only chance at liberty."

"I know."

"My hand is his, but my heart is yours. Can that not be enough?"

"Hearts change," I say. "They speed, and slow, and stop. That ring is yours until he dies, or you do."

Her face goes cold. "I have been married before."

"I know. I just—" I tip my head back, staring at the ceiling. It has been painted with a fresco of Mars and Venus intertwined: clouds and blue sky, gilt and fantasy. Like everything in this place. "I can't do it, Cecilia. I can never have you, because if I do, I will lose you. And I couldn't bear to lose you again."

From the direction of the staircase, I can hear muffled laughter and music: the sounds of another world, one I can never enter, and one I must send her back to.

I know that if she must marry, then Sir Grey is the least objectionable choice there is. I know that if she must live freely, then marriage is the only solution. But I know that if I must love her as I do—unthinkingly, foolishly, without redemption—then I must do so from afar. Then, when she forgets me, nothing will change.

I look back at her. She has extended her arm, palm flat: offering me her hand. "David," she says.

I step forward and close her hand for her, curling my fingers beneath her own until she makes a fist. Her arm drops.

"Farewell, Lady Grey," I tell her.

Ten days.

On the first, I work. I eat. I go with Jan to Mother Tiffin's, conduct a halfhearted flirtation with an Italian, and then refuse his invitation to go home with him. On the second, it is an alehouse rather than Tiffin's, and I drink until I am sick.

On the third day, Jan comes by and nurses me through my hangover. He doesn't ask questions. He looks at me as if I am on the verge of dissolving, like paper in the rain, and he insists on staying for the remainder of the week. He stays for Shabbat, and on the fourth day—the day of rest—I read and sleep as he works on his accounts. I am waiting for the time to pass, praying for the time to pass, so I will be released from this threshold I am hovering upon, desperate to step forward, desperate to step back.

Time does pass, albeit slowly. The fifth day, the sixth, the seventh. On the eighth, the Myddletons call me back to their townhouse. I go, because I must, and they rain praise upon me for Master Myddleton's improvement. There is a young woman there with them, plump and pretty, who is introduced to me as Dear Ellie by Mistress Myddleton, and who is carrying Master Myddleton's baby. Mistress Myddleton seems exceptionally fond of her husband's lover, cooing over her as I do a general examination of her health. When I tell her all is well, Mistress Myddleton presses a kiss to Ellie's cheek and cries, "Marvelous!" as Ellie flushes.

Perhaps, I think as I leave, *I have misunderstood something fundamental about Christian marriage.*

On the ninth day, the day before Cecilia is to be married, I cancel my evening appointments and visit a pair of graves.

The Jewish graveyard in London is tiny, tucked between sev-

eral alleys, surrounded by leaning houses that seem on the verge
of toppling over. It was a garden only ten years ago, and it still
carries that legacy in the scattered trees and flower beds. It is
quite lovely, and few enough of us have died here that it still carries vast stretches of open space. There are no walls or gates yet,
although the community is raising funds. Father donated often.

His gravestone is simple. His name is inscribed in both Hebrew and Portuguese. There are many pebbles left piled upon it;
he was well loved by the community here. He saved many lives
over the course of his career. And, only a few paces away, there is
Manuel's grave, too—just as well tended, stones stacked precari-
ously. Several of them are mine.

I place the two stones I have brought with me—kidney-shaped
and smooth—beside the others, one on Manuel's grave, one on
my father's. Murmuring a brief prayer, I step away. Meanwhile,
the graves watch, silent and inscrutable.

I have a curious urge to say something, but who would listen?
I cannot convince myself my father is present, that Manuel is
present, as much as I wish they were. In the distance, a church
bell rings—I wonder what Cecilia is doing tonight, in preparation for the wedding. A Jewish bride would be washing in a
mikvah, purifying herself before God. Do gentiles do something
similar? I realize now that I do not know. I know nothing of
Christian weddings except that they take place in a church, with
a priest, and without a chuppah. Nothing above the couple except those towering, vaulted ceilings, nothing to cover them—
something about that thought seems terrifying.

It is very late. The sun ought to have set entirely by now, but
when I look west, it still glows faintly in the sky, red and flicker-
ing. I frown and peer closer. The light seems different somehow
from all other dusks I have seen. As bright, but somehow broader;

CHAPTER SIXTEEN

David

I run home.

We can't yet see the fire from our window—when I tell Elizabeth Askwith, she insists that it shall pass—but I am uncertain. The houses in this city are ripe targets for flames, wood boxes pressed against each other like overcrowded teeth. The fire is distant, but I doubt it shall be for long.

I am correct. By the next morning, it has reached London Bridge. My house is off the main road, but when I walk to the corner, I find myself surrounded by an exodus. A great crowd of people have been pushed out of the city center by the flames, and they are now making their way east, carrying whatever detritus they have managed to salvage: a pair of laundresses walk by with washing pots hung from their necks, clattering like castanets; a family with at least a dozen children trundles along the cobbles, their cart laden with oranges; a scribe clutching rolls of paper weaves furtively through the horde. I notice a young man with burns on his hands, and I offer him a poultice, but he refuses and runs away from me.

The sky goes dull and dark with soot. A warm, ashy wind whips through the streets. Every Jew in the neighborhood comes to my door, in the typical way that news spreads in our community, with clandestine knocks and furtive gazes. "Will the ashes bring disease?" asks Master Pinto, the banker. "It is as if we are in Gomorrah," the rabbi tells me. On the street itself, people stand outside their houses to watch the conflagration grow, shrieking and gasping and pleading to God. For hours, it continues: black sky, red city, and prayers accompanying screams.

I am terrified for Jan, whose home almost certainly has met the flames. I decide that if I hear nothing from him before the sun sets, I will go east to search for him. Meanwhile, I go to the doorstep and remove the mezuzah. In times of disaster, it is risky to display our faith so openly. No doubt some will blame Jews for the fire and come to enact revenge.

In the early evening, someone knocks on the door. It is Jan. The moment I see him, he sags forward, over the threshold, and I catch him. He yelps in pain.

I hold him upright; his lip is split, jaw bruised, and one leg is hovering awkwardly over the ground. Across his back, he has a large bag, stuffed so full it can hardly close. "What happened?" I ask, horrified.

"Riots," he says. "Foreigners are being blamed for starting the fire—I wanted to warn you."

"Are they heading this way?"

"Not yet. But the flames are."

"You are injured," I say.

"I was caught in a crush on the way. I think my ankle is broken. It took me hours to get here." He shakes his head. "It is bad, David. It spreads too fast. I had to leave my house. I fear it will reach you, also."

"Do you know how it started?"

"No one does," he replies. "But it hardly matters now."

I look over his shoulder. The red glow in the sky has spread further, stretching upward, like blood seeping through a bandage. "I'll treat your wounds, first," I say. I open the door wider and gesture for him to come inside. "Then I think we ought to leave."

He puts an arm around me and follows me indoors, leaning heavily on my shoulder. In the kitchen, Elizabeth Askwith helps me prepare a poultice for Jan's cuts. She is even more churlish than usual, pacing the kitchen while I set his ankle, glaring at the window. "I shall not leave, David Mendes," she says, "until you and Master van Essen leave, also."

I am touched. "Thank you, Elizabeth."

She looks nervously at Jan's ankle, which is swollen purple-red. "'Haps I should seek a cart to hire."

"You can try," Jan says. "But there are few to be had. I heard some are charging more than forty pounds for passage."

She blanches, but says resolutely, "I'll negotiate."

"Return within the hour if you have no luck," I tell her. "Take no risks."

She nods curtly and disappears into the hall.

Jan presses a finger to his split lip. "It's all gone, David," he says quietly. "All my things. And the city . . . the cathedral, the bridges . . ."

I wrap my arms around him. He shudders and presses his wet eyes into my shoulder.

We begin packing the things too precious to leave: recipe books, medical equipment, the tefillin, mezuzahs and the menorah, clothing for the winter, and what ingredients I can keep dried. Eventually, Elizabeth Askwith returns stone-faced. There are no carts to be had. Resourcefully, she had also gone to the river, seeking a barge; the only one available wanted two hundred pounds to take us. I don't make so much money in a year.

Someone knocks again. This time it is Sara, who lives only a few doors down from us. I feel ashamed I hadn't thought of her earlier. I *haven't* thought of her, I realize, since I sat shiva for my father; grief has made me callous.

She looks over my shoulder to see the bags stacked by the staircase.

"You are leaving?" Sara asks me.

"Soon."

"Where will you go?"

"I don't know. Anywhere there is ground to sleep on, I suppose. You?"

She pauses, gives me a long, inscrutable look, and says, "That depends. My cousin's home is in Mile End, and he can house me. I can walk there."

"You should go, then."

"I—" She swallows, looks away. "But I could also stay here. With you."

I don't know what to say. I hover in the doorway, the city in flames around us, and I can think of no better response than, "It is dangerous."

"Yes, obviously," she snaps. Then she rubs her neck, clearly ashamed at her own annoyance. "It is a bad time for me to ask you this—"

"Yes, it is."

"—but I must. I have been giving you time, after your father . . . I know, of course, how difficult it is. But I am beginning to feel as if you have been avoiding me. As if you will never give me an answer to my proposal, unless I demand one face-to-face."

"I haven't been avoiding you."

She shakes her head. "I wish you would be honest with me," she says. "Sometimes I cannot tell when you are. You are a terrible liar, David, but not so when you are lying to yourself."

"Sara . . . I . . . You are very dear to me," I say. "Forgive me for not speaking with you sooner. I am glad to have you in my life, and I do not want to lose you."

She makes a frustrated sound. "What does that *mean*?" she demands. "I have asked you to marry me. You must either agree or refuse. Do so now, and save us both the grief of waiting longer. The city is on fire. This may be the last time we see each other."

I bow my head, contrite. "I—I cannot marry you, Sara. I would be a terrible husband to you. We both know that."

"What makes you think so?" she asks, raising a brow. "If you are refusing because you think you are somehow undeserving, you are misguided. You're a good man, David. I would be proud to marry you."

"I know, but—"

"Love grows with time. Marriage is a beginning, not a culmination."

"Yes, but still—"

"Of course, I will accept your refusal. It's just—I don't want you to refuse for such a ludicrous reason—"

"I was in love with him," I say, interrupting her. "Manuel."

She blinks at me, falling silent. I await some further reaction—disgust, or shock, or anger—but after a long moment, she simply says, "Oh."

It is the first time I've said it aloud, the first time I've truly acknowledged it in front of anyone else. It is ridiculous—the city is on fire, Cecilia is getting married, and I am about to lose everything—but I smile.

"I was in love with Manuel," I repeat. It feels as if I have had stones stacked upon me, like the graves I have visited, and they have suddenly been lifted away. "And now I am in love with someone else. So I cannot marry you, Sara. I hope you understand."

"I understand," she says faintly. "Did—did he know?"

"I never told him. I don't know if he knew."

"I see." She tugs at her collar as if she might somehow lengthen her gown and cover herself with it, hide herself from me, and spare us both the agony of the conversation. "I had no idea."

"I know."

"He loved you, too," she says. "I don't know if it was in the same way, but he did. And"—her voice cracks—"when he died, you were there. You understood. I felt like you understood, when no one else did. Now I know why."

"Sara, I am sorry," I say. But, to my shock, she leans forward over the doorframe, wrapping her arms around me. Hesitantly, I return the embrace. Her tears dampen my shirt.

"I want him back," she whispers into my collar. "I want it all back. I want everything to be as it was."

"I want that, too. But we can't go back. Not anymore."

Sara sniffs and pulls away. She rubs her cheek with the heel of her hand. "I am angry with you," she says. "You owed me an answer sooner. But—I don't know. I don't know how to feel."

"Forgive me."

"Stop apologizing," she replies, scowling. "It helps neither of us, and it is extremely aggravating."

"Pardon," I say. Then I laugh, as does she.

"Does it hurt?" she asks gently. "That he'll never know?"

"I was happy to have him in my life, regardless."

She nods. "You love very quietly, David."

"Perhaps I should have been louder," I say.

"I don't think so," she replies. "There's no need to be loud, if you are with someone who can listen."

There is a shriek from a nearby street. We both flinch and turn to look. The light in the sky has grown deeper, brighter. When our gazes meet again, Sara's eyes are wide with fear. She shakes her head, as if to return herself to reality.

"Go to your cousin in Mile End," I tell her. "We'll be fine."

She looks uncertain. "You'll be leaving soon?"

"Yes. As soon as possible."

I don't tell her about Jan's ankle. I take her hand, squeezing it. Sara squeezes back, and kisses my cheek.

"Farewell, then," she says, and she hurries back down the street.

I watch her leave, uncertain whether I will ever see her again. The fire is coming, and we cannot know who will survive it. I do not want to feel the grief of it all—what has happened, what will happen—not now, not when there is still so much to be done. I take my sorrow and bind it up, stitch it closed, place it somewhere secret so I can ignore it until it inevitably bursts its seams.

In the kitchen, Jan is still sitting on the counter. When he sees me enter, he says, "David, you should leave me here."

"Don't be absurd," I say.

"What are you intending to do? I can hardly walk. Will you carry me down the street, in that crowd, in such a panic—?"

"If I must," I say. "But we have crutches, somewhere, that my father once used. You can take them."

"You should leave me here," he repeats. "I can go at my own pace, once the pain lessens."

"If you stay, I stay."

He scowls at me. I scowl back. He says, "You are being an idiot."

"And you are being a stubborn ass. What sort of friend would I be if I abandoned you?"

Jan sighs. "You would never abandon me, friend or not. That is why you are so extraordinary, David."

I clear my throat. There is no time for tears. "Stay here," I say. "We will continue packing. I will fetch you when we are prepared to leave."

He nods reluctantly. I embrace him, then go to salvage the last few items I can take with me. In the parlor, father's wood carvings, which I save in favor of the porcelain; in my bedroom, my Talmud, my herbal, and my best hat; in the garden, the strings of glass beads on the hooks, warm to the touch and coated in a thin film of ashes. I take a moment to look at my plants, my ailing basil, my rosemary, my fist-sized lettuces. My throat tightens. Living things, all of them—my life's work, my greatest achievements—and I am leaving them to the flames.

In the storeroom, Elizabeth Askwith has found a traveling case and is filling it with medicines. She has opened the window, understandably so, as the room is unbearably warm. But it is a lost cause, as the fire has made the wind hot and dry. It gusts in, ruffling my hair as I help her pack. It brings the scent of char with it, and I imagine what the city will be like once the fire is gone, once only a carcass remains—I picture the skeletal beams of the burned-down buildings, and the ashes that will pour out of the empty doorframes, like blood from leaking veins. Soon that smell will be all that is left: a passing whisper of memory, the ghost of a city near gone.

I go to my father's room last. I know there is little here that I can take with me, but I go all the same. It is the first time I have opened the door since my shiva, and I find a memory trapped in amber: all as it was, bed rumpled, cases full of clothes peeking out from under the bed. I go to his desk and open the drawers,

wondering if there might be something small of his I have forgotten, which I can now take with me—a pen, a pin, perhaps
even another wood carving. But the drawers mostly contain papers, old accounts and patient notes. I rifle through them regardless, then spot a hint of color. Curious, I pull out a heavier
sheet of vellum, high quality, on which is penned a large chunk
of Aramaic text. The borders are hand painted in green and red,
roses and pomegranates. Signatures have been left in faded
brown ink at the bottom.

It is my parents' ketubah, their wedding contract. I had no
idea my father kept this all these years, hidden at the bottom of
a drawer. To hold on to such a thing, even after the divorce—
I cannot imagine what he was thinking. Or perhaps I can. I
remember those first few weeks in London, the incremental fading of the hope in his eyes every time he said, *Ana will be here
soon, Davi. Your mother will be here soon.*

There is only one line in Hebrew on the contract, just above
the signatures: *Ani l'dodi v'dodi li.* I am my beloved's, and my
beloved is mine.

I take the ketubah with me, and I close my father's door for
the final time.

CHAPTER SEVENTEEN

Cecilia

I stand before the mirror in my wedding dress.

"There now, Cecilia," Margaret says, tucking a lock of hair behind my ear. "Have you ever seen a lovelier bride?"

I remember the woman in the pageant, smiling at her husband, haloed with gold. I think that a bride must be in love to be truly lovely. You can paint a face and cinch a waist, but you can't put joy into someone's eyes.

When I married Will, my dress was blue, also—a paler blue than this one, which is true cornflower, the color of a sapphire in sunlight. I had flowers in my hair, but they were tiny daisies and wilting columbine; the purple aster and larkspur that crown me now are resplendent, regal, the sort of thing I might expect of an empress. Diamonds around my throat, pearls strung over my shoulders. I am a widow no longer. I am reborn.

I make no reply to my sister, but she doesn't care. Her mind is elsewhere: on the myriad arrangements she has made for the afternoon, the procession to the church, the ceremony, the feast, the smiling speeches. Sam and I are to be tugged about like kites on a string. *See how they fly!* Margaret will say, before reeling us back to earth.

There is a knock on the door. The maid is outside, nervous, bearing a dish with a letter on it. The seal is obscured from me, but it must alarm Margaret, because she tells me, "Don't touch your hair, you'll ruin it," before disappearing into the corridor, shutting the door behind her.

I meet my own eyes in the mirror. The blue of my dress only makes them look more gray, darkens them, gathers a storm where the sunlight should be.

For a moment, I wonder what would happen if I didn't marry him, if I found some other way to escape this place. A convent; a faked death; and then what—live on the streets? Sell Sam's mother's diamonds and leave for the New World?

I sigh and turn away from the mirror. I look to the window instead, and I frown. I can see the glimmer of red light on the horizon.

Margaret reenters the room. Her face is flushed. "I have extraordinary news."

I point to the window. "What is that?" I ask her.

She ignores this. "The *king* has agreed to come to the ceremony," she says, breathless. "Can you believe it? He won't be at the banquet—thank the Lord, we couldn't have possibly changed the menu at the last minute—but Mistress Myddleton mentioned it to him, and he has deigned to offer a blessing—"

"I think it's flames," I say.

"What? Are you even listening to me, Cecilia?"

"Yes, I—I know, it's extraordinary, but—*look*."

She finally looks out the window. "Yes, there's a fire in the inner city. Apparently, some Catholics started it yesterday. It's impressive that it still burns."

"It must be enormous if we can see it from here. Won't it spread?"

"There are firebreaks made near the park," she says. "We are too distant regardless. It spreads east, last I heard."

"East," I echo. Toward Aldgate.

"It shouldn't have much bearing on the wedding, thankfully. Most people are fleeing via the river."

"What about those without a barge?"

She frowns. "Well, I imagine they'll have to go by foot, as I doubt there are many carriages to be had. Did you touch your hair? It looks a little lopsided."

"Won't they lose their homes? All their things? How will they carry it all?"

"The Lord works in mysterious ways," she says airily. "Perhaps it'll do them good. Adversity is food for the spirit."

Someone knocks on the door again: It is the same maid as before. "My lady, your husband has returned from court," she says to Margaret.

"He is early," Margaret replies.

"He requires your presence. He says it is urgent."

She grimaces at this, but says, "Very well. Cecilia, I shall return soon. And don't—"

"—touch my hair," I reply. "I know."

She leaves with the maid. Outside the window, the sky is swathed in gray clouds. The faint glimmer of the fire is barely visible, miles away from here. It sparkles in the glass; it is almost beautiful. And it travels east, toward Aldgate. Toward David. I picture the flames. I picture the heat and the chaos they will bring with them. Where will he go? How will he escape, without a carriage or barge of his own? He is so clearly foreign—a target for rioters and looters—and meanwhile I am here, swaddled in silks, pearls in my ears, preparing for a masquerade. My wedding will be no better than theater, really. Sam and I will be actors, playing pretend while London burns.

I remember Will and me in London last year. I dragged him into the bookstore, the one with the tabby cat and the Florentine history. A fire started that day, invisible and endless and cruel, and it has been burning within me ever since.

I will die before I see David burn, too.

I remove my delicate, coral-studded slippers, trading them for my walking boots. I don't have time to remove the gown, but I hitch my skirts up, remove the collar of diamonds. Then I leave the room and sneak down the corridor toward the stairs, aiming for the kitchens. On the steps, I pause, as I can hear Margaret and Robert speaking in the parlor.

"...Absurd," Margaret is saying. "The king is coming. We are distant enough that we are safe."

"I am not suggesting we *cancel* it, my love, only move the ceremony a little later, once the panic has subsided—the streets are difficult to navigate, and the crowds are scattered—"

"It won't reach us," Margaret says. "God is with us. Whatever quarrel he has with the rest of the city, surely we are not to blame?"

I creep away. In the kitchen, the cook is at the hearth, stirring a pot that smells strongly of cloves. There is a delicate marzipan sculpture on the opposite counter: for my wedding feast, I presume. It is of a unicorn, spiral horned, rearing upward. Its mane has been painted with gilt.

The cook doesn't seem likely to move. There is nothing for it; I must bolt past him. I take a deep breath, dart forward, rush past the unicorn—the dish catching on my sleeve—and then through the back door, ignoring the cook's cry of surprise. There

is a crash in my wake, the marzipan tumbling to the tiles. I barrel
into the alley with the momentum of a cannonball, almost slam-
ming into the opposite wall.

No time to pause. I continue running until I hit the main
road, which is mostly deserted; there are no wanderers in London today. But at least dogged Katherine is still present with her
flower stall, glancing warily up at the ashen sky as she rearranges
a posy.

"Evening, mistress," she says, smiling at me. I expect she still
hopes I will buy a flower. I must continue to disappoint her.

"Forgive me," I reply. "But I must ask—how far away is Aldgate?"

She blinks. "There is a fire," she says.

"Yes, I know. What if I went via the river?"

"Not long—a half hour, at most. But there aren't any barges to
be had." She pauses. "As there is a fire," she repeats.

I thank her, ignoring her put-out expression as I run away.
Someday I shall return and finally pay her for all her help.

It feels odd to come back around to the front of the townhouse; I am terrified that Margaret will burst from the gate and
pull me back inside. But the street is empty, and I reach the
house opposite the Edens' without complication.

A footman answers the front door. Thankfully, he is so
alarmed by my anxious countenance and state of dress that he
permits me inside without protest, leaving me to wait in the
parlor. Moments later, Sam descends the steps. He was clearly
in the process of dressing, as he holds his wig in one hand, and
his outfit is a resplendent suit of peach-tone velvet. His bare
head is covered in a buzz of brown bristles the exact shade as the
wig.

"Cecilia!" he says, and then he gives a little shriek and covers his eyes with an arm. "You are in your wedding gown! I'm not supposed to see you beforehand. It's bad luck."

"Yes. About the wedding—"

"Did you hear that His Majesty is coming?" Superstition already forgotten, his arm falls in favor of a wild gesticulation. "Isn't that exciting?"

"Very. Look, I must beg a favor."

He jams the wig lopsided onto his head. "Of course. What is it?"

"I need to borrow your barge. To go into the city."

"Really?" he asks, frowning. "Are you certain? I heard there is a fire."

"Yes, I know," I say, tamping down my annoyance. "Hence why I must go, to see if David—Master Mendes—is all right. I want to help him. His house is in its path."

Sam nods slowly. "Pardon, to clarify— You wish to go *into* the fire?"

"Beyond it. To Aldgate."

"Where in Aldgate?"

"I don't know."

"It is a large neighborhood," he says.

"Yes."

"It is likely quite dangerous."

"Yes."

"It is our wedding day. We'd miss the ceremony."

"Yes," I say again.

He pauses to consider. We stare at each other. On the floor above us, there comes the faint, rhythmic yip of Duchess's barking as she finds some new household object worthy of her derision.

Sam shrugs. "Well, all right," he says. "If that's what you want. Let me fetch Duchess, then we can leave."

"I don't think we should bring Duchess, Sam," I say.

"I suppose you're right. She might jump into the water. Pevensey!" he calls.

A butler in red livery appears in the foyer. "Yes, sir?"

"We are taking the barge."

"Where to, sir?"

"Aldgate."

"Ah." Pevensey presses his lips thinly together in poorly veiled consternation. "Is it your intention to miss your wedding ceremony, sir?"

"Less an intention than an unfortunate requirement, I'd say. But Cecilia is with me, so I don't think she'll mind."

Pevensey gives me a hard stare. "Indeed. But—I don't think we will find a bargeman willing, sir, without an extortionate fee. Considering the conflagration."

"I don't care what it costs. Just be quick about it, please."

"Very well," he says dubiously, and he bows before he leaves.

"I'm so grateful," I say to Sam.

"Oh, no trouble at all," he replies cheerfully. "Honestly, I was very nervous about the wedding, so it's something of a relief. I do hope Master Mendes is well, and that His Majesty won't be too insulted. Let's pray the flames slow, so they don't reach Aldgate before we do."

A bargeman is secured impressively quickly, although he is no doubt charging the equivalent of a year's wages. I ought to feel guilty about incurring such an expense, but I am too relieved to care. Peering outside the window, I see a number of panicked servants rushing in and out of the Edens'; looking for me, I expect. They don't even consider the fact I might be hiding in my fiancé's home.

Soon enough, we are on the water. Sam's barge is small but beautiful, an impressive confection of turquoise-painted wood and plum-colored canopy. The crest of his family is emblazoned on the side in gilt. As we begin to move forward, we stare at each other—me in my wedding gown, him in his fine suit—and we both laugh.

"Forgive me," I say. "I've ruined the day, haven't I?"

"Of course not! This seems much more important than the wedding."

"You and I are the only ones who will think so."

"Yes," he replies. "Well—we are the bride and groom, after all. I think it should be up to us, in the end, what we choose to care about. You look very pretty in your gown, did I mention that?"

"Thank you," I say, touched, and I raise a hand self-consciously to the pearls dangling from my ears.

It is testament to the panic of the city that few bother to stop and watch us as we pass by; the banks of the Thames are thick with boats and people, swarming like flies over carrion, desperate to escape the approaching flames. Their voices buzz and swell, punctuated with the occasional shriek or groan. Above us, the seagulls circle with purposeful vigilance, as if they intend to scavenge from the flames.

As we continue, the crowding only gets worse. The river teems with other boats, slowing our passage considerably. In the distance, the glow in the sky grows ever brighter.

"Gosh, it *is* busy, isn't it?" Sam says, looking out over the other barges. "Much of the court is here. I suppose they want to see the fire. Oh look, there's the king!"

"*What?*"

Sam points to an enormous barge in the distance, canopied in red velvet, populated by an impressive crowd of people. Sam waves to them. A tall, dark-haired figure spots him, and waves back.

"Shall we go greet him?" he asks me. "Apologize for not show-ing up to the ceremony? It's likely he's already forgotten about it, to be frank. He often responds to invitations and then neglects to go. Perhaps it is his French blood."

"We can't, Sam," I say. "There isn't time. We must continue to Aldgate."

"Very well," he replies, unbothered, and pats my shoulder.

We continue down the river, past the Strand, past Temple Bar, where I am relieved to see the coffeehouse remains un-touched. But then we see the fire itself, and all relief disappears. It is a storm, a fury, a rapture: the flames whip upward like fin-gers clawing at the sky, made dark with soot, and that darkness then made ragged with light. Every so often, a collapsing build-ing echoes like thunder, and the fire rises in response, snarling and vengeful. Even from the distance of the water it feels as if the heat of it touches me. It is radiant, ravenous. It is the mouth of God, crushing London between its teeth.

Sam says, "Oh." When I look at him, he is crying.

My own eyes prickle, and I swallow wetly. Once I resented this city, but seeing its ruin fills me with a hollow sort of dread. It meant so much to so many. Now, it is ashes.

We continue the journey in silence. Eventually, the gray-and-white stone of the Tower comes into view. We spend a good while trying to find a spot to dock; when we do manage it, we are crowded by other boats on every side, each filled with people trying to leave, clutching bags to their chests and cramming shoulder-to-shoulder on the seats. One barge almost tips side-ways, overweighed with people, and there is a great cacophony of shrieking.

Sam and I clamber onto the dock. On my suggestion, he in-structs the bargeman to take the boat to the center of the river, as there are a number of people here who might attempt to requisition it for themselves. Meanwhile, we make our way into the streets.

"Do you know how to get to Aldgate?" I ask Sam.

"Yes, it's only minutes from here. But I couldn't say where Master Mendes might be."

"We'll find him eventually, even amid this chaos." I take his arm. "Let's go."

Chaos is too mild a word for London this evening. It is utter anarchy. Although the flames haven't yet reached this area, many have still taken it upon themselves to loot storefronts and smash windows; the cobbles seethe with people and carts, boot soles and wagon wheels crunching against shattered glass. Sam and I navigate as best we can, but several times we are forced into a different direction by the crowd, like grains of sand in a tide. By the time we reach some of the quieter residential streets, I feel battered and bruised.

Sam looks as shocked as I am. His wig has almost fallen off. He adjusts it, pulls fretfully at his cravat, and says, "Where do we begin?"

"I don't know."

"We must go back and forth, I suppose, and hope we see something. But if he is inside a building—"

"Cecilia!" someone shouts.

I turn around. It is Johannes van Essen, loping down the street toward us on a pair of crutches, waving frantically. I wave back, overjoyed.

"What are you doing here?" Jan demands, once he reaches us. "You are in terrible danger!"

"I came to find David."

His face softens. "Of course you did."

"Are you all right? Do you know where he is?"

"My ankle was wounded in a crush, but otherwise I am fine.

And yes, I know where he is. I have been helping him pack. I left briefly to make another attempt at finding a cart, but . . ."

"Sam has a barge."

"Who?" he asks, mystified. Then he notices Sam behind me. "Oh."

Smiling, Sam gives him a small bow. "Hello. You must be a friend of Master Mendes. I am Sir Samuel Grey, of the Kent Greys."

"Johannes van Essen."

Sam extends his hand for him to shake. "A pleasure to meet you, Master van Essen. A Dutchman, I presume? You know, my father led a contingent at Dole—" Jan takes his hand and kisses it. "Goodness."

Jan grins at him with such charisma that even I feel a little flustered. "I am enchanted, Sir Grey," he says. "Please, call me Johannes. Or Jan, if you are willing."

"Goodness," Sam says again.

"If I may ask—why is it, Cecilia, that you are wearing a garland? And such an extraordinary gown . . ."

"We were going to get married today," Sam says brightly. "But we came here instead."

Jan drops Sam's hand, eyes widening. "Right. Well, then, I suppose . . . if you have a barge, I must take you to David—both of you." His mouth sets grimly. "This way."

We follow him through the streets until we arrive at a narrow road crowded with latticed, white-plaster houses. One house has its door open; a dark-haired woman with an apron and a dour expression is dragging bags out onto the road.

Jan goes to help her. As we approach, David emerges from the same door.

He looks tired and anxious, sleeves rolled to his elbows, dark hair loose around his ears. His beard is less neatly trimmed than usual, but it is still short enough I can see the arrowhead-angle of his jaw—was his neck always so broad? Were his arms always so tightly corded, his hands so large? Perhaps his brief absence since that night at the Myddletons' has changed him somehow; or perhaps it is me who has changed, that sees more of him and wants more of him with each moment in his presence. It is impossible to tell.

David says something to Jan in Dutch, then he notices me. His face goes slack with astonishment.

"Cecilia," he says.

I hadn't realized, until this moment, how terrified I have been for him; how much I had believed that we would never meet again. I lurch forward and fling myself at him.

David catches me, stumbling with my weight, steadying himself with one hand on the doorframe. I tighten my arms around him, burying my face into the crook of his neck. "I thought I'd never see you again," I say. "And the fire—the fire—I thought the fire . . ."

"Cecilia," David says again, and he returns the embrace. "How . . ."

I press a kiss to his jaw, and then another against his cheek. He makes a wounded noise, but he doesn't release me.

Behind us, Jan coughs. "Forgive me for interrupting," he says. "But, David, surely you want to bring more than this?"

"I doubt we can carry more," he replies.

"There is plenty of room on the barge," Sam says.

David stiffens and drops his arms. Reluctantly, I step away from him.

"Sir Grey," David says. "Forgive me, I did not notice you."

"Oh, that's quite all right. I am glad you are well, Mendes. Cecilia was so worried!"

David blinks at him, flummoxed. "You—I—yes. The barge?"

"Yes, that's how we got here. It is waiting in the river. I am certain we can take you, and Master van Essen, and . . . pardon, mistress, what was your name?"

"Elizabeth Askwith," the maid says gruffly.

"And Mistress Askwith. It might be a little crowded, but I'm certain we shall manage."

"But . . . Where will you take us?"

"Well, home, I suppose," Sam says. "Where else? There is more than enough room. Unless you think the fire will reach Saint James's?"

David sags with the weight of his relief, leaning heavily against the doorframe. "It shouldn't, considering it spreads in this direction. Sir Grey, I can't thank you enough."

"Oh, it is nothing, really. It was Cecilia's idea to come. And I enjoy entertaining."

Jan laughs. "Sir Grey, you are a treasure. I shall go collect more things to take with us."

Sam glances between David and me. "Good idea. I will help you."

David maneuvers us out of the doorway. Sam goes inside, and Jan follows, the maid trailing behind them both with a long-suffering expression.

Once we are alone, I look at David imploringly. "Forgive me," I say. "I came here without asking. I know I may be unwanted."

"You aren't unwanted, Cecilia."

"Even after what happened at the Myddletons'?"

"I wanted you then, too," he says. "That was the issue. But—the wedding—

"We aren't married. We came here instead."

"But . . . Why?"

"Because I am in love with you," I tell him. I know that if I don't say it now, I might never do so. "I love you so desperately, and I know you want me to let go of you, but I can't. I just can't."

He says, "Cecilia, this is impossible. We are impossible."

"I don't care about that. The entire city is burning around us, David. If there was ever a night for impossible things, this would be it."

"And what about tomorrow?" he asks. "When morning comes?"

"I don't know. But we needn't think about it today." I lay a hand on his chest. "Please. I am to be married—if not today, then someday soon. After this, I may never see you again. The city could be ashes; neither of us may ever return. I accept that. Just—let me forget it, just for a little while. For one day, let me forget."

He sighs in surrender and pulls me back to him, pressing his lips to mine. I wind my arms around his neck. It is less desperate than it was the last time, despite everything: slow and sweet and searching. It feels like an apology. It feels like a promise.

When he pulls back, he says, "I am so grateful you are here, and that you are safe. Thank you."

Jan appears in the hallway behind him. "David, if we are to take all the bags . . ."

David flushes. "Yes. Pardon."

He squeezes my hand before disappearing into the house. I wait with the bags on the road, feeling a paradoxical mixture of delight and anxiety.

Everyone soon emerges. We begin the journey back to the river, all of us laden with bags. David knows a route that doesn't require taking the main road; that is a mercy, as I can't imagine how difficult it would be for us to navigate the crowd. Once we reach the water's edge—it is just as busy as it was when we arrived—Sam begins hopping up and down, waving his arms about to gain the attention of the barge floating idly at the center of the river. Thankfully, he is arresting enough in his peach coat, and soon the boat makes its way toward us.

Jan is impressed by the barge. "That is yours?" he asks Sam.

"Yes. I had another, but I crashed it into a wharf."

"You can sail?"

"Oh, not at all. That is why I crashed it."

This response makes Jan wheeze as if someone has punched him in the stomach, and he murmurs something in Dutch. David gives him a chiding look.

We get onto the barge. The maid—Elizabeth—sits at the front, and says to Sam, "If it isn't too much trouble, sir, I should like to be dropped across the water."

"Are you certain, Elizabeth?" David asks. "Will you be safe?"

"My ma is in Borough, David Mendes. I want to be with her."

"Very well," he says, although he still seems uneasy.

We set off. Jan sits beside Sam and listens to him tell the long and complicated anecdote of his boat crashing. Meanwhile, David and I place ourselves at the stern.

David looks warily at Jan and Sam. "We should keep Jan away from Sir Grey, I fear."

"Why? He is smitten. I think it's sweet."

"You don't mind?" he says, surprised.

"It would be quite hypocritical of me to judge," I reply. "I've hardly acted with much propriety myself when it comes to wanting those I shouldn't."

David swallows. He reaches over and takes my hand in his own. "The wedding . . ."

"It didn't happen. The ceremony was supposed to take place late this afternoon."

He looks relieved. "Does your sister know where you are?" he asks me.

"No."

"She will panic."

"Yes, I know," I say. "I'll deal with it tomorrow."

"Tomorrow," he echoes, frowning.

"Yes. I could stay at Sam's tonight. With you."

"Cecilia . . ."

"I could send a messenger to Margaret," I say, "telling her I will come in the morning, that Sam and I have eloped. There'd be little she could do to retrieve me."

"But why?" he asks.

"Because I want to," I reply. "Isn't that reason enough?"

"No. As much as I would like it to be—it isn't."

The uncertainty in his eyes frustrates me, and my response emerges more harshly than it should. "What am I supposed to do?" I say. "You never believe me when I tell you what I want; you seem to think you know it better than I do. I find it demeaning."

"I don't mean to demean you. But you were very unwell when we first met. You are better now—I am so glad—but still, your attachment to me is grown from grief, and from desperation. You have been vulnerable, and perhaps I have taken advantage of that."

"I am not as fragile as you think. I know that I have been unwell, but you haven't somehow tricked me into wanting you."

He asks, "How can I know that? How can I be certain?"

"How can we be certain of anything?" I reply. "My own mind works against me so often, David. There is so much of myself I dislike, and so much of myself I don't trust. There are days when every thought I have feels like a lie. But this—you—has always felt real. I have never questioned it. I can't prove that to you, but I am asking you to believe it. If we had met some other way, at some other time, nothing would change. I would want you just the same."

His grip on my hand tightens, and the barge sways beneath us. The glow of the city behind us gilds him like a saint. He doesn't speak his acquiescence; he doesn't need to. In the soft, half lidding of his eyes, his surrender is as clear as any answer could be.

"Ani l'dodi," he says. I don't know what it means.

The boat stops at the other side of the river, and Elizabeth leaves. She shakes David's hand, promising to search for him once the fire ends. Then she takes her things and stomps out into the streets.

"Will she be all right?" I ask David.

"I think so," he replies. "She is tenacious."

We continue to sail west in silence. As we near the fire, even Sam ceases speaking. It is worse than before. The heart of the city is entirely devoured, and the smoke billows in great clouds, swaddling the sky in soot. David stutters a breath that seems more powerful in its grief than any weeping could be; I press my arm against his and offer what futile comfort I can.

Something falls against my bare shoulders, a light touch, like a lover's caress. I glance up to the sky and gasp softly. Ashes are falling over us, gentle as snowflakes. They dust David's hair white, coat the blue silk of my wedding dress in a silver sheen. For a long moment, I can do nothing except watch them spin in the air, entranced by the dancelike quality of their movements.

Eventually, I look back to David. He is watching me and smiling, with a gentle sort of regret.

"I shouldn't say this," he says, "but you look beautiful—as if you have risen from the flames."

Throat tightening, I twine my hand in his, and we turn back to the city. The fire burns so high that it seems it could set the sun itself alight and burn it away, make the sky brighter than any day, prevent the night from coming. Time itself has ended. There will only ever be the river and the fire, and myself and David between them, watching London burn.

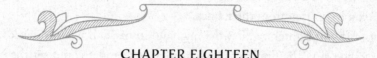

David

The first time I fell in love, I was eleven. My father was invited by a physician's guild to give a lecture in Granada. He was very glad to accept: our ancestors had been from Andalusia, and they had fled west when the Spanish Inquisition began. The Inquisition in Portugal had started a generation later. My grandfather had often joked that if we were destined for a pyre, it ought to have been in the shadow of the Alhambra, not the gutters of Lisbon. "Men like us," he'd say, "deserve to burn in the most beautiful place on earth!"

There was never a pyre for us. Our false conversion had assured that much, at least. But the unfulfilled promise of Granada lingered, the pomegranate ripped from our hands. My father saw this lecture as an opportunity to show me part of our history, and soon we were making our way south. I remember very little of the journey itself. We went by ship to Malaga, and from there north to the city, on mules and by coach and foot.

But I remember Granada. I always will: It was my first love, after all. I understand why my grandfather wanted to die there.

Our family has always been doctors, and it feels like a physician's city. The twisting streets rise and fall like breathing lungs, the canal's veins flowing between them, to the heart of the cathedral. Above these organs rises the rib cage of the Albaicín, a neighborhood that holds the last dregs of non-Christian rule. Once home of the Moors and the Jewish quarter, it still remains as it was five hundred years ago, stretching across the hills in strands of whitewashed walls and terra-cotta rooftops. From its heights, one can see the palace of the Alhambra as it colors the land gold.

My father and I could see it all from our balcony. He told me stories of princesses and conquerors, the great sultans and the Jews who advised them. This was once a land, he said, where our people and the Moors drank together, from fountains of milk and honey.

They were fairy tales, but I believed them. I thought of those fountains, and I imagined that the milk and honey remained within my veins. From the moment of my conception, the blood of Granada itself was inside me. All the princesses and conquerors and sultans paraded along my fingertips. At night, I would run beside the canal clutching my candle, watching the windows of Alhambra blink at me, another mote of light in an ocean of stars. I screamed and cried when we had to leave.

I used to dream of returning. Even after coming to London, I would constantly imagine making the trip, standing in the streets of the Albaicín and watching the land turn gold again. But recently even memories of Granada feel lost to me, and the thought of seeing it again is as futile as diluting the sea. All things are ephemeral: I am reminded of that as I watch the fire swallow the place I call home. Even cities don't stand forever. Perhaps one day, Granada will burn, just as London has.

Grey's townhouse is astonishing. It is a monument to bad taste, all damask and gilt furniture. It has more character than the Edens'—one can feel the presence of the owner, at least, in the haphazard layout, the endless vases of flowers and paintings of court beauties. But still, I have never been fond of these suburban homes, in which so many of my clients shut themselves away like kings in moated castles. Why come to London, to live in such an isolated place? The joys of the city feel so distant here. But the tragedies are distant, too, I suppose. Tonight, that is a blessing.

We are safe, finally. I feel so indebted to Grey that I can't stop expressing my gratitude, to the point where he eventually claps me on the shoulder and says, "Mendes, I am honored, truly, but you needn't thank me further." Still, it feels as if I should. He has a room set up for Jan on the ground floor, so he needn't ascend the steps on his crutches, and he takes Cecilia's request for a room of her own without a moment's confusion nor suspicion. He provides us all with an enormous meal and tells us to stay as long as we need. I have rarely seen such generosity of spirit.

The sun sets, but the fire continues to rage. After supper, Jan, infatuated, manages to draw Grey into a game of whist. I beg leave to sleep, as does Cecilia. We all part ways in the corridor. Then I light a candle and pace around the guest room Grey has offered me, nervous, confused, wondering if I ought to be doing something else, making some decision I haven't yet made. Should I find her—Lord, no, I shouldn't—but I can still feel her hand in mine, still hear the way she said, *I would want you just the same.*

I must mourn the David I once was, who valued caution and temperance above all else, and who—like the David of old, watching Bathsheba from the rooftop—has now been committed to his grave. But I no longer have the strength to refuse. It has been an ugly day, full of horrors, and if she comes, I cannot deny her. Not tonight.

Eventually, the door opens. Cecilia hovers at the threshold, hesitant, peering from the side of the doorframe. It reminds me of the day we met, when she watched me from behind the linden tree. Our gazes meet.

"Should I leave?" she asks me.

"No," I reply.

Neither of us move. We only stand there, actionless, staring at each other. The awkwardness of it makes us both laugh.

"Pardon," she says. She enters, closing the door behind her, and she comes to stand in front of me.

"Cecilia," I say, "I—I don't know if . . ."

"You needn't know anything, David, except that you want me." She takes a step closer. "As I want you. Do you?"

"Yes," I reply. I put my hands around her waist and draw her close. Her hands fall to my shoulders.

She leans in and brushes her lips across my neck. I shudder. "Since that night at the park, I have thought of this so often," she says against my skin. "It is shameful how often I've imagined it."

"There is no shame in that."

"It is a sickness," she replies. "You are an affliction, David Mendes. I can't be cured of you."

I say, "You are in need of a physician."

"I found one, but he only seems to have made the matter worse."

I kiss her. She sighs and kisses me back, undoing the buttons of my shirt with stumbling hands. Her cold fingers trail over my collarbone, nails just sharp enough to scratch.

"Are you certain?" I ask her. "We needn't . . ."

"Yes," she replies. "Are you?"

"Yes."

She gives me a smile that slips beneath my skin like a needle. This is likely the only night we will ever have together. I wish it could be something more than this, an indulgence before an inevitable farewell. I wish I could tell her how much I want her, that I could show it to her without the agony of trying to put it into words. I would remove my heart from my chest and give it to her, if she could somehow find proof through its dissection. I would hand her the scalpel myself.

I can't make it more than it is, but I can do all I can to make it worth what will come after. I chase her lips as I pull away clothing and hairpins, whispering endearments to her, moving with such slowness she is reduced to begging by the time we are undressed. Then we are skin upon skin and lips against lips, and we fall to the bed entirely entangled.

She lies beneath me, flushed and willing. "What do you want?" I ask her.

"Touch me," she says. "Please."

She watches my face until I do so, my hand pressing between her thighs, and then her eyes flutter closed. She sighs in pleasure.

All thought is gone, all fear, all hesitation. I am lost to her. I was from the moment we met. She is a promise I hadn't known I'd made myself, now fulfilled; an answer to a question I hadn't known I'd asked; Cecilia, as she is and always has been, whispering my name as she bucks against my fingers. She has discovered me, as I have her, in this unfamiliar bed, in the darkness and the silence of a room we will never return to.

I take my time, and with each passing moment she grows louder, gasping and desperate. I kiss her quiet, letting her breath fill my lungs. Then she is moving my hand away and pulling me closer, aligning our hips. I watch her face as I push into her.

"David," she sighs.

I cup her cheek in my hands and whisper her name as we move together. I trace her jaw and nose and hairline with my lips. I learn her, like I have learned the chambers of the heart, or the slicing of chicory root, reading her skin like letters on a page, swallowing her sighs like measures of medicine. She becomes a part of the herbal, a recipe to be memorized. She is both a sickness and a cure. She is part of me now.

We sleep intermittently, each waking the other with wandering hands and soft words. At one point, I open my eyes to a dark room, and I feel her lips against the back of my neck. I shift, and she sighs, burying her nose into my shoulder. She whispers something unintelligible. Perhaps she is dreaming.

When I turn to look at her, Cecilia's eyes are closed, breaths slow. The clock on the mantel ticks softly; it is still very early. But she is so beautiful, and the morning so terrifying to consider, that the thought of returning to sleep feels agonizing. Slowly, so I don't wake her, I slip out of bed and pull on my clothes. Then I leave the room.

I intend to go to the kitchens for a glass of water, but I don't know the layout of Grey's home. I soon find myself lost. Monotone in the darkness, the place is overdecorated and cavernous, some sinister quality of sentience in the furniture's ill-defined bulk. Wandering aimlessly, I turn a corner and bump into someone. Alarmed, I rear back to find that my assailant is Grey himself, half dressed in a silk dressing gown and slippers. He yelps like a cat that has been trod upon.

"Oh, Mendes!" he says once he has recovered. I shush him reflexively, and he repeats, "Oh, Mendes," much more quietly. "Good evening. Or should I say night! You couldn't sleep? I hope the room is to your liking?"

"It is excellent, thank you. I only wanted a glass of water."

"Ah! This way."

I follow him down the corridor. He is not wearing his wig, and it feels illicit, somehow, as if he is naked.

"I couldn't sleep, either," he says to me as we walk.

"Why is that?"

"It is a common affliction of mine. My thoughts sometimes grow very loud and numerous, and I can't stand the noise. I toss and turn and then must resort to activity, or else go mad."

"Have you seen a physician?"

"Oh, dozens," he says. "I am accursed with restlessness. Not much to be done. But it could be worse, I suppose—better too many thoughts than none at all."

We enter the kitchen. Grey has running water—an extraordinary luxury—and we both drink in an awkward silence. "Look," he says, suddenly. "I have a mind to show you something. Unless you are desperate to return to bed?" I shake my head, and he grins at me, teeth flashing white in the darkness. "Excellent. This way."

He takes me up several sets of stairs and into a large room, which seems to be mostly used as a storage area. It is filled with vases and statues hidden beneath tarpaulins, as well as several mountains of dusty books. One wall has three windows, giving a beautiful view of the river and the night sky. It faces south, so we can't see the fire; the city looks misleadingly peaceful.

Grey claps his hands together. The sound echoes through the room. "I wished to hear your opinion on something."

He strolls over to one of the cloth-colored shapes and pulls the tarpaulin away. Beneath it, there is a curious object: metallic, tube-shaped, balanced on a large tripod. It gleams invitingly in the light.

"Do you know what this is?" he asks me.

"A telescope," I reply. I have seen them in illustrations, although I have never had the privilege to use one myself.

"Yes, exactly! Have you operated one before?"

"I admit, I have not."

"Ah," Grey says, disappointed. "No matter, then."

I make an amused noise. "Were you hoping I could instruct you?"

"Well, you are the educated sort, Mendes."

"Thank you, sir."

"My father left this to me," he says morosely. "He loved astronomy. But I can't understand how to use it. I believed one merely had to look through the eyepiece, but all I see is darkness."

I walk over and attempt it. He is correct: The view is nothing but black, despite the other end of the telescope being pointed to the sky. "Hm," I mutter, and I inspect the object more closely. I had some experience with microscopes at the academy in Lisbon, and it seems this might function similarly. I adjust one of the rings on the tube and peer again. The moon suddenly appears in the lens, blown to enormous proportion.

It is so bright that I almost flinch. Then my vision focuses, and I wonder at the detail. It had always seemed so perfect from a distance, but enlarged, the moon is flawed and cracked, like impasto on a painting.

I step away. "Try it now," I say to him.

Grey leans forward to look through the telescope. He makes a choked noise, and says, "Oh goodness," before going entirely quiet.

For a few minutes, I stand in silence as he stargazes. Then I hear him sniffling.

"Are you crying?" I ask.

He moves back from the telescope. "Pardon," he says, rubbing his face with his sleeve. "It's very beautiful. I am grateful to you for showing it to me."

"It was no trouble." I look at his face; his cheeks are flushed, and his eyes are sparkling with unshed tears. "May I ask you something, Sir Grey?"

"Of course."

"Do you love her? Cecilia, I mean."

Grey says, "I am very fond of her—she has become a dear friend."

"But you do not love her."

He sighs. "The marriage . . . Until Lady Eden has a child, I am also my uncle's heir, you see. And if *I* don't have an heir, all of it—the Eden and Grey estates both—go to my sister, who has married into another family. It leaves the line extinct, which is something I don't care much about, but Robert cares about it a good deal. Dynasty, and all that."

I consider this and feel a revelation dawning, unwelcome but insistent. "You still need to marry her," I say slowly. "Just as much as she needs to marry you."

Grey stares at me, and I stare back at him. His wide eyes have an extraordinary naïveté about them; they lend his face an unsettling earnestness. Although we are likely near the same age, he seems very young.

"You love her," he says. "And I don't."

I don't respond.

He continues, "It just—it all feels so terribly unfair."

Again, I remain in silence. Does he expect me to agree with him? Of course it is unfair. Only someone desperately accustomed to privilege would be surprised at that. For a moment, I imagine myself as Grey—I imagine what it would be like to be born as he was—to whisk Cecilia away from this place and shower her in comforts, to spend each night with her as this one was spent, to live without fear or shame. But the fantasy is futile at best, and self-destructive at worst. It is like picking at a scab or scratching a new scar. It is so tempting to imagine loving her, and having no questions to ask, nor to be answered, except whether she feels the same. But the return to reality is more painful than I can bear.

I don't want to feel anger toward Samuel Grey. He is a good man, and in marrying her, he would be doing a good thing. My thoughts on the matter should end there; if only they did.

"We could elope," Grey says. "Then Cecilia could leave immediately. There would be no need for the ceremony. And she would be my wife only in name; that was always my intention. It would be nothing more than the signing of a contract."

"Why would you enter such a marriage?" I ask him. "Refuse the chance to take a wife you love?"

He clears his throat. "I've never had much desire for a wife, regardless," he says with a familiar sort of shame in his eyes, and my heart clenches in sympathy. He turns back to the telescope, fiddling with the stand. "In truth, Master Mendes, I often feel rather useless. Each morning, I wake up and look at the ceiling, thinking to myself: Well, Samuel, what have you accomplished thus far? And the answer has always been—nothing." He sweeps his arm, gesturing to the room. "Such is the sum of my existence. Vases and telescopes and marble busts. In that sense, nothing I have ever done has been truly selfless. Coming to London, befriending Cecilia, even going to Aldgate today—it has all been an attempt to feel as if I am a man of value, a man who can be of worth to other people. I am so grateful to you, and to her, for entering my life. Helping you will be the only good thing I have ever done."

"Sir Grey," I tell him. "Samuel. You are more than a man of value. I believe you are one of the most exceptional men I have ever met."

He sniffs. Clearly he is near tears again. "Don't say such a thing. Not before I warn you of the rest."

"The rest?"

"I am required to return to Kent for the winter, to manage the estate. Considering what has happened in the city, I will likely leave very soon."

"You would take Cecilia with you."

"If she is willing," he says.

"It would be good for her, I think. To get away from her sister."

He replies, "I think so, too. But listen, there are ways—you might visit, perhaps."

I shake my head. "I appreciate the offer," I say. "But if you truly want what is best for Cecilia, you will encourage her not to see me again."

Grey looks aghast. "Why is that?"

"She will be happier without me," I say.

"I sincerely doubt that."

"You don't understand," I reply, voice sharp. "It isn't as simple as you believe. We are too different."

Grey says, "I know that you are different. But that doesn't change what I have seen."

"What have you seen?"

"The two of you together," he replies. "Perhaps I am naïve. I know that I am. I know people can be cruel; I know I often underestimate that cruelty. But it is the least we can do, I believe, to allow ourselves a little kindness."

A lump forms in my throat. I can no longer look at him. I turn away.

He approaches and lays a hand on my shoulder. "Summer in London," he says. "I always summer in London. If she agrees, we will return next year. It is time enough, Master Mendes, for you to change your mind."

"Perhaps."

"Time enough," he repeats. "I know it is. All will be well again."

And—for a moment—I almost believe him.

I am not in the mood for stargazing now. I bid Grey farewell, and I return to the bedroom.

As I walk the townhouse's crowded hallways, his words echo in my mind. He is correct: There is time enough, certainly, for things to change. Eight months—nine? More time than I have known Cecilia at all.

Cecilia is still sleeping. It is almost dawn. The light streams through the window and pools around her. It illuminates her skin, the halo of her hair. I sit on the mattress and watch her.

She is ivory and gold. She is Granada; she is the mezuzah on the doorframe. And someday, perhaps, things will change: The fire will end, a new summer will come, the linden will bloom again.

But, until then, I cannot touch her. I cannot return to her.

I have to let her go.

CHAPTER NINETEEN

Cecilia

I awaken to an empty bed and a knock on the door. I have only a moment to look at the space beside me, shocked and woeful, before the knock repeats. I am forced to answer.

It is Sam. He enters and sits beside me, taking my hands in his. He speaks. He explains. He suggests we elope this very morning.

I have no answer for him. I tell him I must think upon it, and I ask him to bring me somewhere else. I cannot stay in this room, surrounded by my memories of the evening, haunted by the emptiness of the bed. He takes me to a music room instead, where he leaves me alone with his harpsichord. It is an extravagant thing, wood and black enamel with gold inlay. The underside of its raised lid has been painted with a dawn sky. Despite the fact that no one in the house plays, it has been kept tuned.

I play "Go, Lovely Rose." When I am finished, I look up to see that David is watching me from the doorway.

Relief slices through me like a sword. "You weren't there this morning," I say, accusatory, at the same time he says, "Forgive me."

Irked, I play a discordant chord, and he winces. "It was cruel of you," I say, "to leave me to wake up alone. I thought you had left."

"I know. I am sorry, Cecilia. I—I was—"

"You were being a coward," I say.

"Yes."

He enters the room, standing beside me, staring down at the harpsichord keys. He taps a high note.

I echo the note back to him. "Sam thinks we should elope."

"I know. Will you?"

"I don't love him."

"What does that matter?"

"I love you, David," I say.

He gives me a pleading, anguished look, and repeats, "What does that matter?"

I flinch. "It matters to me."

"You should go with him. Go to Kent. Get away from this place."

"Get away from you, you mean."

"That, too, yes."

I make an awful, pitiful sound, precluding a sob, and I am so ashamed of it I slam my palm down on the keys in frustration. The harpsichord hollers as if it is in pain.

"Did last night mean nothing to you?" I ask.

"It meant everything, but—"

"Everything, and yet not enough, clearly."

"Cecilia, please," David says. "What choice do you have? What choice do we have? At least, in this way, you will be free. We won't have to fear our discovery."

I scowl at him, blinking back tears. I breathe in shakily to prevent myself from sobbing again. "It is cruel to be so cruel," I say, "and frame it like that, so I am not permitted my anger."

"I am sorry."

"Don't apologize," I say. "Leave me to my grief, if you believe it so necessary. Be harsh so I will resent you, and so resent your leaving less."

"You want me to hurt you?"

"Yes. I want to despise you. Make it so."

"I don't know how," David replies.

I say, "That is because you are awful."

"I know."

"You are an awful person, David Mendes. I am glad I am leaving. I wish I'd never met you."

"I know," he repeats.

I pull him in for a kiss. He kisses me back, desperate, pressing me into the harpsichord. The movement sends notes scattering through the air like ashes in wind. Yet another loss to bear— another memory to make, to carry like a lodestone with me— and you would think I would have learned by now how to suffer such things without weeping. But it is a lost cause. Tears well and fall. David soon tastes like salt, and he pulls away to swipe his thumb across my cheek.

"Things will be better soon," he says. "You will be happier."

"You could come to see me in Kent."

"I cannot."

"But why?"

"You need me to tell you again? All the reasons we cannot be together? I would have thought you would be sick of it, by now."

I smile bitterly and say, "I am finished with others telling me what my life ought to be like, and what I ought to want."

"I know. I am sorry."

"I will come back to London," I tell him. "I will be here. And you will be here, also."

"It is a large city."

"I don't care. When summer returns, so shall I. And I will find you again."

He shakes his head. "You will forget me," he says. "I know you think otherwise, but once you are gone . . ."

"I swear I won't forget you, David," I reply.

"You can't promise that."

"I can, and I do. Will you forget me?"

"Of course not."

"You must swear you won't," I say. "As I have sworn to you. Unless you promise to remember me, I will not leave."

He makes a wounded sound. "Don't say that. How can I promise now, knowing that refusing will keep you with me?"

I seize his wrist. "If that is how you feel, then choose otherwise. Tell me to stay instead."

For an agonizing moment, he stares at me, and I at him, and neither of us says anything at all. Awfully—selfishly—I wish I could transport myself to the past, when he was coming to the townhouse to treat me, and I could be certain of his presence. When he was mine because he had to be. When neither of us had the choice to make.

"If I asked you to stay, I would cage you again," David says. "Lock you away in your sister's home. I cannot. You are meant for greater things than that. Go with Sam and be happy with him. Live, Cecilia."

"I will," I reply. "I will be happy. I will live, and soon, we will meet again. I know that we will. We are meant for each other, David Mendes. I am my beloved's, and my beloved is mine."

He exhales shakily, eyes widening in surprise. I press my lips to his once more, quickly, harshly. It is not a good kiss, as much a reprimand as it is affection. After, my head drops to rest in the crook of his neck, and his arms close around me. One of his hands rests upon my back, and the other cups the base of my skull. His skin is very warm.

I pull back to look at him. "Say you love me, David. Give me that, at least. Lie, if it is necessary."

"I cannot lie to you," he replies.

"Then—"

"*Te amo*," he says. "*Ani ohev otah*. I love you. That is why I must ask you to leave. Promise me you will, querida. Swear you will."

I swallow my tears, collect myself, look at him directly. I see myself in his eyes; a hint of reflection—something gold, something pale—in the pools of black.

"I swear," I say. "And I swear, also, that I will return."

I step away, scrubbing at my face with my sleeve. David drops his arms.

"Farewell, Cecilia," he murmurs, whispering it like one of his prayers.

"Farewell," I reply.

I turn back to the harpsichord. I cannot stand to watch him leave. Waiting until I hear the door moving, I allow myself a sob. I play a note, and then another; suddenly I am so furious, so enraptured by my own grief, that my hands are moving by instinct. I am angry at David for leaving, at myself for letting him leave, at the world for forcing us to part. I slam my fingers across the keys, hardly knowing what I intend to produce. Then I hear a familiar roll of notes, and I realize this is the toccata I have been attempting for months now, which I have never been able to finish, never been able to perfect.

This piece is monstrously difficult, but that was never why I had trouble with it. I could play it, technically, but it lacked the flourish all toccatas require to soar. It is too dark a song for joy, and yet too fast for sorrow. Now I understand that what it needed was anger. It requires its player to wield it like a weapon. I sound each note as if it is battlefield surgery, as if I have blood on my hands. It is labored and painful and violent.

It is flawless. It is the greatest performance I have ever given or will ever give. And when I look up, David is gone; my only audience is the silence he has left me.

There are three Cecilias now, whom I have been and have become.

The first: Cecilia Lockwood, whose fifteen-minute delay left Margaret with the dowry and herself with an abundance of precociousness. Youngest sister, youngest daughter. The sort with the cheek not only to covet another's fiancé, but to marry him, also; who went to church in feathered hats and pastel gowns simply out of a desire to be interesting; who laughed while she danced at her wedding and ate so much cake she was sick with it.

Then came Cecilia Thorowgood, whose swallow heart swooped from joy to grief and back again. She knew the greatest happiness of all my lives, and the greatest sorrows, also. For all her fragility, she survived plague and fire and heartbreak. But she could not survive herself, and the decisions she made. There is some irony in that.

Because now I am Cecilia Grey: elevated higher than any of her predecessors, and laid lower, also. The afternoon after the fire, David leaves with Jan in a borrowed carriage, braving the ashen streets rather than remain with me. An hour later, I marry a friend for no reason other than convenience, signing my name on a contract witnessed by a single well-paid priest and my new husband's butler. Afterward, we have a feast of partridge and wine. I eat only three bites, stomach squirming with grief and guilt.

"Sam, this is too much," I tell him, staring down at my plate.

"Oh?" He looks over the groaning table. "Yes, I suppose you're right. You needn't finish it all."

"I didn't mean the food. I meant—what you've done for me."

"Nonsense, Cecilia," he says. "The house in Kent is such a lonely place usually. I did not want to spend Christmas alone, and I am so glad to have company. I already told you, I never wanted to be married; I'd much rather have a friend than a wife. And now you are both, and yet not both—it is odd, I know, but I am glad of it."

"Very well," I say uncertainly. His smile looks genuine enough, but the guilt is suffocating, still. I spend the rest of the meal fiddling with my cutlery, unable to eat.

Once we are finished, I retire to the harpsichord room. The house is abuzz with activity as the servants pack things up for the move to the estate. Instead of playing, I sit on one of the audience chairs, my head in my hands, listening to the chatter and rumble of their work.

I do not know how long I am there for. I am silent and not weeping; it seems the well of tears has finally run dry. But the sun does eventually set entirely, and I am soon concealed by darkness.

A beam of light emerges from an open door. Someone enters the room, a little uncertain in their open-backed mules, pink-ribboned stockings bunched at the heels.

Sam sits next to me and lays a hand on my back.

"Let me tell you something," he says.

I never imagined he would ask for permission to say anything. I give him a sideways glance. "What is it?"

"Well," he replies. "I think I ought to tell you everything."

Then Sam squares his shoulders, stares directly at the harpsichord, and tells me everything. He tells me about a boy from a noble family in Kent, whose fevered mother refused to pass him to the midwife for inspection once he was born—knowing, perhaps, that she would not live long enough to see the sunset that night. So Sam was raised by his father, who was distant and often absent, and by governesses: a great crowd of them who came and left as quickly as mayflies.

"The only time Father ever wished to see me," Sam says, "was when he had made a discovery. He considered himself a natural philosopher, you see. He was always showing me illustrations from books and new inventions. He spoke Arabic and Hebrew and dozens of other languages." He paused. "It was a disappointment to him, I think, that I didn't inherit his mind. He tried to teach me mathematics once and got so frustrated at my failure he almost cried."

"Like my mother," I reply. "When she wanted me to sing."

Then, in stuttered and hesitant terms—prompted gently by the occasional question—I describe my own upbringing: my sister and my mother, our women's house, how centered our lives were around Maggie's marriage, Maggie's beauty, Maggie's income. And when Sam replies to speak of his father's death, and his first days at court—the terror he felt, the sense of unworthiness—I talk about Will. I tell Sam how I loved William Thorowgood from afar, about my joy when we were finally married. I tell him about the wedding and the dancing and the awful portrait. About our brief and wonderful life in the Thorowgood manor, which was not perfect, but still happy.

I tell Sam about Will himself, who had a gap-toothed smile and a ceaseless reservoir of joy. "He was sunshine," I say. "He was laughter and comfort. He was so young. We both were." I describe how Will hummed as he walked, how in the evenings he would read plays aloud and do different voices for each character. I tell Sam how Will grew sick, how the buboes came, the shuddering, the seizing, how his sisters and I all huddled about the door and said, *Soon, it shall pass*. How Will slept and slept, and how it happened, finally, while I was sitting beside him, reading, holding his hand.

I tell Sam that I felt as if it was my fault. I knew it was not, but I felt as if it was. Sometimes I feel that way still.

It all pours out of me. I cannot prevent the words from escaping in a great torrent, while Sam listens with his chin resting on his fist, patient and fascinated. I describe how I continued to live in that house like a ghost, and how Margaret had at first seemed to offer some escape from my grief. But then Will remained with me, and the memory of him filled my belly so I could not eat, and Margaret offered no solace at all.

And then I tell him about David, about the linden and the canal, the coffeehouse, the night in Saint James's Park. How I began to love him, despite it all; how his leaving feels like an amputation. How I do not know who I am now that he has gone.

At that, finally, Sam responds.

"You are Cecilia still," he says. "David leaving doesn't change that, I think. And marrying me doesn't change it, either."

I wipe a tear from my face. "You really think so?"

"I know so," he replies. "And I know it is a privilege to be your friend. You have been very brave. I could only aspire to such courage."

"You are brave, too, Sam."

"Oh, I hope so. I haven't faced a tenth of the trials you have, so I suppose it is difficult to tell." He smiles at me, earnest and eager. "We are going to have to spend a lot of time together; I am happy about that. You are my best friend. We haven't known each other for very long, but I think you are."

"You, too," I say. "You are mine."

"Unhappiness comes, invited or no. The fire alone is proof enough of that. But I think what you've taught me, Cecilia, is that happiness needs to be searched for. We've got to take it, when it's offered. We can't wait for it to arrive."

I throw my arms around him. Into his shoulder, I mumble, "Thank you."

He returns the embrace. "That's all right."

"I am sorry I am sad. I don't mean to be ungrateful."

"You aren't ungrateful. Far from it." He pats my shoulder. "Hm. How to comfort you? Let me show you one more thing. I think you will like it."

And so we leave the music room and go through the corridor, up a set of steps—and another, and another—until we are in an attic of some sort. The room has many windows, angled toward the sky.

Sam points at a strange device that has been set up pointing toward the windows, a sort of metal tube on a tall tripod. "That's a telescope," he says proudly. "I have just learned how to use it. Come look, through this end."

Dubious, I approach, and crouch to peer through the lens. I see only blackness.

"I don't think it works," I say.

"Oh." He runs forward and starts fiddling with one of the rings around the tube. "Perhaps now?"

I look again. The moon peers back, radiant, enormous; I gasp in astonishment.

"I can see the moon," I say.

"Marvelous. How does it look?"

"Extraordinary."

"I know!" Sam exclaims. "I could hardly believe it when I first saw it. Isn't it perfect?"

"Not really," I reply. "It isn't perfect. It is covered in craters. And it isn't full, either, see? It is waning. Nearly a sphere, but not quite."

"Imperfect, then. But beautiful, all the same."

I say, "Like a barroco."

"What's that?"

"A pearl. One that's better for its imperfection."

"Like us," he says.

I smile. "Like us."

CHAPTER TWENTY

David

Our house is gone. The blaze's furthest point was two streets beyond ours.

Jan, also homeless, pools his resources together with mine to lease a small, three-room flat in Mile End. Rents are exceptionally high—of course, they must be, when half the housing in the city is gone—but the flat is owned by Sara's cousin, and his charity allows us both the rooms and the small patch of garden behind the building, which is drowning in weeds and rotting roots. I go there sometimes, considering planting something new; but the task seems so monumental, the chances of failure so high, that I keep my seeds in their packages and start making medicines using purchased ingredients. I am forced to let Elizabeth Askwith go, but when I try to give her the pay for her final month, she refuses it. "Once you have a household again, David Mendes," she tells me, "you know where to find me."

A week after we move in, Jan and I return to the city center to walk through the wreckage. We are accompanied by a roving crowd: looters, the dispossessed, and those—like us—who survey for curiosity's sake. The remains of a charred, massive building dominate this section of the city. We pause to look up at it.

I ask, "That was the shopping gallery, no?"

"Lord, yes, it was. It is hardly recognizable now." Jan shakes his head. "Do you remember the time the beadles refused you entry? Now no one can enter at all. There is some satisfaction in that, I suppose."

"It is a shame. It was a beautiful building."

"Ah, buildings can be remade." He loops an arm about my shoulders and steers me away from the remains of the gallery. His ankle has healed well, and his limp is nearly imperceptible. "But retribution," he says. "That, surely, is eternal. An eye for an eye, is that not what the Good Book says? An eye for an eye, a tooth for a tooth."

I kick a chunk of wood blocking our path, gone black and brittle in the flames. It skids away. "Suffering for sinners, without salvation for their victims. Little satisfaction in that."

"Ah, you should be crueler," he replies, and I sigh. "You are permitted some comfort in avoiding another's misfortune. It is a pillar of humanity."

"Call me a beast, then," I tell him.

He gazes across the crowd. "It is a horrid thing," he says. "All that has been lost."

"Yes, it is."

"Is it possible for us to return to the way things were?"

"I don't know," I say. "Perhaps it will be better if we do not."

To that, he has no response. We continue to walk in silence. There is enough around us to keep us distracted. There are the sounds of the crowd: gasping, praying, prurient laughter. There are children playing within the creaking shells of the gutted houses. There are gulls shrieking as they swoop toward the

Thames. Life continues, as it always will; it doesn't matter how much has been destroyed. London will always survive, despite what it has lost.

By October, the city is rebuilding. I am not. When I walk the streets, they are crowded with scaffolding, beams bursting from the ground like saplings, people scurrying across them like aphids. Bricks and mortar, wood and tile. London is stitching itself together.

Work continues. Life continues. I continue, in a half-dream haze, unchanging and unaware. The events of the previous summer feel almost imaginary. Some days it is as if Cecilia never existed; some days, there comes a knock on the door, and I open it expecting it to be her. Perhaps I am mourning her, but it doesn't feel like grief. I grieved Manuel, and I grieved my father. This feels like impatience, except hollow, pointless: waiting for something I fear will never come. From the moment I last left Samuel Grey's house, I have been telling myself I will never see her again. I must tell myself that, I must expect her promises to be false. But sometimes I remember the determination on her face when she promised to return—and I am tempted, for a moment, to believe otherwise.

In November that year, Sara marries Joseph Alvarez. The ceremonies are small, as they must be in our community. We are less than fifty families, all in all. It is well known that Sara and I were once together: At the wedding, some look upon me with pity, presuming I must be jealous. I am not. But after the contract is signed, the prayers are made, and we return to Sara's home for celebration, I find myself momentarily despising her and her new husband. I cannot look at them; they seem to blind me. Sara is radiant in a gown of turquoise silk, beads of gold wrapped in her hair. Joseph is just as handsome, near a decade younger than his new wife, with a sprawl of brown-red hair and a beard that curls wildly around his chin. He looks at Sara as if she is summer itself, come to keep the cold outside at bay. I watch them watch each other, and something inside me aches.

Leaving the room, I go outside to sit on the front steps of the house. It is almost dark. Inside, the candles are lit; squares of orange cast by the windows glow and sputter on the cobbles in front of me. There is something strangely violent about the movement of the light. It almost seems as if the building behind me is on fire.

Sara emerges from the front door and sits down beside me.

"You will ruin your dress," I tell her.

She shrugs and pats her skirts. "It can be cleaned."

I look back to the street. In the house opposite hers, a hazy figure passes across the upstairs window.

"You are upset," she says. "What's wrong? Joseph thinks you are jealous of him, but we both know that isn't true."

"I am glad you are happy," I say.

"Of course."

"I only . . . I wish I was happy, also." I groan, scrubbing my face with my hand. "Pardon. I have had too much wine, I think."

Sara watches me in silence, frowning. Then she says, "You were like this, also, when Manuel died."

"Yes."

"You miss—this person. The one you told me you loved."

"Yes."

"Are they dead?" she asks.

"No. She isn't dead."

"Will she come back?"

"She . . ." I sigh. "I don't know."

Sara squeezes my shoulder and stands, offering me her hand. "Come," she says. "This is not a night for sorrow. Drink more wine, if need be, and speak to my husband. Put his fears at ease. You could be good friends, I think."

I take her hand and stand. "Thank you, Sara."

She kisses my cheek. For a moment, I am transported: She smells like silk and fire and something I lost long ago, which recalls Lisbon and synagogue and Manuel's smiles across the seder table. The smell of home, of community. It lingers briefly, then disappears as she pulls away.

"You will find her again," she says. "If it is meant to be, you will."

Winter comes and passes. The shopping gallery is replaced with a tangle of scaffolding, which I am informed will someday be a theater. Spring begins a slow and uncertain arrival: a scattering of blue-skied days that are interrupted, as a tremor in an arthritic hand, by sudden and violent storms.

On the last day of March, I show Sara out after her appointment, offering her my arm as we reach the staircase.

"Honestly, I am not made of porcelain," she snaps at me. "I won't shatter, should I descend a set of steps unaided."

"I only thought to help."

She grumbles and shoves past me, ignoring my arm. Joseph, who is waiting for her in the hallway, gives me an apologetic look; still, he hasn't the courage to intervene. He kisses her once she reaches him, and says, "It is certain?"

Her expression softens, and she smiles at him. "As much as it can be. David, the primrose oil?"

"It will be ready in the morning."

"I will come to pick it up," Joseph says. "Our thanks, as always. If we have any trouble—"

"Talk to a midwife first," I say firmly. "I appreciate your trust in me, but she will know better than I."

They both sigh—they have more trust in a Jewish physician than a gentile midwife, perhaps understandably so—but they don't complain. After farewells, they leave.

I go downstairs as well, then out the back door, to the tiny patch of garden I have yet to tend. As I go to stare at the soil, berate myself for my lack of industry, I suddenly notice there are small hooks screwed into the crumbling brick wall behind the flower beds. The hooks are rusty with age—once they likely held trellises, but no longer. What metal remains glints in the sunlight, winking at me as I move.

I return inside and retrieve the glass beads Manuel gave me from my traveling case, where they have languished since we moved here. I string them from hook to hook, taking care to turn each bead to catch the light.

Halfway through my work, Jan comes downstairs to watch me. Once I am finished, he steps forward and crouches to put something in the soil beneath the hooks.

"What was that?" I ask him.

"A coffee bean," he says, smiling at me. "Who knows? Perhaps, someday soon, it'll actually start to grow."

By May, the trees begin to bloom. There is a linden in Saint James's Park that bursts open its blossoms like fireworks, sending them spinning in the air. Linden flowers are a sedative; they make you wistful, complacent, dreamy. That may be why my memories feel so unreal, why they linger so insistently, even after months of trying to forget. The courtyard of the Eden town-house, where I first saw Cecilia, was bathed in the stuff. It made the air sweet, my chest light. Perhaps it drove me to madness. It is a comforting thought, and one I consider often. Sometimes I can pretend briefly that my longing for her is a disease that I can treat. That I can cure it with decoctions and troches and electuaries.

One day I return home to see a letter on my desk. I almost break the seal, and then I realize I recognize the handwriting on the envelope, the jagged sweep of the vowels in my name.

I go to retrieve another letter—one I received very long ago, that I saved from the fire, that I have kept in a drawer all this time, despite myself—and I compare it to the one I have just received.

It is undeniable. The letter is from Cecilia.

I sit down in the chair, hand trembling. How does she know where I am? Jan, it must have been—I know he has been corresponding with Sir Grey, lovelorn fool that he is.

I imagine opening the letter. I imagine what it will say. *David, I still love you.* Or: *Master Mendes, I am writing to ensure our parting is permanent.* I don't know which version would be more terrifying.

She is due to return to London soon. I know that much.

I break the seal on the envelope, pull out the folded piece of paper—I can see the dark, illegible imprint of her writing on the reverse, can see the message is brief, curt, direct—and I can't do it.

I put the paper back into the envelope, and I put the envelope into my drawer.

Pacing the room, I seek desperately for distraction. I polish all my pewter plates. Then I make a set of electuaries and prepare all my patients' poultices for the next fortnight. My attempts to scrub the pots afterward are so aggressive I skin my knuckles against the metal, and I must bind them with gauze.

That night, I cannot sleep. I squirm beneath my sheets, and I stare at the ceiling, imagining Cecilia's letter in my drawer hot as a coal, burning a hole in the wood, smoke filling the room. I drift away only when the sun begins to rise, and even then, I rest only briefly. I dream of linden and the water. I dream of fire and the past.

Jan and I wander often nowadays. So many of the places we used to frequent are closed. The coffeehouse on Temple Bar burned down, as did our favorite alehouse.

We usually end up going to the river, where we buy pastries and sack from a street vendor. This evening, many have had the same thought, and a large crowd of people mills near the water. A busker is performing magic tricks with cards. Jan insists on watching for far longer than necessary.

Afterward, we stroll west, toward the scaffolding and char, where the city has begun rising from its ashes. The damage is still arresting to see, despite the rebuilding efforts; a scar on London, a black hollow carved out like excised flesh.

Jan looks up at the skeletal remains of an inn. "Despite all that happened here, there is something beautiful about it," he says.

"How so?"

"The burned buildings, next to those being rebuilt. What has been lost, what has been gained. Perhaps soon we will repair the damage in full, and ultimately be better for it."

"How can we be better for it?" I ask. "So many have suffered."

"I suppose so. But there is joy in our release from that suffering, is there not? Joy in recovery?"

We continue. Gulls swoop ahead, while barges drift listlessly across the water. We pause at the river's edge to watch the sun as it sinks.

"David," Jan says. "I think we must speak of it."

"Speak of what?"

"It has been eight months. You are as bad as you were in September."

"I don't know what you mean," I reply, although I do. Of course, I do.

"You can't run away from this. You can't move on from her if you don't acknowledge what happened."

"There's nothing to move on from."

He makes an aggravated sound and tears a few crumbs from his pastry, flinging them to the river. A crowd of birds descends immediately, eager scavengers, clawing at each other in violent hunger.

His concern stings like lye. And it is childish, I know that, but I turn from him and start walking away.

Jan gives a cry of frustration and chases after me. "For God's sake," he says. "Surely you must realize how ridiculous this is."

He sees something then, and his mouth snaps shut, eyes widening. I follow his gaze. He is watching one of the barges in the river. Like him, I recognize it immediately. It is unusually colorful, made of turquoise-painted wood, with a plum-colored canopy. There are a good number of people crowded on it, brightly dressed and obviously wealthy: gentlemen in wigs and embroidered jackets; ladies in vivid gowns and glittering jewelry, fluttering gilded fans that flash like flames in the light of the sunset. And one of those ladies is Cecilia, like a memory of a dream, tipping her head back to catch the wind.

Even at this distance, I know it is her. She is wearing a low-necked, sky-blue dress, with pink silk slashed into the sleeves.

Everything about her is exuberant, excessive: her hair, tightly curled, springs to escape from its pins; her pearl earrings spin ardently as she turns her head, so large I can see them even from the riverbank; her lips are confected cherry-red with rouge, her cheeks the same. She is almost unreal. For a fleeting moment I recognize her no more than I would a stranger—but she is not one. She is Cecilia, still.

"David . . ." Jan says, laying his hand on my arm, but I am not listening to him. Like a fish on a line, I am pulled to the water's edge, watching the barge as it makes its inexorable journey past us. Cecilia turns to Grey, who is standing beside her; he looks exactly as he did when last we spoke, cherubic and smiling. She says something excitedly to him. He nods and laughs. Neither of them takes notice of me. Why would they? I am only another member of the common crowd, staring at them in envy, imagining himself among the passengers. It is like observing a painting, or a stage play. We are in separate worlds. She is not real.

The barge continues east. The Thames tugs her away from me, smiling, unknowing. I watch her leave from the bank, and my denial leaves with her. Nothing has changed. I am with her beneath the linden, in Saint James's Park, in a bed in her husband's house. I am listening to her music and her laughter and her hushed-voice desperation, as she asks me if I love her.

"David," Jan says again. "David, she is gone. David, listen to me."

He is wrong: She isn't gone. Cecilia is still with me, and she will be always. It doesn't matter what I do. There is no wound to be healed. She is a gap, an emptiness, a limb amputated. If I do nothing, I will live my life around the space that she has left.

I look at Jan.

I say, "Forgive me."

"What? Why?"

"Because you are right," I tell him. "It's time I stopped running."

The next day, I stop at the apothecary and I buy some seeds.

Upon my return, I skirt around the edge of the house in Mile End, waving to Mistress Yorke on the top floor, the sweet, gray-haired widow who is now my neighbor. In the garden, I set to work, pulling weeds, shifting stones. Once there is enough space, I begin to plant.

Fumitory: tiny, pink flowers like pomegranate seeds; small silver leaves no bigger than a fingernail.

Oxeye daisy: ubiquitous, fried-egg blooms, bright yellow and palest white; withstands rain and snow and bitter drought.

Epithymum, or dodder: parasitic. I plant it beside the straggling ivy crawling up the wall, the remains of whoever worked in this garden last. When it blooms—if it blooms—it will spray white flowers across the ivy's vines, stretch toward the sun.

Once I am finished, I return to my rooms and rearrange Father's wooden figurines on the shelf. I have no appointments today. It is Shabbat this evening. I spend the remainder of the afternoon helping Mistress Yorke clean her rooms, and then I go out to buy flowers for the table, as Father used to.

There are foxgloves in the bouquet. I rearrange them in the vase and think of Cecilia saying, *I wouldn't regret loving you,* and I think of her hand pressed against my chest, with my heart thrumming beneath it, and my uncertainty chokes me like a noose.

I think of her letter in my drawer. *Tomorrow,* I tell myself.

As sunset nears, I take out the candles and lay them on the

table, setting only one place. I will spend this Shabbat alone, as I have all Shabbats since my father's death; Jan is out most Fridays working, haggling at port before the merchant ships sail. I ought to have gone to synagogue this afternoon, and yet I haven't attempted to do so even once since Father's passing. I don't have the courage to see the pity in everyone's eyes.

Someone knocks on the door. Confused, I go to answer.

It is Sara, and her husband, Joseph, and Jan is behind them.

I say, "Hello."

"Hello," Sara replies, and she kisses the mezuzah as she pushes past me. "Since you refuse to spend Shabbat with us—despite all our invitations—*we* will spend it with *you*, instead."

Jan and Joseph are both laden with baskets and bottles. Jan grins at me as they walk past me into the corridor. "I decided not to work tonight," he says. "I hope you don't mind me joining, also?"

"Does it matter if I mind?"

"Not at all."

Sara cannot cook, but clearly, Joseph can: He has made fish stew, fried sardines, and sesame seed pastries. Jan has brought several bottles of wine; he sits patiently through the kiddush before pouring himself a glass so tall it nearly spills to the table. I share with them the anise challah I baked the previous day, and the date rolls Elizabeth Askwith dropped off that morning when she came to visit. My irritation at their unexpected arrival quickly diffuses into gratefulness as they laugh and chatter and argue around me. Sara heaps spoonfuls of grain onto my plate. Jan lays a hand on my shoulder as he passes me the bread, and Joseph gestures so widely while he tells a sailing story that he has to sheepishly collect the pastries from the floor.

Once we are finished laughing at this, we fall into a satisfied silence, cheeks flushed from wine.

Then Jan says, "David—I went to the coffeehouse at Temple Bar today."

"Didn't it burn down?" I ask.

"Well—yes. But the land is for sale."

"As is the land in half of London," Joseph says. "How much are they asking?"

Jan sighs. "Too much," he murmurs, and he pours himself another glass of wine. But the slight smirk he gives me, brows raising, makes my eyes narrow in suspicion.

At the end of the night, Sara hugs me and kisses my cheek, as does Joseph. "Keep well, David," she says.

"Thank you for coming."

"Any time." She takes her shawl from the stand, and then pauses. "You are a dear friend to me," she says softly. "You always will be. You know that, don't you?"

I smile at her. "I do."

They leave. Jan is quite drunk. We share a bedchamber, but tonight, his sonorous snores are too much to handle. I retreat out into the living room, lying on the couch. My rest is fitful, the couch being unfit for the purpose, and the ticks of the clock too loud for comfort. When I wake up, however, I find myself oddly soothed by my surroundings. The rising sun breaks through the window. It hits the brass candlestick on the mantelpiece in a glitter of pink and orange. On the shelf, the wooden figurines glow as if they are embers, made warm and living by the morning light.

I listen. I can still hear Jan snoring. When I go into the room to dress, he doesn't wake up. I suspect he will be sleeping all day.

It is Shabbat. I should be going to synagogue now; I should be resting or studying the Torah.

Instead, I go into the garden and crouch to check on my seeds. They remain untouched by birds—I'd hoped as much, and put up netting, but one can never be certain—and I smile. I plant a few more while I am there, some thyme and rosemary for the new season.

I imagine my father beside me, crouching to inspect the soil. *Working on Shabbat, David?*

I must, I picture myself replying. *If I do not do this now, I never will.*

The vision doesn't reply. He just watches me, frowning.

You told me to leave London once, I say to him. *Would you tell me that again?*

He strokes his beard, but he makes no response. His eyes are dark and kind.

I ask, *You were proud of me once. Are you still?*

Still no reply. He offers me his hand. I lean forward to take it.

You wanted me to be happy, always, I say. *Do I want that, also?*

He cannot respond; he is my creation, my dream-golem, molded of my own insecurity. But I find my eyes are prickling with tears still as I let the imagined meeting fade, and I am left alone in the garden once more.

I go inside and take out my recipe book, wondering if there are any ingredients I am missing. I have decided to prepare a decoction. It is one I have not made since summer last, and it will have to wait now until my garden has grown. And as I open to the correct page, I find a little note scrawled in the margin—one of my father's comments, in his sprawling, chaotic handwriting: *plants for the easement of sorrow—a fool's errand.* But then, lower, in a smaller, hesitant addition: *Well. I may be wrong. Eden was a garden, after all.*

I smile. My father and his proverbs.

But now, to work. Daisy, dodder, fumitory—ingredients for my own medicine, one I will take once it is done. It is in some ways a return to the townhouse, where Cecilia and I first met: a beginning and an end. A cure for melancholy, if such a thing exists.

Afterward, I go to my study, and I open the letter.

David,

At sunset on the twenty-seventh of May, I will be in Saint James's Park.
Meet me there.

Yours, always,
Cecilia

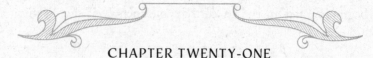

CHAPTER TWENTY-ONE

Cecilia

When we left London eight months ago, we took a gilded carriage. Behind us, people dug through the ashes of a city razed. The houses were charred corpses, the streets filled with a slurry of abandoned things. I felt relief as we left, but regret, also: for the city, for David, for Margaret, for all I had abandoned and been abandoned by. I swallowed my tears and closed my eyes as the cobbles became dirt and the buildings became fields.

In the carriage, Sam spoke excitedly of the estate. He told me how much I would love it in the winter, once the snow fell and the lake froze over. How glad he would be to have company there, now that his parents had passed and his sisters were in France. When we stopped to rest that afternoon, I was referred to as Lady Grey by an innkeeper. For some reason, this made me laugh quite hysterically, and Sam had to apologize on my behalf and explain that I was exhausted by the journey.

We reached the estate by the evening. The Greys own acres upon acres of land, and their manor was built many hundreds of years before this one. It carries that age distinctly, in the narrowness of its windows and the darkness of its brick. Ivy crawls eagerly across the walls of its gardens. It is a haunting place, but a beautiful one. When we first saw it, Sam bounded out of the carriage and stretched his arms wide to greet it. Then he turned to me and said, "Home."

I had sent a courier in my wake to deliver the news to Margaret. She was as furious as she was pleased; we were married, which was what she had wanted, but without her involvement, which decidedly was not. Sam assured me the court considered our wedding to be a romantic elopement, and even the king approved—so the mighty Edens could do nothing except smile and bite their tongues.

Over the winter, Margaret could only communicate with letters, which she sent in great piles. Each one demanded the same thing—that I apologize for my behavior, that I return and speak with her—but their tone swung wildly from demanding to pleading, cruelty to kindness. I never replied. Eventually, they became less frequent, and by spring they had stopped altogether.

Meanwhile, Sam did his best to make me comfortable. He bought a harpsichord and had a spare chamber made into a music room. I was comforted, but I still felt like such a burden to him. It had been so long since I had been given any measure of freedom. And I was surprised by my need to relearn very simple things; I don't know how I had forgotten them, but I had. When I was at my sister's townhouse, it had felt as if my very existence had been an insult, one I had to amend. I had to learn I was permitted simply to be, that I had not betrayed Will by my refusal to follow him. That I had not betrayed Margaret by leaving her. That David wasn't there, and I was still Cecilia without him.

I wanted to remain hopeful and determined, imagining our

reunion, but I missed him. I missed him enough that I cried about it quite often, and I felt a fool each time I did so. Sam had a physician visit, and the man made me decoctions in an approximation of those that David had; I did my best to describe their contents and flavor, but they weren't the same. The doctor had been quite confused by some of my requests. "I fear I will be unable to source epithymum," he admitted to me, chagrined. "It is in short supply, and only the best of gardeners can grow it."

For the first few weeks, I hid constantly in my room, as if to erase my presence from the house entirely. Sam had to coax me out with promises of music and tea and playing cards. It must have been exhausting for him, but he persisted. He had to remind me to bathe, which was the most dreadful thing of all— I remembered how to use water and soap, of course, but I had no instinct for it, no motivation.

"To learn something is commendable," Sam said to me once. "Whether it is for the first time or the fiftieth!"

So I learned again. It took a long time. I was still grieving, as much as I wanted to claim otherwise. And there was no single moment where I was at peace. I often imagined that there would be—I imagined that I would find some sudden symbol of joy, see new meaning in life, and then be happy. But instead, one day in early March, I realized that I hadn't felt despair for some time. Sadness, of course, and grief, and even melancholy—but not despair.

The snow was thawing that afternoon, the sun bright and warm. There was a linden tree at the edge of the estate, and I went to see it. The tree wasn't blooming, not yet, but it would soon.

I went the next day, and the next, and soon it was a ritual of mine, come rain or shine: I would go to see if the linden had bloomed. *Not yet*, I always told myself, *but it will*.

And then, one day in early March, it did. A tiny thing, alone and barely born; but it was a flower all the same, on one of the lowest branches, trembling in the breeze. So I sat beneath it, stooping on a gnarled root—the branch above me, with its single, bud-green passenger—and I took my paper and my pen and began to write a letter.

David,

At sunset on the twenty-seventh of May, I will be in Saint James's Park . . .

On the morning we intend to leave for London, Sam misplaces his favorite hat, and we spend far too long attempting to find it. Eventually we discover it—thankfully unburned—within the fireplace of the first-floor parlor.

"I put it there to prevent myself from losing it," Sam tells me, sheepish, as we clamber into the carriage. "I believe my logic was that the placement was so absurd I would be sure to remember where it was."

I pat his shoulder consolingly. "Sound reasoning," I reply. "Perhaps somewhere less perilous next time."

We pass the journey playing cards, and soon London sweeps us into its grasp, clumsy and eager. Were I a wiser woman, I would be approaching our return with something resembling temperance and dignity, considering I am now a lady of stature. Instead, as we reach the edges of Saint James's, I lean out of the window and nearly fall out of the carriage as I try to peer upward. Scaffolding has erupted from the city's center, like buds on a bough.

"Look!" I say, and Sam leans out of the window on the other side, giving a cry of delight. Then his wig flies away from his head, and I start laughing as he frantically demands that the driver stop so it might be retrieved from the blackberry bush it has tumbled into.

Here is how we have prepared for our return: Sam has packed no less than a dozen cases full of our clothing, including an entire bag simply for Duchess's things, and he has bought us a new carriage with padded seats for the journey. He has had the harpsichord in the townhouse tuned; he has secured us invitations to a number of society events, including a play next week that the king shall be attending; and he has told me, over and over, that all will be well. I want to believe him. Sometimes, I do. But the city has memories, and I still fear they will swallow me whole.

We continue into London, and soon we reach the townhouse. I had forgotten how near it was to the Thames. Did the river always glitter like that? Perhaps the reduction of the fire has caused the buildings to cast fewer shadows upon the water; in the noon sun it glows brighter than anything I have ever seen. From the window of the first floor, it looks like molten silver, poured into the earth. I point this out to Sam. He is taken by the image and writes an awful poem about it, then informs me he has invited a number of his court friends to come on the barge this evening.

"Already?" I ask him. "We've only just arrived."

"To see the city after all the rebuilding! Come, Cecilia, aren't you curious?"

"I am," I reply. "Very well, then."

"And perhaps tomorrow, we might meet with Master van Essen, as he has invited us to a coffeehouse—well, not a coffeehouse, but it *could* be one, you see, if—"

"See Jan?" I ask. "But . . ."

"It would only be him," Sam says. "No one else."

No one else. Of course not.

By the time the sun is setting, we are sailing along the water—in much different circumstances than the last time I was on the Thames.

On the bank, London is a palimpsest, new built over old. People walk through the charred remains without pause, weaving beneath scaffolding, talking and laughing and living. I feel strangely privileged; so few across history will see the city like this, cocooned and metamorphosing.

As we continue past the city center, toward Aldgate, I lean over the edge of the boat, peering out at the wharf where we had stopped the night of the fire. Beside me, Sam presses his hand to my back.

"All is well?" he asks me.

"Well enough," I reply.

This back-and-forth has become a constant between us, and usually it is enough that he will leave the matter be. But this time, he says, "You're nervous."

"Yes. I . . ." Swallowing the lump in my throat, I wrap my fingers around the edge of the barge. The water sprays a light mist against my knuckles. "How many times can someone fall in love, do you think? Does it become impossible eventually? Do we run out of affection to give?"

"I don't think so," he replies. "If David doesn't— I think you will love again, if you wish to, no matter what happens."

"I don't know if I wish to. It's been so long, I . . . I don't know. David never replied to me, and perhaps I'm a fool to still go to meet him." I pause. "You're certain Jan gave you the correct address?"

"I'm certain," Sam says with remarkable patience, as I have asked him the same thing many times before. He squeezes my shoulder. "Whatever happens, I'll be here. You know that, don't you?"

I smile at him. "I do."

I turn to the riverbank, watching the crowd on the shore as they stroll in the evening sun. There are so many people, so many things to see. It isn't a cavernous estate in Kent, where one is invited to linger on the past, to watch the snow fall and the hearth burn and remember what has been lost. Memories or no, London is full of distraction.

Even if he doesn't want me, even if it ends in disaster—maybe here, I will still be able to forget.

That night, Sam and I go to a party at the Myddletons'. Over glasses of port, he tells me about a scheme to open a coffeehouse that I only pay halfhearted attention to, distracted as I am by thoughts of David. We eventually get sucked into a drunken game of whist, and the next morning, we both wake up late, hungover and irritable.

I muster the courage to leave the bed by eleven. Heading downstairs, I see that there is a package in the foyer, clearly having been delivered earlier that morning. It is large and flat and rectangular, wrapped in brown paper; I presume it is for Sam, who is still asleep upstairs. But then I see there has been a note delivered with it, and the note is addressed to me, in a familiar, elegant script. I realize with dawning dread whom the package is from.

I read the note. I know I should not, but I read it anyway.

Dearest Cecilia,

So long since I last heard from you; so long since we spoke. You are across the street, and yet you have never felt so dis-

tant. Whatever slight you have felt I have done you, whatever grudges you harbor, please forgive me for it, and know
that I will always forgive you anything in return. I miss you
terribly.

I hope married life is treating you well. How far you have
come, little Celia. I am proud of you and proud of the match
you have made—my only wish is that you had let me come
to the wedding.

I would like to have another portrait made of you and me,
or you and your husband—whatever you would prefer. It has
been time enough, I think, that the last painting I gave you
be returned. I took the liberty of writing to the Thorowgood
estate, and they were glad enough to send this to you. I hope
Sir Grey does not find it too much of an imposition. I know
how important it was to you. It is my sincerest wish that it
will remind you of all the joys you have experienced in your
life, and all the strength you have derived from their loss,
and how much I—your dearest sister—have always loved
you.

My warmest regards,
Margaret

I drop the note. With trembling hands, I reach forward and
rip the wrapping away.

It is my old wedding portrait. Will and I stand before rolling
grassy hills, me in my blue gown with my pearls in my ears, him
in his navy doublet. His hand is in mine, his eyes are dancing, his
hair gold and curling. I had forgotten how much I looked like
Margaret in it; the woman at his side could have been her, were
it not for the sharpness of her jaw and the narrowness of her
eyes.

I haven't seen it in years, but once this painting was as familiar to me as the veins of my wrist. Will had hung it on our bedroom wall, and it had remained there until the day he died. He was very fond of it. Sometimes he would stand in front of it and smile at our painted faces, humming tunelessly to himself.

But I have always hated it. I hate it still; I hate the way I look in it, expressionless with a face that both was and was not my own. And as I look at it now, I remember how, one morning, I had told him, "It is not very good," thinking to convince him to move it elsewhere.

"Oh, my love," he had replied. "It needn't be good. It is a reminder, that is all."

"Now that I am here, you don't need a reminder. Do you expect to forget me?"

"I shall never forget you."

"Oh, indeed."

"I shall love you for forever, Cecilia," he'd said. "Always, without limit nor ending. If you love another, even then."

And he took me in his arms, and he kissed me, as the wedding portrait watched blankly from the wall.

Now it watches me again. And even though its bride is not truly Cecilia, and it never will be, perhaps I should envy her all the same: She has Will with her, always. She will never know that loss. She will never know any loss at all.

But framed as she is, still and silent as she is—perhaps I should pity her instead. I don't know why Margaret sent this to me. She might have genuinely thought I would be happy, or she might have done it out of vindictiveness—but I think I am glad that she did. For so long, the painting has been trapped in that attic, an image unseen. Better to be made into something new than to remain purposeless. Better to burn and rebuild than to crumble slowly.

I return to the bedroom, where Sam is lying facedown on the mattress, head covered by the pillow.

I pull the pillow away. He groans.

"Sam," I say. "Get up. We have to see Jan."

We go to Temple Bar.

Jan is waiting for us there. When Sam sees him, he lights up brighter than the North Star, and he greets him with a sort of bashful enthusiasm that makes Jan look exceedingly smug. I give Jan a very harsh look, just to put the fear of God into him, but I'm not certain it does very much. He steers Sam around the street with his arm wrapped around his shoulder and his lips right at his ear, and I begin to wonder if I shouldn't just leave.

The building that once held the coffeehouse is entirely gone. All that remains is a foundation of gray stone and a few toppled wooden beams, punctuated at the front by the stone archway that had once framed the door, and has now somehow remained standing. The portal created has something almost arcane about it, as if I might step through it and find myself in fairyland; beyond it, the ground is littered with heavier pieces of rubble too difficult to shift, and a few green sprouts where grass has repopulated booths once full of patrons. It is difficult to imagine the building reconstructed, but certainly, it must be possible. The proof of that is all around us, the skyline full of scaffolding and the street thick with brick-laden carts.

". . . rooms above," Jan is saying to Sam. "And a garden space, too, for spices—we might lease some of the soil to David in exchange for his help."

At David's name I spin to look at them—I had been inspecting the foundations of the back wall—and both men look like they are about to laugh.

"Anything of interest, Cecilia?" Jan asks.

"Well—" My face flushes. "I *did* find something, actually. Come look."

I bring them to the back of the foundations. Beside a low wall, I crouch; they do the same.

"There," I say, pointing. "Do you see it?"

It is a sapling, taking shelter behind the scorch-marked brick.

Jan seems delighted. "How on earth did that happen?"

I reply, "I don't know. It's sweet, though. Jan, do you know what kind of tree it is?"

"I do not, sadly."

"Perhaps David could tell you."

He smiles at me. We all stand. "Perhaps."

"*I* know what kind of tree it is," Sam says, miffed. "I do know some things, actually."

I pat his arm. "Forgive me. What is it?"

"A linden."

I laugh. "Really?"

"Yes," Sam replies with great bravado—and whether or not he is correct, I choose to believe him.

We all return to the street.

"Well?" Jan asks.

"Well what?" I say.

Jan and Sam trade a look. Then Sam says meekly, "Jan would like us to invest in his purchase of the land."

I raise my brows. Jan leaps to add, "I truly do believe it will be a sound investment. The coffeehouse here previously did a roaring trade—all we need is the money to rebuild."

"I'm for it," Sam says without hesitation. "It all seems very exciting. But Cecilia must agree. It's her money, too."

Both men turn to me expectantly.

"Very well," I say, and Sam claps and cheers. I raise my hand. "On one condition."

"Anything," Jan says.

"You must let the linden grow."

He takes my hand in his own, shakes it warmly. "You have my word, Cecilia," he says. "No matter what else happens; that tree will outlive us all."

CHAPTER TWENTY-TWO

Cecilia

I t is the twenty-seventh of May.

I have yet to hear back from David.

I will go to meet him, all the same.

Sam stares out the window and says, "I think it might soon rain. Do you want to take the carriage?"

"It's only a short walk, Sam," I reply.

It feels as if I ought to be panicking more than I am. The lion's share of the anxiety seems to have fallen to my dear husband, who is muttering to himself and pacing fretfully as I dress. Meanwhile, I fiddle with the laces of a gown that I purchased in preparation for our return: It is the color of a dried rose, with gold at the sleeves. My wedding pearls glint in my ears, and I curl my hair into a cascade of bronze and gold. When I look at myself in the mirror, I realize I have never felt more beautiful.

Sam continues to insist about the carriage all the way to the front door, where he finally relents after one of my sternest looks. His expression is as if he is seeing me off to war. He seizes my wrist and releases it. "He will be there," he tells me, but it almost feels as if he is reassuring himself, rather than me.

"I hope he is," I reply. "But if he isn't—we must have champagne tonight, regardless."

I descend the steps; the closing of the gate feels louder than thunder.

As I step into the street, I glance nervously upward, wondering if Sam's advice had some merit. The cloud cover is not entire—patches of sunset-blushed sky peer through cracks in the gray—but still, there is something distinctly ominous about the darkness of them, the bruise-colored blackness. I hope they don't herald disaster.

As I begin to walk, a voice calls my name. I turn around to see that Margaret is standing some distance behind me, staring at me with wide eyes.

My sister looks as well as she did when last I saw her—perhaps even better; there is a flush to her cheeks and a brightness to her eyes that I have never seen before. She is clearly on her way to some event, in an extravagant green gown and a hat dripping in silver ribbons. She looks lovely.

"Cecilia," she says once more when I don't respond. "Hello."

"Hello, Margaret," I reply.

She comes closer and raises her arms as if to embrace me. I take a wary step back, and her arms fall.

"I . . ." she says. "I am so happy to see you. I wanted to visit, but . . ."

"I'm glad you didn't," I tell her. "I mean—I wasn't ready to see you yet."

She winces. "You received the portrait?"

"I did."

She clearly expects me to thank her, but I don't. We are left in an awkward silence.

"I have somewhere to be," I say.

"Oh," she replies, her expression drooping. "But—how is your husband?"

"Fine," I reply. "But I really do need to—"

"I must tell you something," she says quickly. "Something very important. Have tea with me?"

"Margaret . . ."

"It will only take a moment. A few minutes, even. We don't have to drink tea if you don't want to. Just—please, Cecilia. I beg you."

I look again at the sky. I am running early—the restlessness of anticipation—and I had intended to spend the afternoon wandering the park. I could easily sit with her, if I wanted, and still have time to spare.

"Very well," I say. "Lead the way."

The inside of the townhouse is exactly as I remembered. I had not expected it to change significantly, but I did not imagine it would greet me as it does, with all the familiarity of a monarch's portrait. In the foyer, the green wallpaper is exactly the shade of my memories. The sound of my feet pressing into the carpet recalls the moment I first came to this place, more than a year ago, still bloated with grief. The painting of the late Sir Eden on the wall seems to glare at me, as if blaming me for my absence. He was Margaret's father-in-law, a general in the Cavalier army. I heard he died of dropsy while he was leading a siege. What irony, to fall on the battlefield, and yet find your killer your own heart.

Despite the gray skies, we go to the courtyard—perhaps more

out of habit than anything else. The linden here has flowered, too, and it perfumes the air, sweet and cloying. If I closed my eyes, I could pretend it is last summer once more.

For a moment, it is as if I had never left this place at all, and everything past the day I arrived—the fire, my marriage, Kent, David—was only a dream. My stomach lurches, and I pause, chest tightening, in the middle of the courtyard. When Margaret notices my distress, her composure entirely dissolves. Her face crumples and her hand covers her mouth. "Cecilia," she says through her fingers, "I . . . I won't keep you here, if you wish to leave."

"I'll be fine. Just—give me a moment."

I go to lean on the linden tree, breathing deeply, tracing the bark with my fingers. I count the breaths, time them, measure them, until the churning of my stomach subsides.

Margaret has sat down at the table. I go to join her. At some point, a tea service was brought out; I hadn't noticed. I must have spent some time recovering from my panic. When I sip the tea, I can't taste it. There is only the scent of the linden blossoms at the back of my tongue, as if the branches have reached down my throat.

I return my cup to its saucer, porcelain clattering. "You said you have news."

"Yes," Margaret says.

"What is it?"

"I am pregnant."

I am so surprised by this I give a little gasp, and Margaret smiles. "Really?"

"Yes, really. The physician confirmed it. You will be an aunt, Cecilia."

I *must* smile myself at that. "I'm glad," I say genuinely. "And Robert must be, also."

"Yes, very." Margaret shuffles her feet; there are tears suddenly welling in her eyes. "I'm so relieved," she says. "I thought I couldn't . . . I thought I'd never have a child. Robert was—he—he is relieved, also."

I won't pity her. I am determined not to. I tug at the lace at my sleeve, glancing at the clouds above us.

"And I am so relieved to see you now, also," she says. "I have so much to say to you. I regret so much. I—what I did—it wasn't right. I was so afraid, and I . . ."

She is the picture of contrition, hands fisted in her skirts, head bowed: penitent and prepared for forgiveness. "What wasn't right?" I ask her.

"Pardon?"

"What are you apologizing for, specifically?"

"I failed to take care of you," she says. "To keep you safe. I am sorry."

Anger rises. I want to tell her how wrong she is, how she still doesn't understand, even now, how she controlled me, imprisoned me, took my freedom and punished me when I tried to break free. I open my mouth to do so, to snarl and snap, and then—quite suddenly—the fury dissipates.

It may be that nothing I say will ever make her understand. Margaret and I have had years of this game: laughter, embraces, fury; arguments and catty remarks; milk and honey, sweat and tears. I think the only way to win is to refuse to play.

Margaret's face remains a perfect arrangement of sorrow and confusion, soft cheeks drooping, mouth parted in a half breath. Her blue eyes are as lovely and wide as the sky, glassy with unshed tears. She is utterly transformed from the woman who once locked me in my own room, who hated David for no reason more than his very existence. It is almost enough to make me pity her.

Margaret says, "I often think about it, you know. That night here, when you stood in front of the tree shivering and soaking wet, telling me you were in love with a— With Master Mendes. That moment when you asked us to keep going, you looked at me with such defiance. And I felt so monstrous. I felt as if you could never forgive me for it. And . . ." She sighs, stares down at her hands. "I was correct. You can't forgive me. I see it in your face."

"I don't forgive you," I say. "That doesn't mean I never will. I can't make promises either way."

She nods slowly, leans back in the chair. "I think that is fair."

"Good."

"I love you, you know."

"I know. I love you, too. I don't think anything could ever change that."

"But . . ."

"But," I agree.

I stand from the table. My tea remains mostly untouched; the cup sits on its dish, still full, the liquid reflecting the sky and linden above us in a haze of white and gray.

"Will you come back?" Margaret asks.

"Someday," I reply. "But—for now—I have somewhere else to be."

Despite the weather, the park is still full of people. Lanterns glimmer, the rhythmic tread of feet against gravel punctuating the whistling of the wind. As I enter, I take a deep breath of the leaf-scented air, smiling. I will never tire of this place. It is London for me now. Untouched by the fire, by sorrow and by loss; I shall never know anywhere else, I think, so persistent and so joyous.

Standing by the canal, I wait for David. Through the gaps between clouds, the sinking sun scatters light across the water. In the distance, someone plays a pavane on a mandolin, and I can hear children laughing. The lamb's ears rustle in the wind.

Perhaps he will come. I pray that he will. But even if he doesn't, this will all still be here: the trees and the grass; the city and the sky; my home three streets away; Sam and my harpsichord. I have built myself a new world, pulled from the old one's ashes—and I think Will would be proud of me. I think he would stand next to me, by the water, and ask: *Do you think it is fate, Cecilia, that has led you here?*

I don't know, I'd reply. *Perhaps it doesn't matter if it was. Fate is fickle. It is a coward, and it takes as much as it gives. But I needn't be the same. I can be different. I can be brave.*

I know I can be brave; I have proven that to myself. I have experienced so many deaths and births, so many starts and stops. I am proud to have found a life I feel is worth living.

The wind gusts again. A droplet lands on my head. I pull my shawl tighter around myself. *Don't,* I pray, *I beg of you, don't,* but the pleas go unanswered. Within moments, the sky has opened, and we are all subject to the rain.

Chaos comes. The children's laughter turns to shrieks; the music stops; people rush along the canal to find shelter beneath the trees. I spin around, away from the water, thinking to do the same—but then I realize that doing so would make me much harder to find. What if David is here? What if the rain means he won't see me, and he thinks I haven't come?

My mind immediately supplies the result of such a disaster: him, crestfallen, returning to his home; burning all my future letters, kept from me by an act of God. It is much more likely, of course, that he hasn't come at all, but the merest possibility of such a tragedy prevents me from caring about the rain. Instead, I stand by the canal, drenched. I shout, "David!" peering narrow-eyed through the veil of the rain.

I hear no reply except the roar of the canal water meeting its twin; the reflection made uncertain, surreal, a shifting refraction of gray and purple-pink from the patch of sunlight still crawling across the horizon. "David!" I shout again, and then I begin laughing—for what else is there to do? My gold-trimmed sleeves are soaking wet, my beautiful curls weighed flat, raindrops dripping from my chin. There is rain and there is sunshine; I am terrified and I am joyous. It is summer in London, and the fire has passed. David may not be here, but I am. I can shout in a storm if I wish to; I could even dance among the lamb's ears or plunge myself into the canal. There is no one to see me, no one to stop me. I am free.

I shout David's name again, laughing still. And I know, no matter what happens—all will always be well.

CHAPTER TWENTY-THREE

David

On a Monday evening in late May, I go to Saint James's Park to see Cecilia again. Almost a year has passed since we first met. The city was made a phoenix, razed by fire, born from ashes. Despite the fear and the flames, I have loved her, and still love her, as a linden loves the soil.

The sun is setting, but the park is still a riot of noise and light and color. Rarely has a place ever felt so much like *London* to me as this one does on this day. There are so many people here, so many histories. We are all organs in the great, unknowable body of this city. I walk by the canal, the water threading blue through the gravel like a vein beneath skin. The breeze passes over me, the air smells of dry grass.

Many people would be disgusted by my presence here, my purpose here, but my heart is my own. It beats without country nor religion nor name; it is flesh and blood and the air that I breathe; it is mine, and it is hers, and it will always be so. I am finished with fear, finished with hesitation. The fire has taught me that much. Losing Cecilia has taught me that much. I can survive, and I can thrive, regardless of the cost.

At the fountain, children splash and laugh in the water. A pamphleteer waves papers at me. "Sir," he says, "consider the Trinitarians . . ."

I walk past. The sky has grown gray with clouds. Fissures of dim orange light break through the gaps, the sunset scattering itself like gold leaf. As I reach the edge of the canal, a drop falls on my head, and then soon another. Those promenading hurry to find shelter from the coming deluge. The canal itself, a mirror shattered, begins to shimmer with the force of the rain. The grass stoops and the trees shudder. I am grateful for the meager shelter provided by their boughs, which save me from being soaked through. Soon I must pause to hover by the trunk of an oak, thinking to wait out the downpour.

If I believed in Providence, I might see this weather as an ill omen. But it is such a welcome divergence from summer last, when rain was but a distant memory, and the fire was gorging itself on the dry timber of the city. Back then, we had prayed for storms; now, finally, one has come.

I hear someone shout, "David!"

A distant voice—almost inaudible, over the roaring of the rain—but it is hers. I step forward to peer across the canal, water dripping into my eyes, and I see her on the other side. She is drenched, hair uncurled by the storm, but she is laughing. Her hands are curved around her mouth to amplify her voice. I don't think she has seen me yet. She is laughing for the joy of the rain, for the pleasure of surrendering to it. She is so beautiful I cannot breathe, cannot smile, cannot speak. I stand silently, a prisoner to my own heart.

"David!" Cecilia shouts again.

She must be going hoarse, screaming that loud, across all this distance. And so confident that I am here, also; so unashamed in her search for me. I want to shout back to her, but I am so overcome I cannot. Instead, I say, "Cecilia," in a meager whisper, and pray against all odds that she will hear me, too.

Perhaps she does hear; perhaps she doesn't, and it is fate that turns her head. Either way, she looks in my direction, and our eyes meet.

"David!" she shouts again, this time in delight.

"Cecilia!" I reply, my voice regained, and I walk to the edge of the canal. She runs to the opposite edge—the water between us, her skirts in her hands—and she smiles.

Rain runs in rivulets down my back. In the distance, I can hear shrieking and laughter, someone splashing in a puddle, the trundle of a distant carriage.

"Stay there!" I cry to her, and before she can respond, I am running to the end of the canal, boots plunging into the sodden gravel, half blinded by the rain. My hair escapes its tie, which is lost to the wind. I have my medicine case with me—I was at an appointment this afternoon—and it clatters against my thigh. Irritated, I throw it to the lamb's ears and keep running, skidding around the bend, turning the loop.

And then I reach her. *Finally,* I reach her, and the rain has driven away anyone who could see us, and she is as wet as I am, shivering—she will catch cold. She says, "David—" and I take her in my arms and kiss her.

She is burning hot against me, cold water and warm skin, her breath a brand, her fingers coals as they grip my elbows. She kisses me back as if this is a fight she intends to win, harsh and demanding, and I have little choice but to offer her the victory. By the time she pulls back we are both gasping, half laughing, and I feel near feverish for want of her.

She says, "Hello."

I say, "Hello."

Then we are laughing once more. I tug her away from the edge of the canal, to take shelter beneath the trees. I kiss her again, and once more, and then again; but her fingers lift this time to press against my lips and keep me away.

"You didn't reply to my letter," she says, frowning.

"I know. Forgive me."

"Why? You weren't certain you'd come?"

"I didn't read it until yesterday," I reply honestly. "I had convinced myself you would tell me you despised me."

"What? Why would you think that?"

"Because I am a fool," I say, and her expression softens.

"I have missed you," she tells me.

"And I you. Are you well? How is your health? Your appetite? You are eating still?"

Laughing at the question, she replies, "Always a physician."

"Of course."

"It is much better than it was. My panic, also. Sometimes I wake up feeling sick; or I remember something horrible, and the shortness of breath comes again; but it has been a long time since I lost a meal over it. I put on weight in Kent," she says proudly. She spreads her arms out and spins, water springing from the hem of her dress. "I look better now, I think."

"You liked it there?"

"Well enough. And I think I will like London even better, now that I'm not staying with Margaret."

I wince. "Was she very angry? When . . ."

"Yes."

"I am sorry, Cecilia."

"It isn't your fault," she says. "And I am happy now, I think. Happier than I have been in a long time."

"That is good to hear."

"But what about you?" she asks me. "This past year. Have you been well, also?"

"I . . . couldn't say," I murmur. "I suppose—not particularly. It has been difficult."

"I know. I can imagine."

I take a steadying breath, and I offer her my hand. She takes it. "I have thought of you every day since we parted," I say. "Constantly, Cecilia. Every moment of grief reminded me of losing you; every moment of joy reminded me of when we were together. You have become the moon and the water and everything between them. I can't let go of you. I realize that now."

Her eyes widen, her breath stutters. "Oh."

"If you would have me—"

"If I would have you?" she asks incredulously. "David, I love you—have I not made that clear enough? I am in love with you, just as I was when I left."

"But that is not all that matters, we both know that. You are married, and I am a Jew. We could never be openly together. It is exhausting to stay hidden; I know that better than anyone. Just because Sir Grey is accepting of us doesn't mean that others will be."

"I know that."

"But I love you," I say. "I love you so much that it has made me selfish. I think of everything that could go wrong, and yet . . . none of that seems worse than losing you."

Cecilia opens her mouth to reply, but she doesn't say anything. I kiss her softly.

"I have been a coward," I tell her as I pull away. "I have been so frightened of grief that I have refused myself happiness. If this ends—when it ends—at least I will know that I have been brave."

Cecilia says, "All things end. I have lost things before, David, and I will do so again. If I didn't think love was worth the risk, I would have buried myself with Will and spared myself the struggle."

I lean forward and press my forehead against hers. "I love you," I say again, because nothing else feels adequate.

At our sides, she presses her fingers to the inside of my wrist, and I do the same to her. I feel her pulse thrum in time with my own.

"What does this mean?" she asks me.

"Everything," I reply.

And then I look at her, as she looks at me, both of us smiling in a storm.

Meanwhile, outside the shelter of the trees, the wind howls, the clouds roil. The city mourns and grows and rebuilds, London washed clean by rain: all its memories scorched into the cobbles, and all its promises rising like scaffolding to the sky. We have rebuilt. We have survived.

I hope that those I have lost can see me.

I hope they know that I am not afraid.

AUTHOR'S NOTE

The Jews were expelled from England in 1290, and permission for them to return wasn't given until the 1650s, nearly four hundred years later. In the interim, Jewish communities across Europe were beset by tragedy and further expulsions, including the sixteenth-century Inquisitions of Spain and Portugal. The Spanish Inquisition was earlier, and it drove thousands of Jews to Portugal—who were then, in turn, targeted by the Portuguese Inquisition decades later.

Faced with a decision between conversion, execution, or leaving divested of their assets, a significant portion of Portuguese Jews became anusim, or crypto-Jews. I have done my best to be faithful to what we know of the experiences of early modern crypto-Jewish Sephardim in this novel. But how these groups approached and practiced their faith was both extremely diverse and understandably shrouded in secrecy. Similarly, historical records of the nascent Jewish population in London in this period are also patchy: Estimates for the city's Jewish community vary, but it likely comprised of fewer than fifty families overall. We know that many of these families were Sephardim who had originally fled the Inquisitions, moved to the Dutch Republic, and then came to England. Whether some were crypto-Jews who came directly from Portugal and Spain, like David and his father, is certainly possible—likely, even—but unprovable.

Attaining absolute accuracy in these circumstances is difficult, and I hope that minor modifications to history will be forgiven. But I have aspired to some element of authenticity in this novel's depiction of early modern London, in all its marvelous diversity and chaos. The Jews who came to London in the seventeenth century were certainly met with their share of prejudice. But the city has always been—and hopefully always will be—a home to those who wander, those seeking safe harbor, those who have suffered injustice and who are determined to fight against it. And all of us, in London and elsewhere, owe it to ourselves to reach for happiness, even in the darkest of times. I hope this novel does something to demonstrate that.

ACKNOWLEDGMENTS

Writing a second novel is somehow both easier and harder than the first, and *The Phoenix Bride* wouldn't be half the book it is today without the unwavering support of my incredible editor, Jesse Shuman—it is such a privilege to work with you and to bring stories like this to shelves.

My utmost thanks also to the amazing agents who've worked with me on projects past, present, and future: Tara Gilbert and Catherine Cho, as well as my amazing team at Dell: Kathleen Quinlan, Megan Whalen, Kathleen Reed, Kara Cesare, Kim Hovey, Jennifer Hershey, Kara Welsh, and Regina Flath.

I must also thank the incredible librarians and archivists at the University College London Special Collections, as well as the University's SELCs and Jewish Studies departments, for giving me the opportunity to handle some of the documents referenced in this novel. I am also thankful for their help with my research, in particular from Alexander Samson and Matthew Symonds. My thanks also to John Cooper and Helen Smith at the University of York, who helped foster my love for seventeenth-century studies.

I am so grateful for my incredible friends who read this book and provided feedback. Evangeline and Hannah, I couldn't imagine doing this whole "author" thing without you two keeping my head on straight. And Susie, you have the heart of a warrior and a bottomless reservoir of kindness; you inspire me every day. Jacob, Grace, Lara, Yasmin, Margarida, Becky, Julia . . . You all have listened to me kvetch endlessly, and I'm so thankful for your patience and support.

This book is dedicated to my father, Kim—I love you with my whole heart. My love also to my brother, Jonas; my godmother, Belinda; Estela; my aunt Alex; my uncle Jonathan; my mormor, Danielle; my grandpa Jim; and my cousins Malte and Louise. My mother, Caroline, taught me to love books and storytelling, and everything I write has a piece of her extraordinary soul inside it. Thank you, Mom.

Omar: I'm not sure it can be put into words, so I won't try. I love you. Let's go to Granada someday.

THE
PHOENIX
BRIDE

A NOVEL

Natasha Siegel

A BOOK CLUB GUIDE

JOHN DONNE'S ANTISEMITISM

AND *THE PHOENIX BRIDE*

The title of this novel, and its epigraph, was taken from John Donne's "An Epithalamion, or Marriage Song on the Lady Elizabeth and Count Palatine Being Married on St Valentine's Day." This long poem was written in 1613 to—unsurprisingly—celebrate the marriage of Elizabeth Stuart, the sister of Charles I, to a German prince. Although this poem was written decades before the events of *The Phoenix Bride*, I've always found the fire-and-rebirth imagery to have an uncanny prescience about it. The poem is such a perfect encapsulation of England in the seventeenth century: a constant cycle of destruction and creation, unity and division. The image of a "Phoenix Bride" seemed to me a perfect metaphor for not only Cecilia but also for London itself, rising from the ashes of the Great Fire. "A great princess falls, but doth not die."

John Donne is one of my favorite poets—a true master of love poetry in all its forms. He was also an antisemite, as most preachers in the seventeenth century were. His "Holy Sonnet XI" infamously begins with the line, "Spit on my face, you Jews," and doesn't get much better from there; in a sermon from 1627, in which he calls them "The Jews who are afraid of the truth," he echoes the maxim that "The casting away of the Jews is the reconciliation of the world." Many would dismiss the significance of these opinions due to their near ubiquity at the time, or even praise Donne for the relative mildness of his rhetoric, considering what some of his contemporaries were saying. I'm disinclined to do either. He was an antisemite, he believed that Jews were inferior, and if he knew that I'd used his poem to title an interfaith romance novel, I'm sure he would have been furious.

My use of Donne's poem in this book wasn't supposed to be a tacit endorsement of his views—I'd hope that would be obvious enough, regardless—but it's an acknowledgment of the beauty of his writing and the message behind it. Donne's "Epithalamion" shows that love isn't just sweet, it's tenacious, even destructive—but what it destroys, it creates as well. I see his words now as a celebration of a city I love, and a story about people who his words had once cut down instead of honored. So, in that way, I hope this gives his poem something of a rebirth, too.

QUESTIONS AND TOPICS FOR DISCUSSION

1. "The city was made a phoenix, razed by fire, born from ashes. Despite the fear and the flames, I have loved her, and still love her, as a linden loves the soil." Consider the phoenix, a mythological bird that combusts upon death and is born again from the ashes. What do you make of the novel's title? How does it tie in with the story?

2. What connections do you see between Cecilia and David? How do their similarities bring them together, and how do their differences drive them apart? How does your understanding of one character inform your understanding of the other?

3. There are many facets to his self that David conceals: his sexuality, his religion, his true feelings. Consider this: Is it better to live true to oneself even if it means a dangerous existence, or is it better to live safely in hiding? Are we truly safe if we're in hiding?

4. Seventeenth-century London was a diverse city, full of bohemian coffeehouses and verdant parks, but it was also plagued by inequality, disease, and torrid political shifts. Was the city depicted as a place you'd like to live? Did the author convince you that London has always been "a home to those who wander, those seeking safe harbor"?

5. What did you make of Cecilia's decision to marry Sir Grey? Did you approve of this choice? If you didn't approve, did you understand it?

6. How did your understanding of Margaret, Cecilia's sister, shift throughout the novel? Did you empathize with her or find her villainous?

7. Discuss the significance of music in the novel. How does it reflect the interior states of the characters? Why do you think that music, perhaps above other art forms, tends to reflect and project our emotional states so accurately?

8. Cecilia's grief, manifested as sickness, is not understood by the physicians of the time. How did her psychological ailments present as physical? Do you think we consider and treat this kind of anguish better today? How do you think we, as a society, view pain? Why do you think we often dismiss it?

9. In what ways did Cecilia learn to empower herself? Do you consider *The Phoenix Bride* a feminist book?

10. What do *barrocos* represent in the novel? Do you think imperfect things are capable of being beautiful? Is a bit of imperfection necessary to reach perfection?

11. One of Natasha Siegel's missions as an author of historical fiction is to give marginalized characters the dignity of a happily-ever-after. Whose stories have we lost to history due to fate or circumstance? If a trove of papers were discovered tomorrow, what about history would you hope they reveal?

12. Was there any character you wished to see more of? Discuss characters such as Sir Grey, Jan, Sara, and Margaret. What do their perspectives add to the story and our understanding of London society at the time?

13. Who was your favorite character and why?

14. What do you imagine comes next for Cecilia and David? Do you think their love could ever be? Were you surprised to see a hopeful ending for them?

15. You're casting for a film based on *The Phoenix Bride*. Who is your perfect Cecilia and David?

NATASHA SIEGEL is the author of *The Phoenix Bride* and *Solomon's Crown*, a *New York Times* Editors' Choice. She was born and raised in London, where she grew up in a Danish-Jewish family surrounded by stories. When she's not writing, she spends her time getting lost in archives, chasing after her lurcher, and drinking entirely too much tea. Her poetry has won accolades from the University of Oxford.

natashasiegel.com
Twitter: @NatashaCSiegel
Instagram: @natashacsiegel

ABOUT THE TYPE

This book was set in Caslon, a typeface first designed in 1722 by William Caslon (1692–1766). Its widespread use by most English printers in the early eighteenth century soon supplanted the Dutch typefaces that had formerly prevailed. The roman is considered a "workhorse" typeface due to its pleasant, open appearance, while the italic is exceedingly decorative.

RANDOM HOUSE BOOK CLUB

Because Stories Are Better Shared

Discover

Exciting new books that spark conversation every week.

Connect

With authors on tour—or in your living room. (Request an Author Chat for your book club!)

Discuss

Stories that move you with fellow book lovers on Facebook, on Goodreads, or at in-person meet-ups.

Enhance

Your reading experience with discussion prompts, digital book club kits, and more, available on our website.

Join our online book club community!

f g randomhousebookclub.com

Random House Book Club ™

Because Stories Are Better Shared

RANDOM HOUSE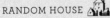